S0-BAF-864

JUN - 2017

Praise for

BURNING

"*Burning* is *Firestarter* for the next generation! Vivid, suspenseful, and tautly wound, this book reads like a love letter to the modern thriller genre. Teens will relate to the accessible, well-drawn characters and tight pacing." —Micol Ostow, author of *Amity* and *The Devil and Winnie Flynn*

★ "Stephen King's *Firestarter* meets Walter Dean Myers' *Monster*. . . . With its subtle yet timely commentary on police brutality, interracial dating, and LGBT rights, the novel addresses contemporary issues without didacticism. A wildly fulfilling and frightening read." —*Kirkus Reviews*, starred review

"*Burning* is an engaging, fast-paced thriller with a science-fiction twist. . . . A blend of *Orange Is the New Black*, *X-Files*, and *X-Men*, *Burning* has great teen appeal and is highly recommended." —*VOYA*

"A captivating story full of intrigue and suspense." —*School Library Connection*

"Everything is creepier when set inside a broken-down institution, and Rollins plays this up, mixing elements of simmering hostility, paranormal abilities, and questionable authority figures all in a confined and unlikable place. She leavens it with small dashes of innocence, friendship, and family love." —*Booklist*

JUN - 2017

Books by Danielle Rollins

Burning
Breaking

BURNING

Danielle Rollins

BLOOMSBURY
NEW YORK LONDON OXFORD NEW DELHI SYDNEY

Copyright © 2016 by Danielle Rollins
All rights reserved. No part of this book may be reproduced or transmitted in any form
or by any means, electronic or mechanical, including photocopying, recording, or by any
information storage and retrieval system, without permission in writing from the publisher.

First published in the United States of America in April 2016
by Bloomsbury Children's Books
Paperback edition published in June 2017
www.bloomsbury.com

Bloomsbury is a registered trademark of Bloomsbury Publishing Plc

For information about permission to reproduce selections from this book, write to
Permissions, Bloomsbury Children's Books, 1385 Broadway, New York, New York 10018
Bloomsbury books may be purchased for business or promotional use. For information on
bulk purchases please contact Macmillan Corporate and Premium Sales Department at
specialmarkets@macmillan.com

The Library of Congress has cataloged the hardcover edition as follows:
Rollins, Danielle
Burning / by Danielle Rollins.
pages   cm
Summary: After three years in juvenile detention, Angela is just months shy of release, but
then ten-year-old Jessica arrives in shackles and is placed in segregation, and while no one
knows what she did to end up there, creepy things begin to happen and it becomes clear that
Jessica and her possible supernatural powers are more dangerous than anyone expected.
ISBN 978-1-61963-738-2 (hardcover) • ISBN 978-1-61963-739-9 (e-book)
[1. Juvenile detention homes—Fiction. 2. Supernatural—Fiction. 3. Horror stories.] I. Title.
PZ7.1.R666Bu 2016   [Fic]—dc23   2015012107

ISBN 978-1-68119-205-5 (paperback)

Book design by Amanda Bartlett
Typeset by Newgen Knowledge Works (P) Ltd., Chennai, India
Printed and bound in the U.S.A. by Berryville Graphics Inc., Berryville, Virginia
2 4 6 8 10 9 7 5 3 1

All papers used by Bloomsbury Publishing, Inc., are natural, recyclable products
made from wood grown in well-managed forests. The manufacturing processes
conform to the environmental regulations of the country of origin.

For Ron, for everything

Prologue

My dad kept his book inside a folder in the top drawer of his massive metal desk, stolen from the basement of an office building where he'd worked as a janitor. This drawer was the only place in our apartment with a working lock.

Sometimes, after he turned out the lights in my room for the night, I'd creep down the hall and kneel on the dingy carpet in front of that desk, squinting into the lock. I'd claw at the edges with my fingernails, trying to imagine what I could use to pick it. One of my mom's bobby pins, maybe. Or a butter knife. I came up with a million plans, but I always chickened out when Dad turned up the volume on the television or coughed or leaned back in his chair in the living room, making the springs creak.

My dad's book was a mythical thing. It didn't look like much, just a few hundred sheets of paper tucked inside one of my old school folders. He wrote chapters on

McDonald's napkins, gas-station receipts, and math worksheets I never got around to turning in. But the best part of the day was right before bedtime, when Dad reached into his jeans pocket and pulled out the tiny silver key to his desk. He'd wink at me and then lumber into the hallway and open the locked drawer.

"Hey, Angie," he'd say. "Did I read you the one about the werewolf?"

Before I could answer, he'd start describing this monstrous, shaggy wolf that roamed the woods behind our hero's bedroom window. The wolf wore a necklace made of children's teeth and couldn't forget the taste of human blood even after he turned back into a man. The next night my dad might tell the story of the clown who lived in the cellar and crept upstairs only at night, to watch our hero sleep. Or he might tell the story of the crows who gathered in the tree outside the window whenever someone was about to die.

"Why are all the stories about monsters?" I asked one night, after Dad finished a gruesome tale about a snake creature that lived in the shower drain.

It was true, after all. The hero in my father's stories was always the same little boy. He was so boring and so dumb that you almost rooted for him to be eaten. Almost. The monsters, though. They were brutal, complicated things. They gambled away their souls at the local racetracks and made bargains with the witches who lived behind the school playground. My father's monsters were works of art.

Dad winked and closed the folder, easing a sheet of paper inside with his thumb. "Monsters are more interesting than heroes," he told me, before kissing me on the forehead and wishing me sweet dreams.

Breaking into my dad's desk to steal that book was my very first crime.

Dad had left for good just a few years after my little brother, Charlie, was born. He'd taken our DVD player and our only working toaster, and, though he'd left the book behind, he'd forgotten to remove the tiny silver key from his pocket.

I was ten years old, and Charlie was three, way too young for the pocketknife Dad left for him, the one Mom hid in her underwear drawer. I slipped the knife out before she got home from work, and I jammed it into the lock, jiggling the blade until I felt something catch, and the drawer popped open.

I know it seems like this story is about the book, but it's not. In fact, finally getting my hands on that book was a letdown. It wasn't magic after all, and I couldn't make any more sense of the words my dad had scrawled across napkins and receipts than I could of the ones written in the real books at school. I don't even remember what I *did* with the book after that, only that I got rid of it before Charlie was old enough to read, so the stories wouldn't poison his brain the way Mom said they'd poisoned mine.

No, this story is about the lock. Or, more specifically, about what it felt like to twist that cheap pocketknife, catch the lock, then click it open. I'd think about that feeling for years after, every time I jimmied the lock on an expensive car or a new house on the rich side of town. It was that feeling I chased, more than the cash. If my dad taught me anything it was what it felt like to want something, whether it was a book in a faded folder, or him, or whatever was on the other side of a tiny silver lock.

But my dad taught me something else too, something that stayed hidden in my memories until years later, when a little girl with black eyes knocked it loose.

Monsters are more interesting than heroes, he'd said. I had no way of knowing then, as I lay awake through the night with stories echoing in my head, that he was talking about us.

He was talking about me.

Chapter One

Peach sneers at us. Somehow this makes her look uglier than usual, which is impressive. Peach is pretty ugly to begin with.

"Frowning doesn't do you any favors," I shout across the yard.

"You say something, bitch?" Peach yells back. We call her Peach because of the thin layer of peach fuzz covering her bald white head. She shaved it all off her second month in, using a flimsy plastic razor with daisies on it.

We're allowed to use the razors once a month, under supervision, to shave our legs and under our arms, but most of us don't bother since the blades are so dull they're almost worthless. Peach must've gotten a sharp one, though, because the guard watching her only turned her head for a second, and when she looked back, Peach had already hacked away most of her thin, blond hair. The guard tried to wrestle the razor away from her, and Peach left a long, thin cut on the guard's wrist.

I hear they sent her to Segregation for three days after that. She went half-crazy inside. No one has requested a razor since.

"That girl is *stupid*." Issie curls her meaty hand into a fist, showing off the tattoos on her knuckles. Issie's cousin convinced her to tattoo "love" and "hate" on her fingers when she was twelve. He made it all the way through "love," but Issie chickened out after he carved an *h* into her index finger. She says it's because she doesn't want hate anywhere on her body, so Cara and I finish the word with Sharpies most mornings.

Today her knuckles say "love" and "hats." Not our best work.

Cara looks up from where she's sitting, cross-legged, on the edge of the cracked concrete.

"If you keep yelling at her, she's going to come over here," Cara says.

"Yeah? Whose fault is that?" Issie says. Yesterday, Peach called Cara a juvie whore, and Cara threw a basketball at her face. Officer Brody gave Cara a demerit and took all our balls and sports stuff after that. He still makes us do our rec time in the yard, even though it's only, like, twelve degrees out here.

Cara shrugs and tucks a frizzy, black hair back under her orange ski cap. She's the only one here who makes the orange ski cap look good, but that's just because Cara makes everything she wears look good.

I tug my ratty sweatshirt sleeves over my knuckles. Technically it's illegal not to provide us with coats when it's below freezing, but juvie coats smell like mothballs and rat piss so most of us double up our sweatshirts instead. I suck in a lungful of air. Cold or not, at least it's fresh, *outside* air. I want to fill my lungs with it and take it with me when they usher us back into the cramped, crowded halls. I want to hold it inside me like a secret.

Snow stretches around us in every direction, all the way back to the smudge of trees on the horizon. It's not pretty snow. It's the slushy crap you see crusted beneath tires in the middle of January. It's like Brunesfield Correctional Facility buys its snow on clearance at Costco, along with scratchy toilet paper and cheap tampons. Juvie girls never get the good stuff.

Issie leans against the metal base of the basketball hoop, her quivering lips nearly purple. I made friends with her my first day inside, picking her out of the crowd because she stands a head taller than every other girl here. Colorful tattoos cover every bit of her dark skin, and a black braid hangs down her back. Caterpillar-thick eyebrows furrow on her forehead. They make her look perpetually annoyed, even when she's laughing.

In other words, she looks terrifying. The perfect juvie BFF.

Issie wraps her "love" and "hats"–covered fingers around her arms. Her teeth chatter.

"I thought you never got cold," I say, clenching my own teeth so tight my jaw aches.

"I'm not cold." Issie bites back another shiver and grabs her belly, making it jiggle beneath her bright-orange sweatshirt. "I'm like a polar bear. I got blubber."

"Don't draw attention to how fat you are," Cara says, flipping a page of the book balanced on her skinny knees. Her mom was Miss Teen Long Island and taught her all these bizarre rules for how to be a proper lady. Never eat more than fourteen hundred calories a day. Never wash your face with soap. Never tell a man he's wrong. "It's like you want people to notice."

Issie snorts. "Nobody thinks I'm a ballerina, girl."

I look out over the grounds while they bicker, trying to find something to distract me from the cold and from Peach, who's staring daggers at us again. But there's nothing out here worth looking at. Brunesfield is a scab in the middle of the snow, just one squat building on a slab of black pavement. Long rows of barred windows wrap around the brick walls. They remind me of a mouth, like Brunesfield is baring its teeth. Chain-link fences surround the facility on all sides, topped with circles of barbed wire that claw at the flat, gray sky.

Cara thinks the grounds are haunted. She says the trees sneak closer at night, and that if you listen, you can hear screams echoing through the woods. But Cara also believes that UFOs crashed here in the sixties and that Bigfoot lives in Canada.

I close my eyes and try to write a letter to Charlie in my head, but the wind creeps in through a hole in my sweatshirt, making my teeth rattle so hard I can't hear myself think.

"You know the girls in Segregation don't have to go out-side?" Issie says. Just that word—"segregation"—sends a zip of fear up my spine.

"You don't want to go there," I say. The Segregation Block is where they put girls who are "a danger to themselves and others," which is juvie talk for "crazy as fuck." Seg girls don't get to go outside because they don't get to leave their dorms. Ever.

"At least it's warm," Issie says, bouncing on her toes.

"When you're in Seg, you spend all your time staring at those pink walls and slobbering on yourself," Cara says. She tugs a thread from her sleeve, and the fabric near her wrist unravels. She spent a week in the Seg Block when she first got to Brunesfield and didn't say a word to anyone for days after she got out. "The only people you get to talk to are the girls who drop off your dinner. That sound *fun* to you?"

"Hey, you guys see that?" I ask before they start up again. A short white bus rumbles along the road twisting out of the trees. It slows to a stop in front of the distant security gate, and an alarm echoes over the grounds. The gate creaks open. Out of the corner of my eye, I notice a few orange-ski-hat-covered heads swivel around. Ellen catcalls, and a newer girl—I think her name is March—presses her face against the chain-link fence.

"The hell?" Cara slaps her book shut. I walk to the fence and lean against the links, watching the bus approach through icy clouds of my own breath. Issie and Cara crowd in next to me. The second alarm buzzes, and another gate jerks open. A few more girls shove in beside us. The bus rolls forward, oily black exhaust trailing behind it.

"That's a drop," Issie says. "Right?"

"Looks like," I say. Drop-offs only happen on the first Thursday of the month. Brunesfield feels like a war zone for days after the new girls arrive. They start fights and try to prove they're bad enough to be here. Just thinking about it gives me a headache. Today's Sunday, but there's no mistaking the short white bus rolling toward the entrance. Issie and I were brought in on the same bus eighteen months ago.

Brunesfield's main doors shudder open, and a guard trudges into the yard. Officer Brody's arms bulge against his too-tight polo, and a gold necklace glitters beneath his collar. He ambles past us, a hand resting on the belt slung around his hips. His watery eyes travel over each of our faces.

"He looks cold," Cara mutters, and Issie snickers into her fist. Goose bumps climb his arms, and his lips are nearly blue.

"Too tough for a coat?" I shout. I don't usually antagonize the guards, but Brody's a special brand of evil. He leaves us out here in the freezing cold for an *hour*, and now he has the balls to waltz out without even wearing a coat, like he's the goddamn king of winter.

"You're asking for a demerit, Davis," Brody calls, jabbing his finger in my direction. Demerits are how we're punished in here. You get three in a week and you lose phone privileges, four and you spend your free time in your dorm; etc. Get enough and you're sent to Seg for the night, but the week's almost over and I only have one. I open my mouth to yell something back, but Cara elbows me in the side.

"Do you want another six months instead of three?" she says. I press my mouth shut again. I was just approved for release, which means I'm out of here in twelve short weeks. Now's not the time to be a smart-ass.

The doors open again, and Officer Mateo steps out, shivering as he zips his heavy coat up to his chin.

"Ooh, it's the new one," Issie says.

"Gross," Cara says.

"What?" Issie wiggles her fingers. "He's *cute*."

I frown, watching Mateo walk toward the bus. He's cute in that too-clean, Boy Scout way. Like how senators and J.Crew models are cute. He looks like he does a hundred push-ups before brushing his teeth in the morning and calls his mother every Sunday. Mateo gives us a subtle nod, his eyes crinkling at the corners. He started about seven months ago, and Director Wu immediately sent him to work in the Seg Block. I study his face. For someone who works around crazies all day, it's kind of amazing that he doesn't have the haunted, desperate look all the other guards have. Yet.

"Why are they both here?" Cara pulls her sweatshirt sleeves over her hands and bounces in place. She looks even skinnier than usual, with all her bushy black hair hidden beneath the ski hat. Officers Mateo and Brody tend to handle the dangerous jobs, like guarding the Segregation Block or breaking up fights. I've never seen them meet a bus for drop-off before.

"Maybe the new girl's feisty," I say.

Metal screeches against metal, and the bus door jolts open. I hold my breath, expecting someone who looks like Issie: huge and terrifying, with colorful tattoos winding up her arms. Or maybe she'll go the homemade-tattoo route. Some of the meaner white girls think it's intimidating to carve swastikas onto their arms and wrists with ballpoint pens. I don't think they even know what the symbol means.

But the door stays empty. Hushed murmurs erupt behind us. A couple of girls start slow-clapping. Ellen catcalls again.

"*Quiet*," Cara says as she loops her chapped fingers through the fence links. "Listen."

The whispers die down, and I hear it: shuffling footsteps, dragging metal.

A girl steps up to the door. Orange scrubs cover her skinny limbs and bunch around the shackles at her ankles. Two huge eyes take up most of her tiny, elfish face.

"Shit," Issie mumbles. "How old is she? Like *seven*?"

"Ten," I say. "She has to be at least ten." Brunesfield only accepts girls between the ages of ten and eighteen, but this girl doesn't look a day over eight. The same age Charlie was the last time I saw him. She hovers at the top of the bus steps, skinny arms raised in front of her chest like she's worried she might fall.

"The chains are too short," Peach says, her voice sounding uncharacteristically normal. She's right; the shackles binding her ankles are too short for the steps. Mateo realizes this at the same moment we do. He moves forward, offering the girl his arm to help her down. Brody's jaw tightens, and he clutches the gun at his belt like maybe he's going to pull it from the holster. Cara stiffens. Peach says something vulgar.

"Holy shit," Issie says, staring at the gun. Brunesfield guards don't carry guns. At least, they never have before. Brody leaves his hand on the weapon until the girl's shackles clank against the concrete.

"Move along," Brody says, falling in line behind her. The girl shuffles forward, staring down at the thick chains hanging from her ankles.

She looks up only once, when she walks past me. Her brown eyes lock on my face and her lips part, like she might say something.

A shiver starts in my shoulders and shoots all the way down to my toes. The wind around me picks up. It moves through the distant trees and I swear it sounds like a scream, just like Cara said it would. I jerk my head toward the woods, half-expecting to see the bare branches reaching out for us, the trees themselves creeping closer. But the woods look the same as ever. Not moving. Not haunted. Just cold.

I turn back around a moment before the facility doors whoosh open, and the girl disappears inside.

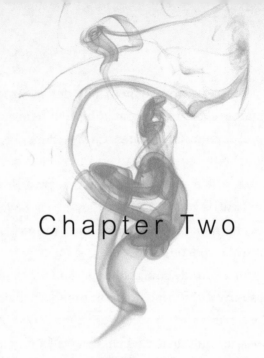

Chapter Two

"What are you waiting for? *Move*." Peach jams her shoulder into me on her way to the door, sneering again so I know it's personal.

"That girl's gonna get her ass kicked," I mutter.

"Not by you," Issie says.

I shrug and glance over my shoulder at the white bus. Another couple of girls dart past me to get to the door. Cara jabs me in the back with her book, and I tear my eyes away.

"Watch it!" Ellen snaps, weaving around me, her hands clasped in front of her. Issie mouths the word "mouse" and points.

"Another one?" I whisper. An involuntary shudder moves through me. *Gross*.

"I saw her catch it at the edge of the field," Issie says. I grimace. The last creature Ellen snuck in was the size of a small fist and made clicking sounds inside her sweatshirt pocket. It escaped in the bathroom a week ago. I never figured out exactly what the thing was, but I picture something like the snake creature from my dad's old stories. I bet it lives in the shower drains and eats our discarded hair.

I move forward, trying not to think of tiny mouse feet and twitching mouse noses. Brunesfield's smell hits me as soon as I step inside: stale air and mold and lemon-scented floor cleaner. If I lived for a thousand years, the smell of this place would haunt me until the day I died. Smudged handprints line the walls, and the floor gleams with off-brand polish that will never remove the scuff marks thousands of shoes have left behind. I wonder if the girls who left those marks still remember this smell.

I wrinkle my nose as the rest of the girls line up according to offense, their hands behind their backs. The low-security girls stand near the front. There are around forty of them now, mostly white girls who clump together, looking at the rest of us like we're monsters. They're all runaways and kids whose parents dumped them because they "couldn't deal anymore." I don't even bother learning their names; they're in and out so quickly it's not worth it. I watch two girls pass a clear plastic bag behind their backs, and roll my eyes. The low-security offenders are always the ones sneaking in drugs.

Peach and the fifty or so crackheads and other druggies shuffle in behind them. They're all here for possession or intent to sell. Peach spots the girls passing drugs and bares her teeth at them. It's technically a smile, but the girls shift away from her, freaked. I don't blame them.

Theft and destruction comes next. Twelve girls huddle in that group. They've been here as long as I have, so by now this is second nature for them. I know them all okay, but they're mid-security, so we don't socialize a lot. Ellen awkwardly moves her arms behind her back, still trying to hide the mouse hidden in her hands. I try not to cringe. *Ew ew ew.*

Issie and Cara wait at the end of the line, with me. They're the only other girls in high security. High security is for the baddest of the bad girls, one step below Segregation. The violent-offenders group. My group.

I move in next to them and twist my arms behind me, touching my fingertips together to create a diamond with my hand. It's procedure, Brunesfield's way of keeping us in line without using handcuffs.

"Orange line, people," Officer Crane barks, moving down the hall to make sure we all have our toes on the orange line painted across the floor. A million years ago someone devised this system of colored lines to keep us in check. Basically, if you want to go anywhere you have to walk on one of the lines. Blue leads to the bathroom, black to the cafeteria, etc. It's completely stupid, and most of the lines have worn off, so none of the other officers enforce it anymore. But Crabby Crane is an old-timer. Rumor has it one of the Seg girls attacked her years ago, and that's where she got the thick red scar that twists over one eye and across the side of her face, giving her a permanent snarl. She's hated the Segregation Block ever since.

She stops when she gets to Cara, Issie, and me, and she stares with one real eye and one shiny glass one.

"Go on—black line," she says. We weave past the rest of the girls without a word. Issie hurries down to the basement, but Cara stops me at the top of the staircase.

"Who's that?" she asks, jerking her head toward the end of the hall. I turn to look.

A tall blond woman stands near the front entrance, a stiff black coat swinging from her shoulders. A girl with shiny, college-kid hair and straight teeth stands at her shoulder, a black binder tucked under her arm. The girl meets my eyes, then looks away.

"Does that girl look familiar to you?" Cara asks. I shake my head.

"I bet they're from the university," I say. Syracuse isn't too far away. Every now and then an abnormal-psych student will come in to "observe" us.

"Maybe," Cara says.

We turn and make our way down the narrow flight of stairs, following the black line through the double doors to the kitchen.

Two guards stand outside the doors. They're both new, and I can't remember their names. The one on the left has a Cabbage Patch face—big cheeks, small eyes, button nose. She would have been pretty except for the mole on her forehead that looks like a third eye. "Officer Sterling," I think her name tag reads. Or "Stanley." I've never been good at reading.

They don't look at us as we walk past, but the new ones never do. It's like they get some kind of training: Don't look the inmates in the eye. Don't think of them as people.

"I'm. So. *Cold*," Issie says once we've made it through the double doors. She jumps in place, sending a tremor through the pots and pans hanging from the peg wall. Officer Stanley or Sterling raps her knuckles against the window on the door.

"Keep it down," she calls.

"Stop it," Cara warns Issie, glancing at the door. "You can't be that cold." When the guard turns around, Issie goes straight to the oven and twists the knob to high, hovering near the door while it heats up.

I turn on the faucet and shove my hands under the stream of hot water, sighing as my icy fingers begin to thaw. Being cold is a small price to pay for looking up and seeing actual sky instead of cracked plaster, but even I have to admit it's been miserable out. It's always cold here, but the past two months have been worse than ever, with blizzards blowing in every other day and wind cutting through your skin like a knife. Like most of the girls at Brunesfield, I'm from New York City—Brooklyn, to be exact. I hadn't realized the northern part of the state would be freezing all the time.

"Come on." Cara nudges me with her arm. "I'm hungry."

I turn the faucet off with my elbow and dry my hands on a rag hanging from the fridge door. Cara, Issie, and I are kitchen staff, which probably sounds strange given what we're in for. You wouldn't think they'd let the violent offenders near hot stoves and knives, but it makes sense, kind of, if you know how things run inside. See, we've all been here longer than any other girl in Brunesfield. We know the rules better than the runaways who were admitted last week, and we're less likely to do something crazy, like the heroin addicts still going through withdrawal. Most of the guards figure that if Cara, Issie, or I were going to start something, we'd have done it a long time ago.

It's lasagna night, so we pull three slabs of preprepared noodles and meat out of the fridge. Gas hisses inside the oven, quickly heating the long, narrow room. A thin line of sweat gathers on the back of my neck as we get to work. The kitchen is always about ninety degrees, and a thin layer of grease covers everything from the black-and-white tile floor to the top of the freezer.

The temperature inside Brunesfield has never made any sense. Some rooms stay boiling hot year-round while others get so cold I swear my toes turn to ice. It drives the guards crazy. The law says they have to keep the building above and below certain temperatures, so they're always cranking the rumbling, spitting radiators up to high or hauling industrial-size fans into the hallways. It never does any good. Brunesfield sets its own temperature.

I peel off my sweatshirt and toss it on the counter. Cara hums under her breath; if you didn't know her you might actually think she was a pleasant person. The heavy scent of meat and cheese fills the air around us. It's almost cozy.

"Who do you think the new girl is?" Issie asks, tugging the tinfoil off a can of tomato sauce. Cara's humming falters.

"We'll find out at dinner," I say, dumping a bag of carrots on the cutting board. I can't think about that little girl without seeing her dark eyes and hearing her chains scrape along the concrete driveway. Cold fingers walk up my back. Brunesfield is a top-security detention center, but I've never seen anyone else wearing shackles.

I walk back over to the double doors, pushing the strange girl out of my mind. "Knife," I call to the guards. Stanley or Sterling comes in, removing a thick key ring from her belt. She unlocks a metal cabinet in the corner of the room and hands me a paring knife. She hovers in the corner, watching me force the knife through the skinniest carrots I can find. The blade's practically dull, and my arms burn as I chop.

Cara clears her throat. "Did you bring the letter, Ang?" she asks.

I slip Charlie's letter out of my back pocket. He's drawn snowflakes along the edges of the paper. The thick, clumsy lines make my chest go tight.

"Here," I say, handing it to Cara. She hops onto the counter next to my cutting board and unfolds it, taking care not to rip the creases. She pulls off her orange ski cap, and more hair than you could possibly imagine frizzes around her face in a curly brown halo.

"*Dear Angela,*" she reads. "*Hi, how are you? I am fine. It's almost Thanksgiving but it hasn't snowed yet so instead of sledding I play Call of Duty. Is it still snowing where you are?*"

"Yes it is, Charlie boy," Issie interrupts, snatching a piece of carrot from my cutting board. I glance at the guard, but she's watching me, not Issie. Her beady Cabbage Patch eyes follow every movement I make with my flimsy knife. I swallow and try to ignore her. I still haven't really gotten used to being watched all the time.

"Did he ever tell you whether he got that hockey stick?" Cara asks, looking up from the letter. Cara's the one who figured out I have dyslexia. I'd never even heard of dyslexia before, but she said she knew a couple of kids with it at her old high school. She's been reading Charlie's letters out loud to me for so long that she and Issie talk about him like he's their little brother too. It's nice. It's been a while since I've seen Charlie, and he's starting to feel more like a character from a book than my actual brother.

"He hasn't sent anything new since before Christmas," I say. Issie hauls a giant sauce pot into the sink and turns on the tap. Most of "hats" has rubbed off her fingers. Now it reads "ha."

"Your release is only three months away," Issie says, her back to me. "You'll ask him then."

I look down at the cutting board, gritting my teeth as I saw through another carrot. Twelve more weeks. That still seems insane. I've been in Brunesfield for a year and a half now. I spent my sixteenth and seventeenth birthdays here. I even got my GED inside. It took me three tries, but I got it.

But at the end of March, I'll be out. I'll be able to use the bathroom without asking permission, and shower all by myself.

I won't have to face another boring day where every hour of my life is planned. *Eight o'clock: breakfast. Nine o'clock: chores. Ten o'clock: morning classes.* In three months, I'll be able to spend all day outside if I want to, just staring up at the clouds.

Cara flips Charlie's letter over, like she's hoping there's something on the back we've missed. Her family never writes, and Issie's letters are always in Spanish. Charlie's are the only ones we all share.

The oven timer goes off. Issie grabs a pot holder and removes a pan of bubbling lasagna while Cara finishes rereading stories of how Charlie got grounded for accidentally kicking the DVD player, and about the girl in his class who keeps throwing balled-up pieces of paper at his head. ("Ooh!" Issie squeals. "That means she *likes* him.") I dump the freshly chopped carrots into a pot of water to cook, then lean past Cara and snag a piece of cheese off the lasagna.

"Angela Davis," someone barks from behind me. Officer Brody steps into the kitchen, letting the double doors slam behind him. "Did I just catch you stealing food?"

Brody narrows his watery eyes. He reminds me of one of those ugly little pug dogs. His eyes sit too far apart, and his nose turns up at the end, like he's making a face. Only he always looks like that.

I called him Officer Grody my first week here. Not my best pun, I admit, but I'd try to look all innocent and say it really fast, so he'd think he heard me wrong. But then the other girls started doing it too, and they weren't as subtle.

Somehow, word got back that I'd started the whole thing and Brody's had it out for me ever since.

I swallow, and cheese burns the back of my throat. "No, sir," I say.

"That's a demerit right there. You think I'm stupid, Davis?" Brody asks. I'm smart enough not to answer that but *dear God* how I want to.

Brody leans against the counter next to me, his eyes traveling down Cara's body.

"Need you to make a tray," he says, adjusting his belt.

"Why?" Cara asks. Only girls in Segregation get dinner trays, and we make those before going outside for rec. There are always three or four girls assigned to take the trays down, and they make this big show of trading good-luck charms and throwing salt over their shoulders before they head out. It's dumb. But I get it. If anywhere in Brunesfield is haunted, it's the Seg Block. Not that any of us would say that out loud.

"We have a new girl in Seg." Brody spits on the floor, then rubs it into the tile with the toe of his boot. "Or were you the only three who didn't notice?"

"The little girl?" I can't keep the disbelief from my voice. Only the craziest, most violent inmates go to Segregation. We're talking girls who really should be in mental facilities, only they get sent here because their families are either too poor or too stupid to hire a good lawyer. Most of them can't sit next to you for a second without pulling out your hair or jabbing you in the eye with their fingers. They're too dangerous to be around the rest of us so they get locked up alone, which only makes them worse. The worst punishment Brunesfield can come up with is sending you down there with them.

"You're joking," I say.

Brody removes an aluminum tray from the stack in the corner and tosses it onto the counter next to me. "Why don't you see for yourself?" he says.

I've been to the Seg Block before. I was on tray duty last fall, before Issie and I got assigned to the kitchen. For a week, it was my job to carry the food to the guard (Crabby Crane, at the time). We'd load the trays onto a rolling cart, and Crane would follow me down the hall as I slid the food through the slots in each door. Crane kept a hand on her nightstick the entire time, and her shoulders wouldn't loosen until we stepped back into the main hall. And Crane's not afraid of anything.

I think of this as I climb down the narrow stairwell, listening to Brody's boots echo off the concrete walls behind me. When you aren't actually there, it's hard to remember why the Seg Block is so creepy. They're small things. Sounds don't behave like you expect them to. Light never seems to reach the corners where light is supposed to reach. You'll hear something skitter across the floor, but when you turn to look, you only see shadows and cobwebs.

Officer Mateo is bent over a crossword puzzle at the door to the Segregation Block. He looks up at the sound of Brody's boots, and a smile crosses his face so suddenly that it takes me by surprise. No one smiles in Brunesfield. Especially not guards. Especially not down here.

"Something wrong?" Mateo asks. Brody loops his thumbs through his belt.

"Miss Davis was getting mouthy back in the kitchen," Brody says, nodding at me. "Thought a walk down the Seg-regation Block would help adjust her attitude."

"Is that right?" Mateo has the kind of smile you could only describe as lazy. It lounges across his face, reminding me of summer and hammocks and sun-drenched days at the beach. He glances at me, and for a second I'm convinced that he doesn't believe a word Brody said. But that's impossible. Guards always take one another's side. Always.

Mateo jabs a button with his thumb, and a buzzer blares down the hall. The security door shudders aside. The smell of urine wafts out from the hall, and I wrinkle my nose. Brody steps into the Seg Block and leans against the cinder-block wall. He crosses his arms over his chest.

"She's in the last cell on the left," he says. I glance down the long, empty hall and feel my first flicker of fear.

"You aren't coming?" I ask.

Brody cocks an eyebrow.

"Right," I say. I've heard rumors that Brody's too scared to walk down the hall himself, so he always sends one of us alone. I straighten my shoulders. *It's just like any other hall,* I tell myself as I walk. The girls down here may seem scary, but there are people who think I'm pretty scary too. They can't be much worse.

Narrow rectangular windows sit inches below the ceiling, each allowing only a sliver of gray light into the hall. Walls the color of Pepto-Bismol stretch out before me, separating cagelike dorms. The Seg Block dorms remind me of the reptile exhibit at the Bronx Zoo. The front walls are made entirely of thick glass, so you can see what's happening inside. The doors are off to one side, thick glass surrounded by a sturdy metal frame. I shuffle forward, tightening my grip on the tray of food. The urine smell grows stronger. Sweat gathers between my fingers even though it's so cold I can practically see my own breath. A radiator hisses uselessly at the end of the hall.

Something moves in the shadows to my right.

I jerk my head around. A skeletally thin girl with stringy hair leans against her door. She runs her tongue along the glass.

"I like new friends." She smiles, revealing teeth the color of rot. Another girl crouches in a cell on the other side of her wall, scratching the cinder blocks. Ragged skin peels away from her hands, and blood dots her fingers. She hesitates, like she senses me watching her, and slowly turns her head toward me.

I flinch and Brody laughs, his cruel voice booming off the walls.

"Move," I whisper to myself. This place feels like the cold apartment buildings where I used to live with my mom and Charlie. Even with the cockroaches and cracked walls, the places weren't so bad when everyone kept their doors shut. But every now and then I'd see light spilling into the hallway as I made my way up the twisting staircase. Occasionally I'd stop, too curious not to peek through the open door. But most of the time I'd just walk faster, closing my eyes so I wouldn't catch a glimpse of what was inside. Some things you're better off not knowing.

I move forward, keeping my eyes straight ahead. Muffled cries and low, panicked voices echo from inside the dorms. I glance back over my shoulder. The distance to the security door seems to have doubled. Like the hallway stretched when I had my back turned. I swallow and hurry down to the last dorm.

A slow, tuneless hum drifts out of the new girl's room, just one note repeated over and over. I step in front of her door, and the humming stops abruptly.

The girl sits cross-legged on a thin mattress in the far corner, her dark eyes fixed on the glass wall in front of her. I'm struck, again, by how normal she looks. She should be in school, entering a spelling bee or signing up for the science fair. Not here.

I don't know her name, so I clear my throat and tap my knuckles against the glass, balancing the food tray in one hand. She rocks in place. Back and forth. Back and forth. She doesn't look at me.

"Okay." The food slot is about a foot from the bottom of the door. I kneel, cringing at the cold seeping through my scrubs. Something skitters across the concrete next to my shoe. I suck in a breath, but the hallway's too dimly lit to see if it was just another roach or something larger.

I flip open the flap and balance the tray on the narrow shelf. The lasagna's gone cold by now, a layer of grease congealing on the fluorescent orange cheese. I lose my appetite just looking at it. I start to push it forward when a shadow falls over me.

I look up.

The girl stands directly in front of the door, staring down at me. I don't know how she crossed her dorm so quickly—I only looked down for a second. I try to swallow, but my tongue feels chalky. Maybe it's an optical illusion, like how the hallway seemed longer the further I walked. I open my mouth to ask her name—then close it again. The girl's large black eyes widen. They grow darker. Her pupils expand to fill the entire sockets.

"Shit," I murmur. I want to move but I'm held in place, frozen with fear. The air around me changes, somehow. It thickens, hanging on my shoulders like a sweater.

Heat, I realize, dumbfounded. It's warm here. The concrete grows hot beneath my knees, and the radiator hisses and thrashes behind me. A prickling sensation starts in my fingers. Then, all at once, the aluminum tray I'm holding *burns*, searing my hand so completely that there's an instant where I can't tell whether the sensation is hot or ice-cold.

I scream and leap to my feet. The tray topples off the metal shelf, spilling to the floor in front of me.

The girl closes her eyes. The radiator pops, then goes silent. Cold air rushes around my ankles and creeps up over my skin.

But my hand still burns. The skin on my fingertips looks red and shiny. Raw.

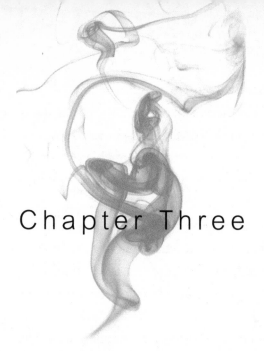

Chapter Three

I race down the hall, the paper-thin soles of my juvie-issued sneakers slapping against the concrete floor. Girls jeer and shout from their cells as I run past, their voices echoing off the walls. I don't stop. In fact, I barely hear them. The blood beneath my burned skin beats like a second heart.

"What are you doing, Davis?" Brody yells. "Get right back there and pick—"

"I can't," I interrupt. I'll get in trouble for disobeying a direct order from a guard, but I'd rather take my chances with Brody than go near that girl again. I tighten my raw fingers into a fist, then release them, cringing.

"What did you say?" Brody asks. I stare at the red scalp beneath his thinning blond hair.

"Go ahead and give me a demerit," I blurt out. "Or make me clean the bathroom with a toothbrush. Whatever."

Usually Brody loves cliché punishments like that, but today he rests both hands on his belt and stares down the hall.

"I don't think so, Davis." Brody's lips stay curled while he speaks, like he's physically incapable of forming an expression that isn't a sneer. "I think this is grounds for a trip to Director Wu's office."

My throat goes dry. A demerit is nothing. The director's office means probation, and probation could delay my release. *God*, I'm an idiot. I wish I could take it all back. The hallway isn't that scary, and the burn isn't too bad, and the girl . . .

The memory of her black, soulless eyes fills my head. I shiver. The girl is horrifying, but I could handle her. Anything to keep from delaying my release.

Brody's hand clamps down on my arm. "Brody, please," I beg at the same time Mateo says, "I think she just—"

"That's *Officer* Brody," Brody says, cutting us both off. "Now move."

I follow him away from the Segregation Block, casting one last glance down the long pink hall before I go. I can't see into the girl's cell from this angle, but her shadow stretches across the hall in front of her.

Like a warning.

I've been to Director Mary Wu's office twelve times in the past year and a half. Mostly for mouthing off and stuff, but I've also been hauled in twice for fighting (once with Peach and once with Cara). The last time was one month ago, to discuss the details of my release in March. During that meeting I sat in front of a panel of caseworkers, probation officers, and board members as Director Wu reviewed every note in my file, all while staring at me over the top of her rectangular-framed glasses.

"And what did you learn from this?" she'd ask, frown lines deepening around her mouth. I heard what she was really saying: *Don't screw up again.*

I hesitate outside her office door. "It was an accident," I say to Brody.

"Don't want to hear it again," he says, his voice practically gleeful. He raps his knuckles against the door, then pushes it open and steps into the office.

"Director Wu? Got another one for you." He closes the door behind him, then lowers his voice to explain the incident. I try to be patient. I count to one hundred in my head. I press my lips together and ball my hands into fists.

A girl stands near the window at the end of the hall, staring at me with wide, milky eyes. I don't recognize her but I smile anyway to be polite. She starts talking to herself in a quiet, urgent voice and gives her hair a violent tug. I flinch as a chunk of it comes out in her hand.

For whatever reason, Brunesfield attracts a lot of crazies. They chill here for a few weeks while they wait for trial or for a spot in a mental-health ward to open up. Or for their parents and lawyers to figure out what to do with them.

Turning my back on the girl, I push my ear to the wood. In Brody's version of what happened, I threw the tray of food instead of dropping it and used some very colorful language when he politely asked me to go pick it up. I grit my teeth, telling myself to stay calm. Arguing will only make things worse.

Then, just when Brody finishes his horrible, overblown, lie-filled story, he clears his throat and adds, "Truth is, she's been mouthing off all day." He lets out a low whistle. "You should have heard the things she—"

"That's not true!" I slap the door, and bright, hot pain sears my burned skin. I'm too blinded with righteous anger to feel it. He's lying! Can't she tell that he's lying?

But that feeling drains from my chest in the silence that follows my outburst, leaving me deflated. Brody opens the door and glares down at me. He looks triumphant. Like I played right into his hand.

"Miss Davis," the director says from behind him. "Why don't you join us?"

Brody inches to the side of the doorway, forcing me to squeeze past the sweaty belly hanging over his belt to make it into Director Wu's office.

"Think I'm tough now?" he says, low enough that I'm the only one who hears. Of course this is about how I yelled at him outside. Brody's just petty enough to think his lies are justified.

A sunken corduroy couch slouches against one wall. Army-green filing cabinets line the other wall, and a beige rug covers the floor. Parts are worn thin enough to see the concrete slab beneath.

Director Wu's desk dwarfs the room. It sits in front of a large window overlooking a flat gray lake surrounded by skeletal trees. The desk's size somehow makes the tiny Asian woman crouched behind it look stately, like she's manning a big, wooden ship. The room itself is a surprisingly comfortable temperature for Brunesfield. I'm confused, until I spot the space heater buzzing in the corner.

"Close the door, Miss Davis," Director Wu says, yanking open the bottom drawer of her ancient filing cabinet. I shut the door on Brody, biting the inside of my cheek to keep from making a face at him. I've already gotten myself in enough trouble today.

Once the door's closed, I notice the tall woman Cara and I saw earlier standing in the corner of the office. Her white-blond hair swoops below her ears and she has a long, straight nose that makes her face look sharp and intelligent. A tiny gold rose is pinned to the lapel of her black pantsuit.

A girl perches on a stool next to her, head bent over a note-book in her lap. We're probably around the same age, but the girl's clothes look pristine and expensive, her fingernails perfectly manicured. A bracelet dangles from her wrist, and the silver charms hanging from it are all shaped like vegetables: A carrot. A turnip. A piece of broccoli. I wrinkle my nose. Why would anyone wear jewelry shaped like vegetables?

"Angela, this is Dr. Rose Gruen and her assistant, Mary Anne," Director Wu says. She pulls a file out of the drawer, then pushes it closed with her foot. Every other time I've been to her office, Director Wu has worn stockings, her scuffed black shoes piled beneath her desk. Today there's a pair of pointed, painful-looking heels on her feet. I look at them, then back at Dr. Gruen.

"Why is she is here?" I ask.

Director Wu glances up, "Oh, she's not here for you. I should have explained. Dr. Gruen is in charge of Youth Services and Outreach for . . . I'm sorry, what's the name of the organization again?"

"SciGirls." Dr. Gruen speaks slowly, her voice as liquidly smooth as syrup. "In the coming days, I'll be speaking with you all about volunteer and leadership opportunities. Today I'm just here to observe."

A smile flashes across Director Wu's face a beat after Dr. Gruen finishes talking. Director Wu never smiles, and her mouth droops at the corners now, like she's not entirely sure how to do it.

"Let's discuss this incident," she says, flipping the folder open.

That righteous anger flares in my chest again, but this time I beat it down. "It's not like Brody's making it sound," I say as calmly as I can muster, sinking into the lumpy corduroy couch.

"*Officer* Brody," Director Wu corrects me.

"Right, Officer Brody," I say. "I dropped the tray; I didn't throw it, and I never said any of those—"

"So you're saying the officer is lying?" Dr. Gruen interrupts. I crane my neck to look up at her, difficult considering she's nineteen feet tall and the couch I'm sitting on has sunken practically to the floor. I gingerly touch two of my burned fingers together.

"Exaggerating," I say. "Not lying."

Dr. Gruen nods, and her expression softens. She gives me a very small smile before glancing back at Director Wu. Mary Anne stays bent over her notebook, shiny hair covering her face. Her charm bracelet jingles as she writes.

"Fine," Director Wu says, her voice clipped. Out of nowhere, the space heater next to her desk sparks. She flinches as the motor whirs to a stop. For a second it looks like she's going to kick it. "Damn thing never works," she mutters, turning her attention back to my file.

She flips through the pages, and a frown line appears between her eyebrows. "Oh dear. I see you were up for release in three months."

Were. I hear that word like she shouted it. I think of Charlie sitting at the kitchen table in our tiny apartment back in Brooklyn. I like to imagine him writing letters to me or doing his homework or even playing *Call of Duty*. But the boy I picture is only eight years old, with hair that sticks up in the back and two front teeth missing. Charlie from two years ago. I have no idea what he looks like now.

I swallow the lump forming in my throat. "Like I said, it was an—"

"Accident," Director Wu finishes for me. Her eyes flick to the top of her glasses. "Miss Davis, I wish we could forget about this whole thing, I really do. But any incident that goes unreported can be used against the entire facility."

I think she glances at Dr. Gruen, but I could be wrong.

"I'll do what I can," Director Wu continues, easing the folder shut. "But if they decide to open your case for review again, I can't promise we'll be able to keep you on schedule to release in March."

"Right." The word cracks in my mouth. "I understand."

"As for punishment," Director Wu continues, "Officer Brody recommended cleaning the Segregation Block for the next week. I think that's fair, don't you?"

My chest clenches. Of *course* Brody suggested that. I focus all my attention on keeping my face impassive. Cleaning the Segregation Block is way too large a punishment for accidentally dropping a tray, but I don't want to risk getting in any more trouble by arguing.

"Yes ma'am," I say. Director Wu gives me a tight-lipped smile and leans over to stick my file back into the metal cabinet. I nod at Dr. Gruen and head for the door. Mary Anne pushes her hair behind her ears and gives me a polite smile.

"Just one more question." Dr. Gruen crosses her arms in front of her chest, tapping her long, pale fingers on her elbow. There's black ink smudged around her thumb and fingertips. "You said you were in the Segregation Block when this happened. Why were you there?"

I pause, tightening my grip on the doorknob. My burned skin tingles, but I ignore it. "Brody—I mean *Officer* Brody asked me to deliver a food tray."

"Just one? To Jessica Ward?"

"Is that the little girl they brought in this afternoon?" I ask.

Dr. Gruen nods. "It is."

"Then, yeah, I brought the tray to her." I start to pull the door open, but Dr. Gruen places a hand on the wood, holding it shut.

"And you just *dropped* it?" she asks. I meet Dr. Gruen's eyes, and it occurs to me that it was strange of her to start working here today, on the same day Jessica was brought in.

Director Wu clears her throat. "You can go, Miss Davis," she says.

Dr. Gruen blinks and takes my hand from the doorknob. She turns it over, glancing at the raw pink skin on my fingers.

A thin smile stretches across her face. "Yes," she says in her smooth, syrupy voice. "You can go."

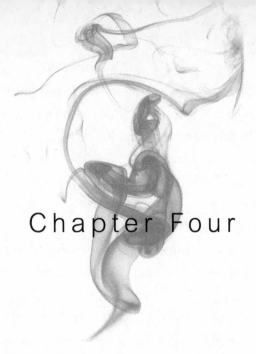

Chapter Four

"I'm just going to say it," Issie says from the bunk above me. I can't see her, but I hear paper rustling and feel the steel bed frame shift. "You are so lucky."

"Are you out of your mind? I have to clean the Segregation Block for a *week*." I frown at my wall. My dorm's previous occupant wrote "Jesus sav" next to my bed. It's creepy. Like something happened to her before she could finish carving the word into the paint.

I try to scratch it out with my thumbnail. Jesus won't save me from a week of icy-cold rooms and crazy girls muttering horrible things under their breath. "Anyone else would've gotten a demerit," I say.

"Yes, but you're special," Issie calls down. I lean onto my elbow and watch her attach a folded frog to the ceiling using tape and cinnamon-flavored dental floss. Issie loves origami, but she's only mastered the one shape. Dozens of blue and yellow frogs hang from our ceiling, bobbing just above our heads.

"You're still sleeping in here, right?" Cara shoots me a look over the top of her book. "You don't have to *stay* down there."

"No, I get to come back after. I just go down to clean."

Cara's expression doesn't change, but some of the tension leaves her shoulders. I expect her to say something else about Seg, but she just ducks back behind her book.

"You guys are forgetting that Officer Mateo guards the Seg Block." Issie flicks her latest frog, sending it spinning above her. Now her knuckles read "ham!" Her idea—apparently she's been craving it all week. "He of the bulging biceps and world's most perfect smile. I'd *kill* for that punishment."

"Apparently you just have to drop a food tray," I say. I open and close my hands, testing the burns on my fingers. The nurse gave me some lotion to rub on them, but they're still sensitive. I dig my teeth into my lower lip to keep myself from reliving that moment again.

Stupid. If that creepy little girl ever gets out of Seg I'm going to *kill* her.

"Can we be done talking about this?" Cara rolls over on her bunk, making the mattress springs creak beneath her narrow body. Our dorm room's so small that every movement echoes off the walls. "Describe this doctor person again."

She stretches on her belly across the bed, her crossed ankles leaning against the wall while she flips through a book on alien abductions. Her hair seems to have grown two sizes. Or maybe she's just decided to stop brushing it. Her mother would be furious. Cara once told me her mom used to make her chemically straighten it and brush it one hundred times every day, like some sort of black Marcia Brady.

"I don't know," I say, absently touching my own hair. It doesn't curl as nicely as Cara's, but I wear it natural anyway and keep it cropped close to my head. My mother never would have coughed up the money to straighten it. "She was tall."

Cara taps a slim finger against her alien book. *Tap. Tap. Tap.* "Like, how tall?" she asks. "Freaky tall?"

"Dr. Gruen isn't an alien," I say.

"I didn't say that," Cara mutters, flipping a page in her book with more force than necessary. Ever since I mentioned Dr. Gruen an hour ago, Cara has attacked me with a nonstop string of questions. *What was she wearing? What did she look like? What did she sound like? What did she say again?*

We don't get a lot of visitors at Brunesfield.

"She was just a person." I've described Dr. Gruen in as much detail as I can remember, from her pointed face to the tiny gold rose pinned to her suit.

"She was *fancy*," I add. That's what I really noticed. She was way too fancy for a place like Brunesfield, where the director can't even afford a new rug.

"So they want someone to watch over us?" Cara says. Issie snorts. When Cara says "they," she means the government—

people in black suits with perfect gelled hair who carry brief-cases instead of guns and can ruin your life with a few strokes of their thousand-dollar pens. Issie and I make fun of her, but I kind of get it. Cara was solidly middle-class before ending up here. She never fell asleep to the sound of gunshots, like Issie and me. She's used to people who hurt each other in different ways.

"What about the other one?" Cara adds in a quiet voice. "The girl?"

"Mary Anne," I say.

"Right. What's her deal?"

I shrug. "She didn't say much."

"I don't want to hear any more weirdo government crazi-ness," Issie grumbles. She turns over in bed, and the bunk sags above me.

Officer Mateo's voice echoes outside our door. "Lights off!"

A mechanical *click* reverberates through the hallway, and the lights go off as one. Cara makes kissy noises.

"Shut *up*," Issie says. A white flashlight beam sweeps through our door, and both girls fall quiet. Mateo's heavy boots thump past. For a long moment there's silence.

"He even looks sexy in the dark," Issie whispers.

"I just vomited in my mouth," Cara says.

"Are you two going to talk all night?" I roll over and bury my head in my pillow, trying to muffle the sound of their voices.

"I'm not tired yet," Issie says. "Tell us a story, Ang."

Cara groans. "I want to *sleep*."

"I know you like hearing them too," Issie says. "Go on, Angela. Tell it."

I've been telling Issie stories since our first night at Brunesfield, when it was just me and her in the dorm. Issie was freaked because it was her second time here, and she was convinced she was never getting out. Her brothers are all Los Niños Malos gang members. They'd never let her join, but she was born into a life of drugs and violence.

That night, I made up a story to make her feel better. I used to do it with Charlie too, when we were kids. He wanted to know why Dad left, so every night I'd tell him a new reason. Dad joined the circus. The government needed Dad for a secret mission to save the world. Dad didn't actually leave; he just turned invisible and lost his voice.

I wait for Cara to protest, but she sucks in a breath. "What story do you want to hear?" I ask.

"Tell the one about us," Issie says.

"That's not really a story," I say, tilting my head so I'm no longer talking into the pillow. It's the same story I told our first night here, but Issie never gets tired of it. "It's what's going to happen when we bust out of this place."

"How are we going to do that?" Issie asks. I hear the smile in her voice. This is part of the story too, the part where she doesn't believe me. I chew on my lower lip, trying to come up with something new.

"I was thinking we could steal a soupspoon from the kitchen," I say, my voice hushed. "And we could tunnel through the floors. That concrete in the corner near the window is all crumbling now. Wouldn't take us more than a month or two to make a hole."

"Or we could try the fences," Issie adds.

"Oh yeah. We'll go over the fences one day at rec." This is Issie's favorite way of escaping, probably because it doesn't involve any planning or waiting.

"We'll climb up the fences really quickly, right?" I continue. "And we'll just crawl over the barbed wire. I don't think it looks that sharp. The guards probably just put it up there to scare us. So we'll climb over the barbed wire, and by the time they figure out what we're doing, it'll be too late. They'll open all the security doors and shit and try to run after us, but we'll make it to the woods first."

I pause, and in the silence I hear Issie inhale.

"The woods are really deep," I say "All the guards think we'd be too scared to try and live out there, because of the wolves and wild animals."

"But the wolves in the woods aren't any worse than the wolves in here," Issie adds. It's part of the story I always tell, the part she likes the best.

"Exactly," I say. "The wolves in the woods aren't any worse than Officer Brody or Peach or Crabby Crane. We could handle them. And the best part is that the woods are big. Huge. We could get lost there."

"And no one would ever find us," Cara whispers, so quietly I almost don't hear her.

I'm the only one who knows why Cara was arrested. She whispered the story to me on a night like this, when Issie was in the infirmary with the flu.

She told me how she set the alarm on her phone for two o'clock in the morning and crept out to the garage to find a hammer. Then she snuck back inside, to where her stepdad was passed out on the couch, and she smashed both his kneecaps.

When I asked her why she'd do that, all she said was, "I wanted them to take me away."

I was supposed to tell her my story next. But I didn't. I never tell my story.

The blankets on Cara's bed rustle as she turns to face me. The moonlight outside our barred window reflects off her eyes. I never asked her why she wanted to be taken away, but it's easy to guess. Most of the girls in here have sad stories.

"Right," I tell her. "No one would ever find us."

I pause, letting the words hang in the darkness. I don't really believe we'd be able to dig through the concrete floor with a soupspoon, and Issie doesn't believe we'd survive in the woods for longer than a week before dying from hypothermia, and Cara doesn't believe there's a place in this world she could run where her problems wouldn't find her. But I think we tell the story for the same reason people pray. Because we want so badly for it to be real.

"How?" Cara says into the quiet. I'd just started to drift off, but her voice jars me awake again.

"What?" I murmur.

"How would we live out there?" Cara asks. "In the woods."

"I guess we'd have to find a cave to hide out in." My eyes flutter closed. "We could wait there until Brody and everyone stopped looking for us. And we'd have to steal a bunch of stuff from the kitchen before we left. Stuff that wouldn't go bad."

"We could steal all the frozen peas," Issie says. Cara laughs under her breath.

"Yeah," I agree. "We'll steal a bag of frozen peas, and we'll heat them over a fire."

There's a beat of silence, and then Issie sighs. "Maybe that doctor person will be good for this place. Things could get better."

"Don't count on it," Cara says. I don't say it out loud, but I agree with Cara. It would take a lot more than a volunteer program to make this place better.

The flashlight flickers into the hallway again, and the dim beam sweeps through our room. We all go quiet. I listen to the *clomp, clomp, clomp* of Mateo's boots outside our door. The flashlight illuminates our room for three seconds—just enough time for Mateo to count our heads and make sure we're all there. Then the light disappears. Mateo's footsteps echo down the hallway.

I ease my eyes back open, but I don't start the story again. Instead I imagine what it would be like. Hiding out in a cave in the snow while the Brunesfield guards searched for us. Heating frozen peas over a fire. Listening to the wind howl just outside. Never, ever going home.

My eyes droop. I hear tree branches scratch at the narrow window near our ceiling, but that's impossible. The trees are miles away. Their branches don't reach this far.

This thought circles through my head as sleep pulls me under. I dream of trees tiptoeing through the snow and wolves circling the woods and helicopter propellers beating against the sky. We're running away, but I hear the Brunesfield guards crashing through the woods behind us. They're going to catch us. Of course they're going catch us.

But at least we got to feel the wind in our hair. The snow crunching beneath our feet. For a little while, we were free.

Officer Crane shows up after breakfast the next morning. "Miss Davis," she says in a voice of steel. She stops at the door to the kitchen and folds her arms behind her back, a soldier coming to attention. Her glass eye stares at the wall behind me, like it sees something I don't.

"Whoa," Issie says. "You look totally FBI."

I frown, staring at Crane's outfit. The guards usually wear a polo and khakis—like camp counselors. But today Crane's dressed in a button-down and black slacks. The silver patch attached to her shoulder reads "Brunesfield."

"New uniforms?" Cara asks. Officer Crane gives her a curt nod, her eye still on me.

"I'm to take you to the Segregation Block," she says. "Diamond on your back, please."

I drop the sponge I'd been using to scrub the breakfast dishes and put my arms behind my back to make a diamond with my hands. Crane absently touches her scar with her thumb as she tucks a gray lock of hair behind one ear. I wonder if she's thinking of the girl who attacked her.

"Say hi to my boyfriend for me," Issie whispers as I shuffle past. I give her a quick thumbs-up behind my back, then make a diamond again before stepping into the hallway.

We're not allowed to talk while our hands are in diamonds, so I keep my mouth shut as we make our way to the basement. Brunesfield looms around us. It strikes me that no one, at any point, tried to make this place pretty, or even pleasant. Clumpy paint covers the walls. It's so cheap that it dusts your hands with white and comes right off when you drag a fingernail over it. Girls have chipped things into the paint over the years. Mostly just their names: Katie, Kendra, Lucy, Jane. Like they don't want this place to forget them. I stare at the names now, and I'm hit with an eerie feeling that Brunesfield swallowed these girls whole.

"Down the stairs," Crane says when we reach the stairwell. The stairs aren't steep, but climbing down without holding the handrail feels strange, like I might fall onto my face at any second. I concentrate on keeping my fingers together behind my back and take the steps one at a time. If Crane's annoyed that I'm going too slow, she doesn't mention it.

The hall leading to the Segregation Block twists off to the right, into the darkest part of the basement. No one's scratched their names into the wall down here. Probably they were too scared. These walls might scratch back.

As we get closer, I swear I hear the prisoners in the Seg Block mumbling, but that's impossible. There's still a thick steel door separating them from me.

"Officer Mateo," Crane says when we reach Mateo's post. "I have Miss Davis reporting for her probationary duties."

Officer Crane's always so official when she talks. It makes me feel like I should curtsy or something. I shuffle up next to her, nodding at Mateo since my hands are in diamonds—I'm not allowed to say anything. He's wearing the same fancy new slacks and shirt as Officer Crane, but on him they look, well, *good*. I memorize every detail to share with Issie when I get back.

"At ease, soldier." Mateo climbs down from his metal stool, setting his crossword on the seat. "Seriously, Jackie, she doesn't have to have her hands behind her back. I can handle her."

I blink, then turn to Officer Crane. *Jackie*? Crabby Crane's first name is Jackie?

"That's highly inappropriate," Crane says to Mateo. A vein throbs in her temple, and I *swear to God I see her blush*. I press my lips together to keep from grinning like an idiot. I didn't even realize Crane *had* a first name. She seems like one of those people who've only ever been called "Mrs." or "Officer" or "Ma'am."

"Oops. Sorry, *Officer* Crane," Mateo says, flashing her a smile that shows off approximately six hundred perfectly straight white teeth. "But I can handle this one. You're free to head back."

"Very well," Officer Crane says. She pauses halfway to the stairs and looks over her shoulder. "*Ben.*"

I don't know whether to be more in awe of the fact that Crabby Crane made an actual joke, or that Officer Mateo's first name is *Ben*, which is adorable. Issie's going to completely freak when I tell her. I smile so wide my cheeks hurt. Best punishment ever.

"So. The director mentioned you were supposed to be on cleaning duty," Mateo says, nodding at the thick steel door to the Segregation Block. The smile slips from my face.

"Yeah," I say.

"Don't look so thrilled." Mateo jabs his thumb into the red button that unlocks the door, and a loud buzz echoes down the hall. "The girls in Segregation aren't allowed out of their dorms, so the actual hall doesn't get too dirty," he explains.

I nod, trying to ignore the anxiety rising in my chest as I shuffle forward and push the heavy security door open. The burn on my hand tingles, reminding me of what happened the last time I was here.

The hall looks the same: Pepto-Bismol-colored walls, gray light slanting in from the windows at the ceiling. It's snowing again. I wait for the radiator at the end of the hall to explode in a shower of sparks, or for the hall itself to kaleidoscope into a new shape. But nothing happens. Thick fluffy flakes drift past the windows, sending shadows across the dimly lit floor. It's almost peaceful.

Someone left a mop and bucket leaning against the pink wall just inside the doorway. I reach for the mop, then flinch at the sound of metal dragging across the concrete behind me. I spin around and see Mateo pulling his stool into the hallway. The security door thuds closed behind him.

"What are you doing?" I ask.

Mateo settles himself on the stool, smoothing the crossword on his lap. He lifts his eyes without moving his face.

"I'm guarding."

"No, what are you doing in here?" I motion to the hall around me. "Don't you have to stand outside the door?"

"Ah." Mateo folds the crossword puzzle and nods, like I've asked him a real stumper. "Yes, technically I'm required to stand outside the door at all times. But, unlike Officer Brody, I don't feel comfortable being on the other side of a security door when you're in here. Some of these girls are dangerous."

I know I should just shut up and count my blessings—I don't want to be in here alone either—but my mouth likes to do this thing where it blurts out whatever I'm thinking without actually consulting me first.

"You could get in trouble," I say.

"Are you going to tell on me?"

"No." I pull the mop out of the bucket and slop it on the floor. Brown suds spread across the concrete and soak the paper-thin soles of my shoes. The burns on my fingers still feel tender, making it uncomfortable to hold the mop. I grimace and try to shift so I'm holding the mop without closing my hand, but it's impossible for me to push it down the hall that way. Guess I'll just have to grin and bear it.

I nod at one of the bulky black cameras staring down from the ceiling. "What about that?"

"Doesn't work." Mateo hops off his stool and walks down the hall, stopping directly in front of the camera. "It's illegal to videotape minors' private quarters without parental consent. The camera at the end of the hall is the only one recording."

He waves at the camera and makes a face to prove it to me, but I'm not paying attention to him anymore. I turn, quickly finding the camera at the end of the hall. A tiny, red light blinks near its lens.

"That faces Jessica's cell," I say. Mateo stops waving.

"Yeah," he says. "She's a ward of the state so they don't need consent, I guess. Some guys came to fix it this morning. That little light's been blinking ever since, so someone must be watching."

I frown. I told Director Wu and Dr. Gruen about my little accident with the tray last night. They fixed the camera this morning. That's weird, right? That they're watching her?

A chill starts in my lower back and crawls up my spine. I shrug to shake it away. I'm letting the Seg Block creep me out. They probably just want to make sure Jessica doesn't hurt herself or refuse to eat or make a knife out of a toothbrush. There's nothing weird about that.

I push the mop down the hall, leaving a shiny, wet path along the concrete. I'm so focused on the blinking red light that I don't notice the skeletally thin girl in the cell to my left until she skitters across the floor on her hands and knees.

"Pretty," she says, pushing her face against the glass wall. I flinch, and the mop slips from my fingers and falls to the concrete. A girl in the cell behind me claps, and I jump.

"Pretty, pretty, pretty," the thin girl whispers, tracing invisible lines on the glass. Raw, angry scratches cut across her cheeks. She presses her face against the door, leaving behind lines of blood.

"Play nice, Bea." Mateo is right behind me. I flinch again, nearly hitting him in the face with my arm as I flail around. Great. Five minutes in the Seg Block and I've turned into one of those jumpy nervous girls that I hate.

"Bea?" I try to make it look like I wasn't so much flinching as leaning over to pick up my mop. "Is that her name?"

"Yeah," Mateo says. He kneels in front of her door and pulls something from his pocket: a crumpled, half-full bag of M&M'S. He pours a few onto her food tray and lifts the flap.

"Before you ask, this is also against the rules," he says. "But the sugar helps her stay calm."

Bea shoves all the candy into her mouth at once and appears to swallow it whole. She keeps her cloudy eyes trained on me and strokes the glass door like it's a cat.

"Do you want to know the rest of their names?" Mateo asks, nodding down the hall.

"You know them?"

"Yeah," Mateo says. "I made myself learn when I first started. If you don't know their names it gets too easy to think they're just these crazy, scary people."

My cheeks flush. That's exactly how I'd been thinking of them. I clear my throat. "Um, sure. Tell me their names."

Behind us, Bea starts singing a slow, lilting song and tracing her finger along the glass. Mateo follows a few steps behind as I push my mop down the hall. He stops in front of every dorm and formally introduces me. Angela, meet Katie. Angela, meet Lauren. They all have such normal, girlie names. Sarah and Emily and Claire. They're the names of girls who get asked to dances and apply to college. It doesn't seem fair that they ended up here.

"Are they dangerous?" I ask. We've somehow reached the second-to-last dorm. The one right next to Jessica's. I glance down the hallway behind me, wondering how we reached the end so quickly. It seems like there are hundreds of dorms behind us. We couldn't have stopped at every one.

"Yeah," Mateo says, crumpling the now empty M&M'S bag in his fist. "Some of them are very dangerous. We're the only center in the county that has the budget for counseling, so we get all the girls who need psychiatric care."

I dunk my mop in the bucket, trying to ignore the pain still burning my fingers. Something flickers at the corner of my eye. I turn, and—*bang!*

The girl in the dorm next to me throws herself at the glass wall. "Boo!" she shouts.

I lurch backward. My knee buckles. I try to put my hands out to catch my fall, but I'm not fast enough. My elbows slam into the concrete and pain shoots up my arms. Black spots cloud my vision.

I blink a couple of times, and when the black clears, I see Jessica huddled in a ball on her mattress in the cell in front of me. She uncurls her arms and stands.

She looks so normal now. No black eyes, no humming and shaking. She's separated her thick black hair into two braids, but she must not have a ponytail holder to tie off the ends, because they stick out from her head at odd angles, making her look like she has antennae.

She touches the glass door with her fingertips. "Are you okay?" she whispers.

Emotion ripples through me. Fear first, then curiosity. Pity. Without thinking, I lift my arm and stretch my fingers toward the glass. Jessica's eyes crinkle at the corners, like she might smile—

Then Mateo wraps his arms around my torso and drags me across the floor until I'm no longer in Jessica's line of vision. I try to pull my feet beneath me so I can stand, but this throws us both off and we fall backward together, landing in a puddle of soapy water.

"What the hell?" I'm lying against Mateo's chest, so close that I feel his heart beating against me. I quickly push myself away from him, cringing at the water seeping through the seat of my pants.

Mateo clears his throat and pushes himself back to his feet. "Sorry," he says. His cheeks burn red. "God, I'm sorry. Are you okay?"

"Peachy," I say. Mateo looks like he's about to offer his hand to help me up, but then his blush deepens and he pretends he was just brushing something off his pants. He averts his eyes as I stand. I glance down at myself.

Water plasters my thin cotton scrubs to my skin, highlighting every—and I do mean *every*—curve of my fairly curvy body. I groan and try to pull the cloth away from my skin.

This. Is just. Great.

"You're okay, right?" Mateo asks. "I didn't hurt you or anything?"

"No," I say, glancing up at him. He's blushing so hard that the tips of his ears are red and he appears very interested in a speck of dust on his shoe. "So, what was that about?"

"I'm sorry," he says again. "I overreacted. It's just that some strange things have been happening around that girl's cell."

My fingers sting when I remember my burn. "What kind of strange?"

"Let's just say that you weren't the first person to run screaming down the hall after coming here."

He glances up at me, then immediately looks at the floor. "You, um, should probably go get changed," he says. "I'll call Crane to walk you back to your dorm."

He clears his throat and makes his way down the hall to the metal stool sitting near the security door. I follow, but I can't help casting one last glance at Jessica's cell.

She's pressed against the glass door. Watching us.

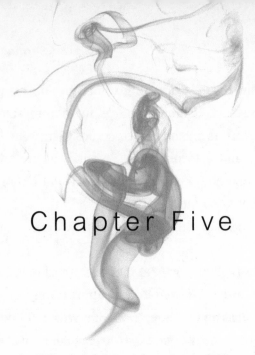

Chapter Five

I head to the library during free period that afternoon. My morning in the Seg Block has put me in a strange, jittery mood. I take the steps to the basement two at a time, going so fast that I don't notice Officer Sterling standing around the corner. Her entire body tenses when she sees me coming.

"Davis, *walk*," she barks, and I skid to a stop. She grips the nightstick at her belt so tightly her knuckles turn white. The mole stares out at me from her forehead.

"Jeez, sorry," I mutter. Sometimes I forget how freaked we make all the new guards. It's like they think one of us is going to start a riot or burn the place down.

Officer Sterling loosens her grip on the nightstick. "That's a demerit. I see you running again and you're getting a visit to Wu's office," she says.

"For *running*?" I try and fail to keep the shock from my voice. I thought Brody was being an asshole for dragging me into Wu's office after the thing with the tray, but this is insane. "No one gets a demerit for running."

Officer Sterling straightens her new uniform. "Things change," she says.

"Apparently," I add. Then, just to be obnoxious, I walk to the end of the hall so slowly my muscles burn.

I nod at Issie when I round the corner to the pay phone. A line of annoyed girls twists down the hall behind her. Aaliyah releases an exaggerated sigh and pretends to study her cuticles. Peach shoots a green rubber bracelet at her back.

"Hey, Angela." Issie tucks the receiver beneath her chin. Aaliyah gives her a dirty look. "You say hi to my boyfriend this morning?"

"Oh yeah," I say. "We talked about you the whole time."

"Hurry up, bitch!" Peach yells. Issie flips her off over her shoulder. An angry-sounding voice echoes from the receiver.

"*Un momento, Mamá!*" Issie says into the phone. I start down the hall, but Issie grabs my arm. "Where you going?"

"Library."

"Issie, come *on*," Aaliyah says.

Issie rolls her eyes. "*Chill*, girl. You don't have nowhere to be."

"Catch you later, Is," I say. Aaliyah shouts something in Spanish and she and Issie start arguing. I hurry down the stairs to the library before it gets out of hand. I can't afford to get in another fight.

Calling the dank basement room a library is borderline delusional. Air ducts twist across the walls, and pipes hiss in the corners. The ceiling's collapsing. There are areas where it droops so low that I have to crouch to keep from smacking my head against moldy plaster. And then there's the heat. The radiator down here hasn't worked in years, but the temperature still manages to creep past eighty-five degrees. Two industrial fans whir in the corners, making the books' pages flutter.

Ellen crouches over the rickety desk in the corner, cooing at something in the top drawer. I cringe, trying not to think about the mouse's tiny pink hands and twitchy nose.

"Hey," I call. Ellen's head snaps up. She slams the drawer shut.

"Oh. Hi, Angie. You checking something out?"

"Maybe." Metal carts stacked high with books line the room. I run my hands over their broken spines as I walk past. Cara used to read them out loud to me, but her throat gets scratchy when she talks for too long, so she doesn't offer anymore. I tried reading one myself. I only got twenty pages in before I threw it across the room in frustration.

"Anything new this week?" I ask. We sometimes get donations from church groups and thrift stores, but Ellen's not always good about unloading the boxes right away.

She shakes her head. "Not since before Christmas. Hey, Carla said you're cleaning the Seg Block. That true?"

I don't think I know who Carla is, but Ellen's in for destruction of property, so Carla's probably another vandalism freak.

I try to picture her, but I can't. I don't even know if she's black or white. "Just for a week," I say.

Ellen shudders. "That place is *creepy*. They make me take the library cart through once a month, and I swear the shadows *whisper* to me." Her eyes widen and she nods solemnly, like we're sharing a secret.

"It's probably one of the Seg girls," I say. "They say things when you walk past their rooms."

"No." Ellen shakes her head. "It's the *shadows*."

I offer a weak smile. Something squeaks inside the desk. Ellen flinches and turns her attention back to her mouse. I think of what Mateo said, about how we're the only center in the area with money for counseling.

Clearly we need more.

I make my way to the folding table in the back of the room, where we keep all six audiobooks that the library owns. A girl huddles in the corner behind the table, giving herself a homemade tattoo with a ballpoint pen. Blood winds around her wrist, and stringy hair hangs over her forehead, hiding her face.

She looks up when I approach. "Badass, right?" she says, showing me her arm. It says "satin" across her wrist in crooked blue letters. The skin below is red and inflamed.

"Looks infected," I say. "And you spell 'Satan' with two *a*'s." I'm dyslexic and even *I* know that.

"Fuck off," the girl mutters, bending back over her arm. I cringe and turn around so I don't have to watch.

Sweat trickles down my back as I flip through the audiobooks. I've listened to them all at least five times, but a book I've heard before is still better than no book at all.

"There you are," someone calls from behind me. I turn as Cara gallops down the stairs. "Mail call!" she says, waving two envelopes.

My heart flip-flops inside my chest. "Charlie?"

"Yup." Cara holds out a white envelope covered in Charlie's familiar, clumsy handwriting. "And one from someone called Patricia Parks. Who's that?"

I freeze halfway through ripping open Charlie's envelope. My mother's handwriting stares up from the envelope clutched in Cara's fingers. *Patricia Parks.*

She was always Patricia to me. She never wanted to be called Mom, especially in public. I take the letter from Cara and shove it into the back pocket of my scrubs without looking at it. I already know what it's going to say. Then, before Cara can ask about Patricia again, I tear Charlie's envelope open and tug out the sheet of notebook paper inside. I unfold it, carefully.

A silly drawing takes up most of the page. Charlie always illustrates his letters to me, knowing that the words can be hard for me to read. In this one, two stick-figure dinosaurs eat waffles in a diner. The smaller dinosaur (a stegosaurus with tiny triangles for scales) has ten candles in his waffle. His eyes are shut to make a wish, and Charlie drew wiggly breath lines coming out of his mouth to blow out the candles.

I run a finger along Charlie's messy waffle sketch and wait for the familiar prick in the corner of my eye. This was our birthday ritual. Every year, I'd wake Charlie up an hour before school and take him to get waffles at Neptune, the diner down the street. Last year was the first time I ever missed it. His birthday's at the end of March, and I thought for sure I'd be out in time to take him—I *promised* I would be. But, once again, I messed up.

If I were ever going to cry about anything it'd be this, but instead I just feel a kind of dull, familiar disgust with myself. After years of failing to live up to people's expectations you get really used to the crushing guilt that comes with screwing up. Again. My little brother is the one person in my life who still believes me when I make a promise. Or, he used to be.

"Did you want me to read it?" Cara asks. I move my eyes from Charlie's sketch to the loopy, childish handwriting below.

"Later," I say. I fold the letter and shove it into my pocket with the envelope from my mother. Cara frowns, studying my face.

"They're delaying your release, aren't they?" she says finally. "You aren't getting out in March anymore."

I try to keep my voice casual. "Nothing's final."

"All because of a stupid tray?"

"All because of stupid Grody," I say, but I don't elaborate. Cara has a misguided sense of loyalty. It'd be just like her to start something with Brody as payback for what he's doing to me.

I clear my throat. "Did you find a book you want?"

Cara had been shuffling through a rack of oversize non-fiction books. She holds up an ancient hardcover with a photograph of something large and hairy on the cover.

"I don't think I want to know what that is," I say. I grab the first audiobook I can reach off the folding table—*Tuck Everlasting*, which I've heard eight times—and follow Cara to Ellen's desk to log our books in the spiral-bound notebook she uses to keep track of who has what. A stack of glossy brochures sits next to the notebook. I pick one up, staring at the photograph of a teenage girl with a chemistry set.

"Where'd these come from?" I ask, flipping the brochure over.

"That doctor," Ellen says. "The tall, pretty one."

"Dr. Gruen?"

"Yeah. She's really nice. She said I should go to veterinary school. And she gave me this." Ellen flashes her wrist. She's wearing a bright green rubber bracelet with the word "SciGirls" written across it.

"What's SciGirls?" Cara asks.

"It's a club where you do all these science experiments and things," Ellen says. "Dr. Gruen's here to recruit new members, but it's really hard to get in. You have to take a test. I think there are more bracelets. Wait here." Ellen scurries back to the storage room before Cara or I can stop her. Her desk drawer squeaks.

"We're leaving." I grab Cara's arm and steer her toward the door. Cara takes a brochure and shoves it into her book.

"You want to join SciGirls?" I ask, raising an eyebrow.

"I want to search their brochure for secret government messages," Cara says, flipping her book open. "Did you know there was this creature thing living in the woods around upstate New York for a while and the government covered it up and—"

Peach comes out of nowhere and throws her elbow into Cara's gut. Cara doubles over, and her book hits the floor.

"Told you to watch your back, *bitch*," Peach snaps.

I hurry to Cara's side, glancing at the library door as I crouch next to her. Officer Sterling won't be able to see inside from her place out in the hall, but she'll definitely investigate if she hears yelling. She was going to send me to Director Wu's for running. Who knows what'll happen if I'm caught fighting?

I look back at Peach, trying to find any sympathy in her angry, twisted face. "Not now," I say.

"Not now?" Peach says. "Funny, I don't remember you asking me if it was a good time when you threw a basketball at my face."

"*I* threw the basketball at your face, bitch," Cara says. She picks up her book and jumps to her feet. Peach pulls back her arm to slap her, but Cara's faster. She whips the book across Peach's face, and Peach staggers backward, gasping.

One thing I'll say about all those nutsy conspiracy-theory books Cara reads—they're *heavy*.

Cara starts to swing the book again, but Peach spits in her face and Cara hesitates for a fraction of a second. Peach darts forward, raking her nails across Cara's cheek. She leaves behind three thin red lines on Cara's otherwise smooth brown skin.

A low buzzing starts in the back of my head. I'm not the kind of girl who sits out from a fight, especially when my friends are involved. I act without thinking. I grab Peach by the shoulders and slam her against the wall like a rag doll. Peach is mean, but she's skinny and she mostly fights like a little girl.

"You want to take both of us on?" I grab her arm and curl my hand into a fist. I *don't* fight like a little girl.

Peach looks at my fist. To my surprise, she starts to giggle.

"You want me to scream, Angie?" she says. Blood oozes out of the cut Cara made when she hit Peach with the book. A tiny trickle dribbles onto her lip.

"What are you talking about?" My anger has started to cool, leaving me all too aware of what I'm doing. Peach stares at me, her eyes hard and cruel. I look at the door— still no Sterling. I could stop this right now. Just walk away. But Peach doesn't look like she's about to let up. And there's no way I'm leaving Cara here alone.

"You think I haven't heard you all talking?" Peach says. "You can't get into any more trouble, or you won't get released when you're supposed to." She slides her eyes to the door, and her bloody grin widens. "I could start screaming right now. Get Sterling in here to see what's going on. Is helping your little girlfriend really worth that?"

"No one's going to scream," Cara says in a calm, even voice. Nerves crawl over my skin. I drop Peach's arm and turn.

Cara holds a tiny silver knife close to her body. It's not some-thing she fashioned out of a toothbrush—it's an honest-to-god pocketknife, the blade glinting under the fluorescent lights. I stare at it for a beat, almost expecting it to fade away, like a hallucination. But it doesn't go anywhere. It's real.

"What the hell?" I whisper. Possession of a weapon—any weapon—isn't something they take lightly in here. Carrying a knife could get you sent to real prison.

"Peach is going to walk, quietly, back into the hallway and leave us both alone," Cara says. She turns the knife so its blade catches the light. "Understood?"

Peach rips her arm away from me, but her eyes stay locked on the blade. She glances from me to Cara.

"Watch yourself," she says, before ducking back into the hallway.

As soon as Peach is gone, Cara tucks the knife back into the waistband of her uniform. Her hands tremble.

"Cara," I start, but I don't know what to say to her.

"You didn't see anything." Cara heads for the library door, but I grab her arm before she reaches it.

"What are you doing with that?" I ask. "Do you know what could—"

"The words you're looking for are 'thank you,'" Cara snaps. I stare at her for a beat, too shocked to speak. Cara's smarter than this. She reads more than anyone I've ever met. She's the one always telling *me* to keep out of trouble.

She stares at me for a moment, and her expression softens. "Look, I need it, okay?" She pulls away from me and straightens her shirt so you can't see the bulge at her waist. "Don't worry about me."

And, without another word, she slips into the hall.

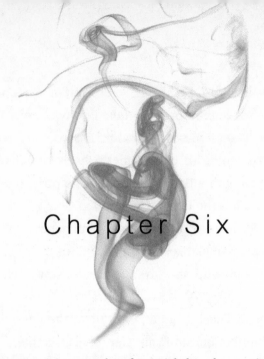

Chapter Six

By the next morning, stacks of SciGirls brochures sit on tables outside Director Wu's door and in the corner of the cafeteria. I hear rumors that a few girls have been called into the new doctor's office to discuss "enrichment opportunities." Whatever that means. And everyone's wearing a green rubber bracelet. Issie has *five*.

I asked her where she got them, but she just shrugged and said, "Around."

On top of that, someone replaced the lightbulbs. Maybe it's dumb, but I've been here for eighteen months and I've almost gotten used to the way the lights in the hallways buzzed and flickered and switched off randomly, like they were being controlled by a team of vindictive ghosts. Now they gleam from the ceilings, steadily illuminating grungy corners that probably would have been better left in shadow.

"I'm telling you, she's some kind of FBI spy," Cara says, jabbing her pointy elbow into my side while we're serving breakfast. "That assistant girl too. They've probably been sent here to check out the criminal element of the future."

I groan and pluck two waffles off the stack with my tongs. They taste like cardboard, but we get actual *butter* to put on top of them, and maple syrup that doesn't taste like maple but is still thick and sweeter than anything else we get inside. It's hard to screw up anything drenched in butter and sugar. Even here.

"No one works for the FBI. Jesus," I say. I drop the waffles on a tray and slide it over to Issie for butter and silverware. "I just don't understand why they're spending so much money on this place all of a sudden."

Cara stirs a giant vat of syrup. "Maybe they want everything in good working condition so they can perform *experiments* on us."

I throw a pat of butter at her, but she dodges it.

"Hey, conspiracy girls, can I get a little help here?" Issie barks, nodding at the line of girls winding away from our counter. Usually it's easy to move them through the breakfast line, but today they mill around our counter like cats. I grab another tray and start to pile it with waffles.

"Come on, Angela, talk. What's up with the new inmate?" Aaliyah asks, raising a black, pencil-drawn eyebrow that doesn't match her bleached-blond hair. Word got out about my punishment in the Seg Block, and now every girl in Brunesfield wants to know what I think of Jessica.

"Don't know, don't care," I say, handing Aaliyah her tray so roughly that one of the waffles slides around the aluminum, nearly falling off.

Aaliyah frowns. "Watch it," she says, nudging the waffle back onto her tray with her thumb. A rubber SciGirls bracelet dangles from her wrist.

"Sorry," I say. I have no excuse for being mean to Aaliyah. Usually the most offensive thing she does is sing old Mariah Carey songs in the shower and doodle kittens on her homework assignments.

"Come *on*." She leans forward and her scrubs top droops down, displaying the oatmeal-colored, juvie-issued tank top she wears beneath. "You *have* to know something. Why is she in Seg anyway? She crazy?"

I shrug and grab another girl's tray.

"Whoever she is, she's *freaky*," a girl named Tyra says. She's short and skinny, with choppy black hair. "I had to bring her breakfast this morning, right? I get up next to her cell and the damn lightbulb *explodes*. Glass flew everywhere."

She thrusts her arm out, displaying fresh nicks on her wrists. Deep, twisted scars crisscross the skin below them. I glance at her arm, trying not to grimace. Everyone knows Tyra has a thing for knives. I wonder what she found to cut herself with in here.

"They had to *move* the girl in the dorm next to her, you know," a girl named March adds, winding her thick ponytail between her fingers. "She kept getting these weird-ass rashes."

"Rashes?" I say, before I can stop myself. "Are you sure they weren't burns?"

March gives me a strange look. "Ew," she says, wrinkling her nose. "Didn't ask for details, thanks."

I press my fingers together. The burns have just started to heal and, as far as anyone else is concerned, I got them from picking up a metal pan that someone left on a burner. I slap two waffles and a pat of butter onto the tray in front of me and hand it to the next girl in line. Aaliyah doesn't move.

"I heard she got locked up for murder." She lowers her voice even though, by now, every girl behind her is leaning closer, listening. Aaliyah drops her voice even further, almost whispering. "She found her daddy's gun, you know? And . . . *bam!*"

Aaliyah slaps her palm against the counter and Issie jumps, dropping a waffle on the floor. Cara snickers.

"She killed her whole family in the same night," Aaliyah finishes with a shrug. "No one knows why. That's why she's in Seg."

"Bullshit." Peach grabs the tray of waffles out of my hands and shoulders past Aaliyah in line. "I heard she was involved in a drug ring that sold crack to elementary-school kids."

"That's so dumb," Cara says. She shakes her head, making her frizzy curls bob around her ears.

Peach scowls. "You say something to me, slut?" she snaps.

Cara leans forward, syrup ladle in hand. Looking her right in the eye, she dumps the syrup on the floor next to Peach's feet.

"*Oops*," she says.

"Bitch." Peach frowns at the syrup puddle and runs a hand over her peach-fuzz hair. "I'm telling Brody you did that."

She deliberately steps in the syrup and smears it across the tile as she walks to her table.

"You do that," Cara shouts after her. "I'll be eating my waffles."

They've been like this since yesterday. Peach hasn't ambushed us again, but every time she walks past she makes a face or says something mean. She won't rat us out, though. Juvie girls don't tattle. She'd rather wait and find a way to fight back.

I cringe at that thought and plop a waffle onto someone's tray. "Brody's going to make us clean that up."

Cara shrugs and dumps another glob of syrup onto a waffle. We haven't spoken about the knife since the fight in the library. We haven't had a minute alone, and I'm afraid to bring it up in front of other people—even Issie. Every single person who learns about that knife puts Cara in danger.

Cara catches my eye, staring just long enough to make me shift and look away. I swear to God, when I first met her I thought she was psychic. She has this way of looking at people. It's like she can see through their skin to the tender, painful secrets they're trying to hide.

I hand another girl a tray of waffles. Erin, I think her name is. She's wearing two green bracelets, one on each wrist. "Are people really signing up for this SciGirls thing?" I ask, nodding at the bracelets.

"Nah. They're just stealing the bracelets," Issie says, dropping a pat of butter on the tray. "It's like a nerd club. All you do is look into microscopes and shit."

"Didn't you hear? It's kind of competitive," Erin cuts in. She yanks at her bracelet, pulling it farther up her arm. "They only take a couple of girls. It's, like, a really big deal to be chosen."

Issie raises an eyebrow. "Really?"

"Angela?"

I look over my shoulder to see who said my name. Officer Mateo leans against the kitchen door. His lazy smile is more of a smirk right now, and his eyes look droopy, like he just woke up.

"Hi!" I say, brightening.

"I thought you didn't work until ten on Tuesdays?" Issie says. She has Mateo's schedule memorized.

Mateo stifles a yawn. "Traded shifts with Brody."

"Another hockey game?" Issie clamps her tongs around a waffle and drops it onto a tray. Last week Mateo worked an early shift so he could watch the Flyers game that night. That's all the information Issie needed. Since then she's gone crazy into research mode, using her measly twenty minutes of computer time a day to research players and teams.

"Flyers are playing the Rangers tonight," Mateo says, grin widening. "New York's going *down*."

"No way," Issie says. "Lundqvist is gonna score on some Flyer ass."

Pathetic, Cara mouths at me. I snicker, but I'm honestly wishing I'd taken a look at some of Issie's notes. She pronounces Lundqvist's name perfectly. She must've found a video that wasn't blocked.

"We'll see," Mateo says, running a hand over his hair. He must not have had time to style it, because it flops over his forehead in messy waves instead of swooping away from his face like it usually does. "Miss Davis, do you have a second? Dr. Gruen needs to see you."

It takes me a little too long to stop staring at Mateo's hair. I blink.

"Did she say why?" I ask. Mateo frowns at me, then pushes the hair off his forehead. My cheeks grow hot, and I shift my eyes back to the tray of waffles. *Stop staring at his hair, you freak.*

"No," he says. "But she's been seeing girls for the past two days, so I don't think you're in any trouble."

I shrug off my apron. It must be time to learn about my own enrichment opportunities. Maybe I'll even get a green SciGirls bracelet.

Cara looks up from the pot of syrup she's stirring and raises an eyebrow.

"Chill," I say under my breath. "Dr. Gruen isn't an alien. She doesn't work for the FBI, and I doubt she's trying to take over the world."

"If you say so," she says. Issie hums the *Doctor Who* theme song. A few of the girls still waiting in the food line catcall as I follow Mateo into the empty hallway, but he pretends not to notice. That easy smile slides onto his face again.

"You all have way too much energy this early in the morning," he says, yawning.

Wind pushes against the windows, making the glass creak. I see movement from the corner of my eye and flinch, spinning around. A cockroach skitters across the wall and disappears into a crack in the concrete. The cassette tucked into my waistband jiggles loose and slips down my leg.

"Oh crap," I mutter, shaking my leg to knock the tape loose. *Tuck Everlasting* clatters to the floor.

"What's this?" Mateo stops and picks up the cracked plastic case. "Is this a cassette tape?"

"Yeah," I say. "Old-school, right? Brunesfield has yet to discover the digital revolution."

"I didn't even know they made these anymore." He turns the cassette over in his hand, studying the picture of the girl in the pink dress on the cover. "It looks like a kids' book."

"It is. My class read it in seventh grade." I'd been planning to pop it into the ancient cassette player in the kitchen while washing the dishes after breakfast. "Or, we were supposed to."

Mateo averts his eyes while I lift my shirt and slip the cassette back in place.

"Why listen to it on tape?" he asks. "Can't you . . . I mean do you know how . . ."

"I know how to read," I say to put him out of his misery. "It's just not easy for me. If I listen to the book on tape I can actually enjoy the story."

"So why bother with books at all?" he asks. "Why not watch a movie or something?"

I glance up at Mateo, and for the first time I'm not looking at his thick hair or smile or the outline of his arms beneath his uniform. Instead I try to imagine him the way he was just a couple of years ago, a teenager at some crappy public school in upstate New York. I wonder if he knows what it's like to be stupid, or to think you're stupid because you can't keep the letters on a page from jumping around in your head.

The corner of Mateo's mouth curls, and I know he wants to smile to defuse the tension. But he doesn't. Instead he clears his throat and presses his lips together, waiting for me to answer.

"You know we're not allowed to have TVs in our dorms," I say, finally. The smile unfolds across Mateo's face. He shakes his head.

"Ah, right. I guess I can't help you there," he says, stopping in front of a thick door. "Here we are."

"Thanks," I say. Mateo nods and starts back down the hall. After a few steps he pauses and turns back around.

"Just so you know, Lundqvist is the goalie," he says.

I blink, confused.

"What?"

"Your friend said 'Lundqvist is gonna score on some Flyer ass.' But goalies don't score." Mateo kicks that smile up a few watts, and a lock of hair falls across his forehead.

"Right," I say, making a mental note to pass that on to Issie later. I push open the door and step into Dr. Gruen's office.

The room looks nothing like Director Wu's. Dr. Gruen's black desk is small and efficient, its surface so shiny I wonder how she works without her papers sliding off. Two equally shiny leather chairs stand guard before the desk, and a floor lamp bathes the room in soft golden light. The air is several degrees warmer than in the hallway, but I don't see a space heater.

Mary Anne stands in the corner, studying a thick black binder like she might be tested on it later. She glances up when I walk in and flashes me a shy smile.

"Angela, please come in," Dr. Gruen says. She sits behind the desk, her hands folded in front of her. She's wearing a different black suit. This one has wide lapels that taper into sharp points of fabric. The same gold rose is pinned to her jacket.

"Okay," I say, suddenly nervous. I didn't notice how beautiful she was before. Director Wu's office has a way of making everyone look shabby and tired but here, in her element, Dr. Gruen's pointed nose and thin face look elegant. Regal, even. She looks like a queen.

I ease into a leather chair. A steel bookcase fills the wall behind her head. It holds only a few books, all artfully arranged by color and height, and a strange twisted sculpture that looks like a burned tree branch. I wrinkle my nose. I *really* don't get art.

Framed photographs take up the rest of the shelves. I lean forward in my chair to examine them. The Dr. Gruen in the pictures looks different from the one in front of me, but just as easily elegant. Instead of a black suit, she wears khaki pants and a white lab coat, and a thick black headband holds back her blond hair. In one photograph she crouches in the middle of a group of girls wearing safety goggles and wide smiles. In another she stands next to a girl peering through a microscope.

Dr. Gruen pivots in her seat, following my gaze to the photographs behind her. Her movements are easy, graceful. Almost like a dance. "Are you interested in science, Miss Davis?"

I blink. Literally no one in my entire life has ever asked me a question like that before. It would be like asking a fish if it was interested in playing soccer.

"Um, sure," I say. Dr. Gruen nods, and Mary Anne leans forward, handing me a glossy brochure exactly like the ones I saw in the library.

"SciGirls is always on the lookout for young women like you," Dr. Gruen continues. "In fact, those photographs are from my work with a local chapter that was doing research on the common cold."

I study the photograph on the brochure cover. Girls holding lab equipment grin at the camera. They all look like Mary Anne: shiny college hair and very straight, very white teeth.

I shift in my chair. I feel almost exactly like I do when I'm struggling to read a book: I understand all the words Dr. Gruen's saying, but they don't add up to anything in my head. Why is she talking to me about science? Erin said this SciGirls program is competitive. They aren't going to want some juvie girl.

"It also looks really good on a college application," Mary Anne adds. Her voice is quiet and higher than I expected it to be. She fumbles with the broccoli charm on her bracelet. "If you're into that kind of thing."

"Mary Anne has been a member of SciGirls for more than a year. She was just recently promoted to my assistant, actually. We consider her something of an expert on the program," Dr. Gruen explains. She studies me, a soft smile parting her lips. "I could see you there. You have the look of a leader."

My cheeks flame. I never learned how to take a compliment. "Is this why you called me in here?" I ask, nodding at the brochure.

Dr. Gruen leans back in her chair. "Actually," she says, "I have another job I thought you might be interested in."

"Job?" I frown. You don't offer someone a job if she's leaving in three months. I place the brochure back on Dr. Gruen's desk. "This is about yesterday, isn't it? My release?"

"Your release," Dr. Gruen repeats, pulling a folder out of the stiff black bag sitting next to her desk. "As a matter of fact, I did speak with Director Wu about that this morning. She confirmed that your latest . . . infraction could delay your release for up to six months."

Six months. All the air leaves the room. I watch Dr. Gruen's lips move, so I know she's still speaking, but I don't hear a word she says. In six months spring will be over. Charlie will have spent another birthday by himself.

And that's if I manage to keep my record clean. I close my eyes, and Cara's knife flashes through my head. How can I stay out of trouble for another six months? It's been hard enough doing it for just two weeks.

"Angela?" Dr. Gruen places her hand on mine, jolting me back to the present. "Did you hear me?"

I open my eyes. "I'm sorry. What did you say?"

"I said," Dr. Gruen continues, "that I spoke with Director Wu and we both agree that would be a terrible shame. I think I have an alternative option. One that could keep you on schedule to release in March, if you're interested."

I sit up straighter in my chair. "Seriously?"

Another smile crosses Dr. Gruen's lips. It's amazing how her entire face changes when she smiles. She seems fuller, somehow. Softer.

"One of the primary tenets of SciGirls is a mentorship program. The idea is very simple. Basically, we'd assign you to a younger girl, and you would mentor her. Show her around."

"It can be really nice," Mary Anne adds. "Almost like having a little sister."

"You've done it?" I ask.

Mary Anne nods.

"Oh yeah. Everyone in SciGirls is either a mentor or a mentee."

"Director Wu was quite taken with the idea, and we both thought you'd be the perfect test case." Dr. Gruen pauses for a moment, like she's expecting me to say something. "Is that something you'd be interested in?" she prods.

I gnaw at my lower lip. "So, you just want me to be friends with one of the younger girls?"

"That's correct."

"Who?"

Dr. Gruen steeples her fingers. "Actually, you've met already. It would be Jessica Ward, our newest inmate."

I think of Jessica's black eyes, and my throat goes dry. "Her?"

Dr. Gruen blinks. "You seem less than thrilled. I'm sorry, I thought you'd be excited about this opportunity."

"*Why?*" The word leaps out of my mouth, and I cringe. I really need to learn how to filter my thoughts.

Dr. Gruen considers me for a moment, then she glances behind me. "Mary Anne, would you excuse us for a moment?"

Mary Anne nods and slips out of the office without a word, closing the door behind her. Dr. Gruen opens her desk drawer and removes a tiny remote, which she aims at a sleek black surface on her bookshelf. I don't realize it's a television until the screen flashes on.

"You like?" Dr. Gruen asks when she sees me gaping. "I'll admit I'm something of a technology snob. My organization has offered to donate some newer devices to Brunesfield, but Director Wu's been a little resistant." She wrinkles her nose at me. "We'll work on her together, shall we?"

"Um, sure," I say.

An image flickers across the television screen. It's Jessica's dorm in the Segregation Block. The little girl huddles in the corner on her mattress, her fuzzy hair sticking out from her head. For a long moment she just stares at the wall, but then a shadow falls across her floor. She jerks her head up, then stands and crosses to the door, lifting a skinny hand to the glass.

That small gesture knocks something loose in my head. I recognize this moment. It happened right after I fell in the Seg Block. You can't see me because of the angle of the camera, but the Jessica on the screen stares right at me. She moves her lips, but there's no sound.

Dr. Gruen pushes Pause and the image freezes. "Can you tell me what happened here?" she asks.

"I . . . I fell."

"Right. And did she speak to you?"

"What?"

"Jessica," Dr. Gruen says, nodding at the screen. Jessica's face is frozen there, her lips slightly parted. "It looks like she's talking. Did she say something to you?"

"She said, 'Are you okay?'"

Dr. Gruen stares at me for a long moment, then she releases a breath and leans back in her chair. "I see," she says.

"I don't understand," I say. "Is something wrong?"

"No, not at all." Dr. Gruen leans forward again, sliding her elbows onto her desk. "It's just that *you're* the first person she's spoken to since she's been admitted. Don't you find that strange?"

I'm not quite sure how to answer, so I shrug.

As though that settles things, Dr. Gruen flips open the folder on her desk, her pale blue eyes narrowing as she examines its contents. "I've recommended that Director Wu take Jessica out of the Segregation Block. I've seen isolation do more harm than good in cases like hers. I was hoping I might recommend she be placed in your dorm room. You have an extra bed, correct?"

"*What?*" I picture that little girl in my room, watching me sleep with those black eyes. I stand so quickly that my chair wobbles back, nearly falling. She's unnatural. I don't want her near me—near my *friends*.

"No," I say, my voice cracking. "You can't do that."

"No?" Dr. Gruen lifts an eyebrow. "I'm sorry to hear that. Does this mean you don't want the assignment after all?"

"Don't want . . . ?" My throat feels dry. I sink back into my seat. "I don't—"

Dr. Gruen reaches across her desk to take my hand. Her skin feels smooth and soft. I can't help wondering what kind of moisturizer she uses. Probably something expensive that she has to special order from Paris.

"I'm so sorry to thrust this on you all at once," she says, squeezing my fingers. "But just think, three more months, and you'll be out. All we ask is that you take Jessica under your wing. Show her the ropes. Be her friend."

Three months. Three months. I let those two words run through my head on repeat, like a song I can't stop singing. I picture the trees just turning green in Prospect Park, and Charlie sitting across from me at the Neptune, shoveling waffles into his mouth. Is there anything I wouldn't give to get out of here in three months?

"What, exactly, would I have to do?" I ask, holding Dr. Gruen's gaze. Her eyes are so pale blue, they're almost translucent. Alien eyes, Cara would say. But on Dr. Gruen they look beautiful. Serene.

Her lips part in another dazzling smile. I blink and look away. It's like staring into an eclipse.

"That's what I was hoping to hear," she says. "Come now. Jessica's already waiting for you."

Chapter Seven

Dr. Gruen's heels clack against the concrete as we make our way to my dorm. Mary Anne follows at her shoulder, easily keeping up with her long strides, but I trail behind them both, feeling like I've shrunk in size. Or maybe the hall itself has grown again. The floor stretches endlessly before us, and the ceiling soars over our heads. I wrap my arms around myself and shiver. It's the new lightbulbs. They make everything seem bigger. Colder.

I picture Jessica in my room, looking up at the frogs Issie hung from the ceiling, and the pictures of UFOs that Cara ripped from her books and taped above her bed. The burned skin on my fingertips itches. I flatten my hands against my legs to keep from scratching.

Dr. Gruen stops beside my dorm. The girl who lived here before me drew a picture of a cute little house and taped it to the door. She wrote "The house that Jesus and Karlie built" in girlie cursive. Someone else scrawled "die bitch" across the house in thick black Sharpie. We leave it up as a kind of tribute to the girls who came before us.

Dr. Gruen barely glances at the picture. "Mary Anne, will you wait out here, please?" she asks.

Mary Anne gives a curt nod and stops beside the door, staring at the wall in front of her. I frown. She has about as much personality as a mannequin. She's lucky she's pretty.

Dr. Gruen taps her knuckles against the door frame. "Jessica," she says in a voice made of honey. "You have a visitor."

I step into the doorway and peek into the room. Jessica perches at the edge of my bed, her skinny legs an inch too short to reach the floor. She twists her hands in her lap. The entire room bends toward her, like she's creating her own gravity. I lean against the door frame, feeling dizzy.

"This is Angela," Dr. Gruen continues. "You met her a couple of days ago, remember?"

Jessica doesn't look up. She swings her legs, casting shadows across the concrete.

"Angela is here to talk to you." Dr. Gruen gives me an encouraging nod and follows me into the dorm, closing the door behind us. My shoulders tense, but Jessica doesn't look creepy right now. She looks scared, just a little girl in a strange new place. I shrug to get my muscles to relax, sinking onto the bed across from her.

Jessica stares at her lap, like I'm not even there. I chew on my lower lip. *Be her friend*, Dr. Gruen said. Easy, right?

"Hi. Um, my name's Angela." My voice sounds the way it does when I talk to Charlie, and I hesitate, feeling like I'm betraying him somehow. But Jessica's legs stop swinging, and she tilts her chin up, just a little. So I continue.

"I remember when they first brought me here. It seems really scary, right? But most of the people are pretty nice when you get to know them."

Jessica moves her hands from her lap to her sides. She wraps her fingers around the edge of the mattress and squeezes until her knuckles turn white. I glance at Dr. Gruen. This is crazy—this can't be what she wants.

But she nods. "Go on," she says. I glance back at Jessica, trying to think of something else to say.

"Okay. Well, things are pretty normal once you learn the schedule. Breakfast is at eight, and then everyone goes to morning chores. Let's see . . . we have classes every day. Math and science in the morning, then a break for lunch and rec, and then afternoon chores and English and history." Calling them classes is pretty generous. Brunesfield is required to educate all inmates under the age of eighteen. But we're all in different grades, so this is mostly impossible. Usually one of the guards just throws on some outdated video and falls asleep.

"After that we have free time until dinner, and then evening chores," I continue. "Oh, and Tuesday night's movie night." Brunesfield doesn't have a lot going for it, but I always thought the movie nights were pretty cool. We vote each week on what we want to watch next so we usually end up with something good. "And sometimes they serve pizza in the caf and that's . . ."

Jessica starts rocking. Back and forth. Back and forth. She hums under her breath. It's a low, tuneless sound. Just one note.

"Jessica?" I ask. Dr. Gruen's eyes narrow in concern.

"Jessica," she says. "Look at me."

Jessica looks up, but her eyes find me, not Dr. Gruen. Her pupils start to dilate. It's subtle at first, like watching someone's eyes adjust to the light. Then I look closer.

Tiny black tentacles stretch across Jessica's irises, seeping into her eyes like oil in water. I think of lightbulbs shattering, of the radiator sputtering and humming behind me. Jessica grips the mattress so hard its springs creak beneath her fingers. The air vibrates, like it's buzzing with electricity. It reminds me of how the sky gets just before lightning strikes.

Black fills Jessica's eyes, blocking every bit of white. Her breathing grows ragged, her chest expanding and collapsing like a paper bag.

I swallow a scream and leap up, stumbling back against the wall. Jessica keeps those black eyes pinned on me. My skin starts to grow warm. Then hot.

Suddenly Jessica shifts her eyes from me to the metal sink in the corner. Something gurgles deep within the pipes and the sink's faucet shoots off, skittering across the room. Water gushes from the hole in the wall, spraying my arms before bubbling over the concrete, still boiling when it hits the floor. Angry marks appear on my skin where the scorching water touched it. The few remaining bubbles dissolve as the water cools.

Dr. Gruen taps a long manicured nail against the wall behind me.

"Interesting," she says.

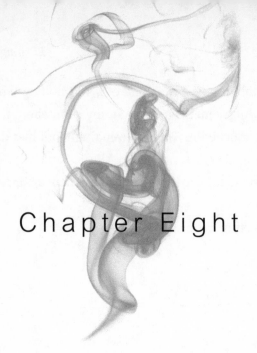

Chapter Eight

I want to run. My skin feels hot and dry, and the sound of the water bubbling up in the pipes plays on a loop in my mind. "You know what she can . . . that she . . ."

Dr. Gruen gives my shoulder a comforting pat. "Walk with me," she says, steering me out of the dorm. She nods at Mary Anne, who's still waiting out in the hall.

"Yes ma'am?" Mary Anne asks.

"Keep an eye on her," Dr. Gruen says. Mary Anne nods and positions herself in front of my dorm. I catch one last glimpse of Jessica before Gruen leads me down the empty hall. The little girl stares at her lap, trembling.

"What is she?" I ask once we're alone. Dr. Gruen stares straight ahead, lips pursed. Her eyes crinkle with concern, but there's a spark to them. She looks almost excited.

"She's a ten-year-old girl," Dr. Gruen says, after a beat.

"I know that. But what *is* she?"

Dr. Gruen doesn't say another word until we've reached her office. She holds the door open for me, and reluctantly, I step inside. Dr. Gruen pulls the door shut behind her.

"I haven't been entirely honest with you, Miss Davis," she says, taking a seat behind her desk. "You're curious about Jessica's ability and, I admit, I've been aware of it for some time. To give you a bit of history, I did my doctoral thesis on genetics before getting involved in social work," she explains. "It's one of the many reasons I was so drawn to SciGirls. The program combines two of my passions—science and helping underprivileged young women."

I slide back into the uncomfortable leather chair. "It's real, then? Jessica is making things hotter with her mind?" I feel like an idiot saying this, but I make myself do it anyway. I'm not good at reading between the lines. I need things spelled out for me. "Like magic?"

"You and I both know there's no such thing as magic," Dr. Gruen says. She taps her fingers on the desk: index, middle, ring; then again, slower. "Jessica seems to be altering the air around her somehow, but we don't know why or more importantly, *how*."

I stare at Gruen's tapping fingers. At first I think it's random, but the third time she does it, the pattern is different—faster. Like she's playing an invisible piano. "And you want to, what?" I ask. "Study her?"

"Goodness no! I left my scientific aspirations behind when I went into social work. I want to *help* Jessica. I've been following her story for some time. SciGirls doesn't usually recruit from inside juvenile detention centers, but when I heard that Jessica was being moved here to await trial, I convinced my supervisors to send Mary Anne and myself as well. I believe we can all help each other, Miss Davis. SciGirls is a prestigious program. It's a fantastic opportunity that many of the girls in this facility would never have access to otherwise.

I clear my throat. "And how are we helping you?"

"Well, I want to learn a little more about Jessica. SciGirls has relationships with some of the best research hospitals in the country. I think that would be a more appropriate place for someone with such a unique ability."

Dr. Gruen stops tapping and places her palm flat against her desk. Her fingertips are black with ink. "The problem is that Director Wu doesn't quite understand Jessica's talents," she continues. "She thinks she's just another dangerous delinquent."

"But she *is* dangerous." Tiny pink dots decorate my arms—burns from where the boiling water hit my skin. They aren't as bad as the burns I got from that metal tray. In fact, they'll probably disappear in an hour or two. But they still hurt.

Dr. Gruen frowns. "I think Jessica's even more terrified of what's happening to her than we are. At times she appears able to control her ability, and at other times it seems to flare up without warning. She shouldn't be here. She should be getting help. Don't you agree?"

"I don't know—"

Dr. Gruen leans forward, and her chair creaks beneath her weight. "Angela, did you notice how Jessica looked away from you when things started to get bad?"

"She looked at the sink," I say. "She made it explode."

"Exactly. Now, I believe that she was attempting to exert some sort of control over herself. Trying to cool herself down, as it were. Because she didn't want to hurt you."

"But—"

"Miss Davis," Dr. Gruen says, cutting me off. "I understand that I'm asking quite a lot of you. But a little girl's future is on the line." Dr. Gruen pauses, letting the words sink in. "I need your help. We both do."

I stare at the hole forming in the knee of my scrubs. "How can *I* help?"

"You can be her friend," Dr. Gruen says. "That's all I'm asking. Get to know her a little. Find out what kinds of things she likes. I can't monitor her twenty-four hours a day, and I'll need to make a compelling case if I'm to get her transferred to a proper hospital. Help me figure out what kind of girl she is. Who knows? Maybe she'll even tell you how this happened to her."

I roll my lower lip between my teeth, considering this. A little girl needs my help. What kind of person would refuse?

"And I'm offering something as well," Dr. Gruen says. "Something you find valuable, no doubt."

Three more months. After a moment, I nod. "I understand."

"Very well." Dr. Gruen flashes me a wide smile. "I believe we have a deal."

She nods for me to go. I stand, starting for the door.

"Oh, and Miss Davis," she adds as I twist the knob. I pause and glance back over my shoulder. She pulls her desk drawer open and removes a rubber bracelet. It's green with the word "SciGirls" written across it in white lettering.

"Here," she says, holding the bracelet out to me. "In case you change your mind about the program."

I cross the room and reach for the bracelet. She grabs my wrist before I pull away.

"I trust that I don't have to tell you this is confidential," she says.

"Confidential?" I repeat.

"Exactly. For now I'd prefer if no one else knew about our little . . . project."

The hall outside Dr. Gruen's office is empty. I pull the door closed behind me with a *click*. Brunesfield no longer feels big. Now it's small—tiny even—like the walls are creeping closer when I'm not looking. Warm air presses against my skin, and a line of sweat rolls down my back. I close my eyes and breathe in and then out, trying to steady my racing heart.

This is nuts-o. Charlie used to say that. He heard it on some decades-old cartoon and thought it was hilarious, so he started repeating it all the time. Homework was nuts-o. Food was nuts-o. It was actually really annoying. It's strange that's the only word that comes to mind when I think about this situation.

"Nuts-o," I say out loud. It's not nuts-o, not really. It's bizarre and dangerous. But it'll get me away from Brunesfield. Away from hallways that change size and rooms that set their own temperature and trees that tiptoe closer at night.

I take my time walking back to my room, relishing my last Jessica-free moments. When I turn onto our hall, I see Cara leaning against the open door to our dorm, talking with Mary Anne. She's actually smiling, which makes no sense. Cara never smiles.

"Hey," I say, walking up to them. Cara flinches at the sound of my voice.

"Oh. Hey." She straightens, and crosses her arms over her chest. "You've met Mary Anne, right? Get this—we used to go to the same high school. Isn't that weird?"

"Yeah, definitely." I peek past Mary Anne, but our dorm room is empty. "Where's Jessica?"

"Bathroom," Mary Anne says. She fumbles with the turnip charm hanging from her bracelet. "You know, I probably should have gone with her. Dr. Gruen told me to watch her. I'll be right back."

Cara frowns. "Who's Jessica?"

"You're about to find out." I turn and watch Mary Anne hurry down the hallway. "The assistant girl is kind of a spaz."

"She's not so bad." Cara drops onto her bunk.

"Really?" I ask. "Then what's with the vegetable charm bracelet?"

"She's a vegetarian."

I groan and toss the green SciGirls bracelet onto my locker. "I love bacon, but you don't see me wearing pig jewelry."

The tiny red blisters on my arms twinge. I bite my lip to keep from cringing and try to slip past Cara so I can run some cold water over my skin. Her eyes go right to my arm, narrowing at the burns.

"What happened?" she asks. *Shit*. I shrug and try to pull my sleeve past my wrist.

"Nothing."

Cara cocks an eyebrow. I can practically see the gears twisting and turning inside her head. "Like how the burns on your fingers were nothing?"

"Exactly," I say. Cara lives for conspiracies and secrets and would give anything for her life to be like one of her books. And now that something legitimately freaky is going on, I can't tell her about it. How's that for fair?

I push my sleeve back up and make my way to the sink on the other side of the room. But as soon as I pass the bunks, I freeze.

Our sink is *gone*. All that's left is a dark circle on the paint, and two crumbling holes in the wall.

"Weird, right?" Cara says, following my gaze. "Somebody came and took it a few minutes ago."

I frown. I didn't think I was in Dr. Gruen's office for that long, but I guess I dragged my heels on the way back. "Why?"

Cara shrugs. "Mary Anne said it was malfunctioning."

"Malfunctioning?" I say. "When have they ever repaired something just because it didn't work? Remember when the toilet in the girls' room wouldn't stop flushing?"

We only have two toilets in the girls' room and for a week one of them flushed every minute and a half (yes, we timed it), making it completely impossible to use. All the guards in Brunesfield knew it was a problem but no one fixed it until it shot a geyser at the ceiling, drenching Officer Crane with toilet water.

The lights in the hallway flicker, distracting me from the missing sink. Jessica steps through the door, clutching a worn teddy bear to her chest. One of her braids has half unraveled and it looks like a frayed wire.

Mary Anne stops behind her. She tucks a strand of hair behind her ear. "I should get back to Dr. Gruen's office. Are you all going to be okay?"

Cara shoots me a look. "What's going on?"

"Yeah. We'll be fine," I say. Mary Anne gives Jessica nudge forward, then hurries back down the hall. Jessica looks at me, and all the muscles in my body tense. I clear my throat.

"Cara, this is Jessica," I say. "She's been assigned to our dorm."

"You can't be serious." Cara lowers her voice but Jessica must hear her, anyway. She shifts her eyes to the floor, and a pang of sympathy shoots through me.

"Come in," I say. "Your bunk is up top."

Jessica glances at the top bunk, then back at me. She shakes her head so subtly that I almost miss it. Crap. She's scared of heights.

"Uh, Cara," I say. "Maybe you should switch with her."

"What?" Cara snaps. At juvie, your bunk is your home. Cara decorated hers with a map of Roswell that she tore out of a library book, funny little sketches of aliens, and a confusing diagram that's supposed to show how the moon landing was faked.

"I think she's afraid," I say. "I could give her my bunk if—"

"Whatever. It's fine." Cara glares at me but grabs her book and starts up the ladder. The rungs creak angrily beneath her feet. I silently vow to help her move her posters later. Jessica shuffles forward and crawls into the bed directly across from mine. She pulls the thin blue blanket up to her chin.

I never had nightmares as a kid, never lay awake at night worrying about creatures hiding under my bed. But now, with Jessica huddled on the bed across from me, I have some idea what that feels like. She watches me with those dark eyes. The tiny burns on my arms flare.

Chapter Nine

Issie dances around the dorm the next morning, wiggling her butt as she pulls a clean pair of scrubs over her hips. She sings animatedly in Spanish, the melody familiar even though the words are foreign.

I stifle a groan and burrow into my pillow. I don't know where she gets her energy. The sun isn't even up. The fluorescent overhead lights make the room feel sterile and cold.

Issie plops onto the edge of my bunk and tugs on her shoes. Her voice gets louder.

"Stop. Singing. *Please.*" I cover my head with my pillow, trying to block out the sound. Issie snickers. For a second, there's quiet. The mattress shifts beneath me.

Then, *"Wake up!"* She leans over me, belting the words into my ear. I chuck my pillow at her, but she catches it before it smacks her in the face.

"Why so grumpy?" she asks, holding my pillow out of reach.

"Not grumpy," I say. "*Tired.*" I doubt I slept for more than an hour last night. The burns on my arms and fingers started to itch every time I drifted off. I'd convince myself that the air was growing warmer, that my mattress was burning my skin.

Then I'd open my eyes and see Jessica sleeping peacefully in the bed across from me and feel like an idiot.

"We're supposed to be in the kitchen in five minutes," Cara says, wrestling her curls back into a ponytail. I kick off my blanket and scoot to the edge of my bunk, fighting to keep my eyes open.

Jessica's balled up in the far corner of her own bed, arms wrapped around her knees. I glance at Issie. She shrugs.

"Jessica?" I say. Jessica tilts her head, but doesn't look up. "We've got to go to the kitchen for morning chores. Wanna come?"

Cara's facing the mirror, but she catches my eye in the reflection. "She can't work in the kitchen. She's too young."

"Right." You have to be at least fourteen to work around the hot stoves and knives. Jessica will probably be assigned something low-key, like sorting letters in the mailroom.

"She could hang out in the caf," I say. "And when we're done working, we can all eat together. How does that sound?"

Cara frowns. "Why would she want to do that?"

"Maybe she doesn't want to stay here alone."

"She'll be alone in the caf while she waits for us."

"*Cara*," I snap. She tightens her ponytail and turns her back on the mirror.

"Jeez, take a pill," she says.

"Have either of you thought about letting Jessica answer for herself?" Issie asks.

Cara and I fall silent. The three of us turn to Jessica. Jessica jerks her head back and forth. *No*.

"That's settled, then," Cara says. "Angela? Ready?"

I hesitate, trying to think of something else to persuade Jessica to come with us. I'm supposed to be her friend, or mentor, or whatever. I'm supposed to hang out with her and show her the ropes. Not leave her in our dorm alone.

I open my mouth to say something, then close it again. Jessica doesn't look like she wants to talk. She looks like she wants to disappear.

"Anyone see my other shoe?" I ask, pulling one dirty white slip-on over my foot. Cara groans.

"Two more minutes before we're late," she says.

"I can't get another demerit this week," Issie adds. "They'll dock my phone time."

"How'd you already get two demerits?" I drop to my hands and knees to look below my bunk. My shoe is in the far corner, half-hidden by the bed's steel frame.

"You kidding?" Issie says. "They're giving demerits out for *everything*. I got one for *laughing* too loud."

"Shit." I turn my shoe over in my hand. Some mysterious creature gnawed through the fabric, leaving a ragged hole in the toe. I stick my finger through the hole and wiggle it at Cara. "Gross. Look."

"Wear socks," Cara says. "Let's go."

I kick off my other slip-on, tug a pair of socks over my feet, and then pull on both shoes. My toe pokes out through the hole. Already, I can tell this day is going to suck. Issie pulls me to my feet and we head for the hallway.

I stop next to the door and glance over my shoulder. "You're sure you're going to be okay alone?"

Jessica doesn't even move her head this time. I knock on the door frame.

"Okay. See you around, I guess."

I do see Jessica around. I see her sitting in the cafeteria. Alone. And walking down the hallway. Alone. And hanging at the edge of the yard during rec. Alone. The other girls don't talk to Jessica or sit with her or look at her. When she walks into a room, it empties.

There are rumors too. Aaliyah swears Jessica killed her family, she just doesn't know how. March heard somewhere that it wasn't her family—it was her entire fifth-grade class. Peach says it was two younger girls who lived down the street. They try looking up the facts online during computer time, but the news sites are blocked.

No one can figure out why Jessica's here, but everyone agrees that weird things happen when she's around. Lights go out. The air gets dry and hot. Once, she walked into the cafeteria and all three industrial-size fans stopped working at the exact same second.

I try to ignore the whispers. People told stories about what I did to get in here too, and none of them got close to the truth. I sit next to Jessica in class and talk to her in the halls and during rec. I ask her questions and tell jokes, but she barely even looks at me.

We're hanging in the dorm one afternoon, just the two of us. Issie's meeting with Dr. Gruen to talk about SciGirls and Cara's off doing Cara things. I've given up on trying to bond with Jessica for the day, and instead I'm trying to fix the hole in my shoe. I got this idea in my head that I could stitch it shut using Issie's cinnamon-flavored dental floss, but my fingers are thick and clumsy and the knot keeps slipping. Frustrated, I throw the shoe—it bounces off the wall and skids across the floor.

Jessica flinches and looks up from the book she'd been reading. Our eyes meet, and she opens her mouth, like she might say something. I smile, sheepishly.

She shifts her eyes back down to the book in her lap.

"Damn, damn, *damn*. Where is my freaking shoe?" I'm on my knees again, digging beneath my bunk for my rat-eaten slip-on. Cara and Issie wait at the door. Irritated.

Cara glances over her shoulder at the clock in the hall outside our dorm. "We have four minutes, Angela. Are you kidding me with . . ."

She trails off as Jessica slips past her and hurries into the hallway. I start to call after her, but she's gone before I get a word out. I heard she got assigned a job in the library. She's been heading down earlier every day, hiding in the stacks during meals and carting dozens of books back to our dorm to read at night. A lot of the other girls won't go into the library anymore. They say she's cursed it.

"Poor little runt," Issie says once Jessica's out of earshot. "You think she talks to anyone at all?"

"I try to talk to her all the time." I crouch down and look behind Cara's locker, but my other shoe isn't there. "I don't think she wants to make friends."

"She wants to make friends," Issie says. "She's just scared."

"Angela," Cara snaps. "Shoes."

"Right." I push myself to my feet and start digging through my locker. I find old notes from Charlie, and an audiobook I forgot I had. No shoe.

Issie frowns, then crosses the room and snatches something off Jessica's locker. "Is this it?"

Before I can answer, she tosses a shoe to me. I lunge, catching it in one hand.

"Yes!" I say, pulling the shoe on. "But why—"

The sentence dies in my mouth. Someone threaded Issie's dental floss in teeny-tiny stitches through the fabric to sew the hole closed. My chest pinches. Cara would never have thought to do this, and Issie's fingers are bigger than mine. I wiggle my toes inside my newly fixed shoe, staring at the tiny stitches. I only know one person with small enough fingers to pull this off.

Jessica sits in a corner of the library, a stack of dusty books piled at her feet. The light above her buzzes on. Then off.

I take a hesitant step into the room. It's empty, except for Ellen and a small group of girls sitting at a bunch of desks, poring over dusty physics and biology textbooks. I frown at them as I walk past, wondering if this has anything to do with SciGirls. They look like some sort of cult, all huddled together, speaking in low whispers.

I hear something shuffling inside Ellen's desk and I move quicker, hoping it's just her mouse.

Cobwebs cling to the ceiling, and half the lightbulbs have burned out, leaving the corners dark with shadows. Something flickers at the edge of my eyesight. I flinch and spin around. Nothing there. *Jesus.* No wonder the other girls think this place is cursed.

I swipe a hand across my forehead and it comes away damp with sweat. It's *boiling* down here. The old radiator—which hasn't worked in more than a decade—rattles and spits in the corner.

"Jessica?" I say. She jerks so suddenly that the book tumbles from her lap. I dance backward, hands out front of me. "*Shit!* Sorry!"

Jessica's eyes don't turn black. The air doesn't buzz or warm. I inhale and lower my hands. My heartbeat steadies. "Sorry. You scared me a little."

Jessica pulls her book back onto her lap. The light flickers.

I sit, cross-legged, in front of her. "You fixed my shoe."

Silence.

I clear my throat. "I wanted to say thank you. So. Thank you."

Jessica shrugs.

"Okay," I say. Everything in my body wants to stand up and walk away. I think about Charlie and Prospect Park in the springtime. I look down at the tiny, even stitches at the toe of my shoe.

"So, um, what kind of things do you like?" I ask. "I know you like books." I nod at the stack next to her feet. Jessica flicks a piece of dust across the floor. I take a book off the pile.

"Horses, huh?" I say, flipping through the book's faded pictures. I take another glance at the stack. *Horses, foxes, lions* . . . "You like animals."

Jessica shrugs.

"You don't want to talk about animals." I pause. "What about . . . food? What kind of food do you like? Pizza? Chicken nuggets? Ice cream? Or music? Do you like music?"

The light above us buzzes back on. Jessica flicks the spine of her horse book.

"Okay. Well, I guess I'll let you get back to reading that." I stand, dusting the library grime off the seat of my pants. One of the girls sitting with Ellen shouts, "Mitochondria!" and everyone at the table bursts into laughter. I shake my head. No one enjoys science that much.

"See you around," I say to Jessica. She tilts her head toward me, but doesn't meet my eye.

"Monster trucks," she says in a very small voice.

I freeze, sure I didn't hear her correctly. "What did you say?"

Jessica draws pictures in the dust with her finger. "You asked me what I like. I like monster trucks."

Two whole sentences. That's the most I've ever heard her say.

"Monster trucks," I repeat. Jessica shrugs. She pulls the horse book back onto her lap, a signal that she's done talking.

It's not much. But it's a start.

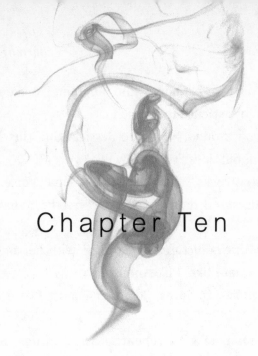

Chapter Ten

I have an idea.

I wait until the free period between morning and afternoon classes the next day, and then I head to the library to find Jessica. She's sitting in the same spot as before, a different book balanced on her lap. Bears this time.

"Come on," I say. "I want to show you something."

She looks up at me. Skeptical. I'm sure she's going to refuse. But she puts her book back on the stack next to her and stands.

I lead Jessica out of the library and up the stairs to the main floor. During free periods you're allowed to wander around on your floor and every floor below you. But high- and mid-security girls aren't supposed to go to the low-security area on the second floor. Thing is, everyone hangs out in the activity center and computer room on the lower floors, so the guards mostly congregate around there. The stairwells are empty.

I hover near the stairs, watching Officer Sterling argue with Aaliyah at the end of the hall. Aaliyah is crying, and gesturing at something in the activity center. Officer Sterling has her back to me. It sounds like they're arguing because someone stole Aaliyah's textbook, but that doesn't make any sense. Who gives a shit about a textbook? I lift a finger to my mouth to motion for Jessica to stay quiet, and I wave her forward. She frowns but follows me up the stairs anyway.

The second floor is empty. I've only been here once before, when I first got to Brunesfield. I was curious, so I figured out ways to sneak around when the guards weren't watching. There are a bunch of dorms on the second floor, a few counselors' offices, and a lounge area with two round windows overlooking the woods. They remind me of wide, unblinking eyes.

I head for the lounge, holding my breath as I sneak past a counselor's office. But it's empty. All the rooms are empty. I stop in front of the window.

"This is what I wanted to show you," I say. Jessica steps up beside me and peers out the window.

The woods stretch for three or four miles, ending near a construction site. I don't know what they're building, but the site's been there as long as I've been here. Most days it's kind of creepy and abandoned, like a ghost town, but today there are dump trucks rolling over the freshly turned dirt.

Bright orange cranes reach across the sky, looking like crazy prehistoric animals.

"I know they're not monster trucks. But they're big." This seemed like a brilliant idea in my head, but now that we're here I see how stupid it is. The whole point of monster trucks is that they're big and loud and they destroy things. You can barely even see the construction equipment from here, and the dump truck is moving dirt around, not crushing another car beneath its tires. "We don't have to stay if you don't . . ."

Jessica pushes past me and presses her face against the window. Her breath leaves misty clouds on the glass. "Cool," she says.

I raise an eyebrow. "Really?"

"They look like dinosaurs."

I crouch down next to her, watching the cranes move beyond the trees.

"Kind of," I say. "Weird ones."

The corner of Jessica's mouth quirks into an almost-smile. "Yeah," she says.

A car with a shovel thing attached to it pushes some dirt to the edge of the site. A crane lowers a stack of steel beams to the ground.

"My dad liked cars," Jessica says. "Trucks and race cars and stuff. He used to tell me the names of all the cars we saw on the street."

"Is he the one who took you to see the monster trucks?"

"Yeah. One time."

I wait for her to say more, but she doesn't. I don't ask her why she used past tense—*liked*, not *likes*—or why her dad only took her to see the monster trucks once or what he's doing now. I know that dads sometimes don't want to be dads anymore.

We watch the construction site for a long time. Jessica doesn't speak again, and neither do I. We don't have to.

I'm in a surprisingly good mood when Officer Crane arrives to take me to the Seg Block. At first I think it's just because of my success with Jessica, but it's more than that. I'm *excited* about my punishment, excited to head to the scariest place in Brunesfield and pull a smelly mop out of an even smellier bucket of water and get to work.

I freeze midstep when the reality of what's happening hits me. I have a crush on Officer Mateo.

I have a *crush* on Officer Mateo.

I have to put my hand on the wall to support myself. This is all kinds of not good. Not only is Mateo a guard, which makes him off-limits, but he's Issie's guard. Issie's had a crush on him forever. We all know she's never going to get him, but that's not the point. In a place like Brunesfield, there aren't many things that are yours alone. Issie's crush is hers, and I refuse to take that away from her.

Whatever this stupid thing is, I must squash it.

Mateo waves at me when I round the corner. He jabs the security door with one finger, not bothering to look up from his crossword. I push the door open and take a second to get used to the Seg Block's shadows and muted quiet. I'm just reaching for my mop when I hear metal chair legs drag across the concrete floor.

"Are you going to pull that stool in here every time?" I ask, glancing over my shoulder. Mateo lets the security door swing shut and scoots onto his stool.

"What's a five-letter word that means 'regretful'?" he asks instead of answering. A lock of hair drops over his forehead and *holy God, he's gorgeous*.

Stop it. He's a guard. He's Issie's guard. "Sorry?"

"No, the first letter has to be *p*."

I drop the soaking wet mop onto the floor, concentrating on the suds to keep from looking at Mateo's face. "Um, that sounds wrong," I say, pushing the mop across the concrete. Even when I'm staring at the floor I can still see him from the corner of my eye. He taps his pen against his chin.

"Maybe," he says, squinting down at the paper.

"Who even does crosswords anymore?" I ask. Mateo was right, this hall doesn't get too dirty. I can still see the soap swirls dried onto the concrete from the last time I mopped.

"My grandfather." Mateo frowns and scribbles something out, then writes a new word in neat, careful letters. "He says it keeps the mind sharp. He's ninety-two years old and still the smartest man I know."

I drag the mop over the concrete, trying to ignore the soapy water soaking through my shoes. "Is he a teacher or something?"

"He was a detective, but he's retired. He started out here at Brunesfield, though. Got a job as a guard when he turned eighteen. Just like me."

I do the math in my head. Mateo started here about seven months ago. He's only a year older than me.

"Is that what you want to do? Be a detective?" I pause to wiggle my foot, trying to shake the lukewarm water from my shoe. Bea stares at me from behind the glass wall of her dorm. I flash her a nervous smile, and she starts to giggle.

Mateo shrugs and scratches something onto his crossword. "That's the plan. It's not easy, though. Only two other guys made detective my grandfather's year and he calls those the good old days. Now it's supposed to be really hard. There are all sorts of tests and stuff."

He tries to keep his voice casual, but I hear the excitement anyway. I've seen people do this before. When the kids at my old school dreamed too big, they'd always kind of shrug it off, like they didn't really want it in the first place. The girl with straight A's would pretend she didn't really want to go to Harvard, that she only applied to see what would happen. Or the six-foot-tall kid who could dunk might say he didn't even notice the scouts who came to watch him play. It's a defense mechanism. When you grow up where I did, you try to keep yourself from expecting too much out of life.

Mateo's shoulders tense up, and a wrinkle appears between his eyes as he bends back over his crossword. It's clear he really wants this detective thing.

"What?" Mateo asks, frowning at me. God, I must've been staring. I shift my eyes back down to the floor, pushing the mop in small, tight circles.

"I can totally see you as a detective," I say. Mateo drops the crossword on his lap and sits up straighter.

"Oh yeah?"

"Totally. You've already got that dark, broody detective hair. Now you just need one of those wool coats and maybe a beard . . ."

The end of my sentence dies in my mouth. I'm describing a real person, this detective I saw after I got arrested. Detective Cass, I think his name was. He came by the holding cell to question me about a string of robberies my ex-boyfriend Jake and I pulled around this really nice neighborhood in Brooklyn. Jake actually did most of them, but I was always in the getaway car. And I was the one who got caught.

My cheeks burn. I was actually counting the differences in our ages, just to make sure it wouldn't be weird if we ever dated. *God*, I'm a freak. I push the mop with a little more force than necessary, sending a tiny wave of soapy water crashing against the pink wall. Bea hisses from her cell, pressing her face up against the door. She taps her fingers on the glass.

"Angela?" Mateo asks. "Are you all right?"

"You got a girlfriend?" I ask. You know how little kids pick at the scabs on their knees, even when they start to bleed? That's what I'm doing. The only way to get this stupid crush out of my system is to make it hurt.

"Uh, yeah, I do," Mateo says. "Stacy."

Stacy. I make myself picture her. Stacy has shampoo-commercial hair. Stacy irons her skirts and wears colorful cardigans that match her shoes.

"What's she do?" I ask.

"She's in school. She's going to be a veterinary technician."

I revise my imaginary Stacy. Now she wears a long white lab coat and she's holding a puppy. I'm not even sure vet techs *wear* lab coats, but I picture it anyway. I put imaginary Stacy next to Mateo in his long black detective's coat. They're standing in front of a little white house holding hands. Maybe the puppy licks Mateo's face.

Despite myself, I smile. Imaginary Stacy is exactly the kind of girl Mateo should be with. There's no competing with her. Besides, it's not like I'm alone or anything. I have Charlie waiting for me when I get out of here. That should be enough.

I'm still thinking about perfect imaginary Stacy an hour later, as I walk back to my dorm after finishing up in the Seg Block. I bet she knows how to cook. No frozen dinners for Stacy. She probably *really* cooks, like with spices and books and boiling water. She probably does all that *Little House on the*

Prairie stuff: darns socks and sews buttons and, I don't know, churns her own butter. I round the corner to our dorm room, walking slowly so I can savor these few seconds alone.

Voices echo down the hall. I frown and walk a little faster. I thought our dorm would be empty but Cara leans against the far wall, and Mary Anne sits on the bunk across from her.

"Oh, um, hi," I say.

Mary Anne stands and clears her throat. "I was just dropping off some brochures." She nods at a shiny stack of SciGirls brochures sitting on my locker.

"Mary Anne thinks I'd be a natural." Cara slides a brochure off the top of the stack and flips it open.

"I should go," Mary Anne says, edging toward the door. "You can hold on to those, Cara. Let me know if you have any questions about joining."

Mary Anne slips into the hall, her shoes click-clacking against the concrete floor. I don't realize I'm holding my breath until she turns the corner and the sound fades.

"What was she doing in here?" I ask.

Cara frowns and nods at the brochure she's still holding. "I told you—"

"No, what was she doing in *here*?" I wouldn't care, but Cara has a pocketknife hidden somewhere in this room. Mary Anne seems nice enough, but Cara would be in deep shit if she found it. Now isn't the time to be hanging out with authority figures.

I lower my voice, always worried someone might overhear me. "Look, we need to talk about the knife."

Understanding flickers through Cara's eyes. "It's hidden. Mary Anne didn't see shit."

"You're sure?"

"Jesus, Angela. I'm not a moron." I try to catch Cara's eyes, but she shifts them to the floor. "Besides, Mary Anne isn't like the guards. She wouldn't say anything."

"You don't know that," I snap. "Just because she went to your high school doesn't mean you can trust her."

"Will you just drop it?" Cara says. "I can handle my own shit."

Normally, I'd let this go. Cara can go from zero to furious faster than anyone I've ever met. It's not worth pushing when she decides she doesn't want to share. In fact, that's the reason Issie and I are her only real friends in here; most of the others can't stand her violent mood swings.

Then again, most of the others haven't seen the real Cara—the one who reads me Charlie's letters and sneaks Issie old math assignments so she can keep making paper frogs. The Cara who still knows all her mom's stupid beauty rules by heart.

Vaseline on your teeth prevents lipstick stains. A dab of apple-cider vinegar gets rid of a pimple . . .

It's *that* Cara I'm thinking about when I cross the dorm and grab her shoulders, forcing her to look at me.

"You *have* to be more careful," I say. Cara tries to pull away, but I'm bigger than her. She meets my eyes, glaring. "If even one person sees that knife—"

"I don't need you to babysit me," she says.

"Cara, will you—"

"Miss Davis. Do we have a problem here?" The voice startles me, and I turn to see Officer Sterling standing in the doorway. Her hand rests on the nightstick at her belt.

I drop my hands from Cara's shoulders and quickly step away.

"No ma'am," I say at the same time that Cara mutters, "No."

"I came to see why you two weren't in the kitchen."

"I forgot my apron," Cara mumbles. She grabs a grease-stained apron from the hook near the lockers, then shoulders past me and out of the room. Officer Sterling looks at me and raises an eyebrow.

"Miss Davis?"

"Yeah," I say, and I follow Cara out of the dorm.

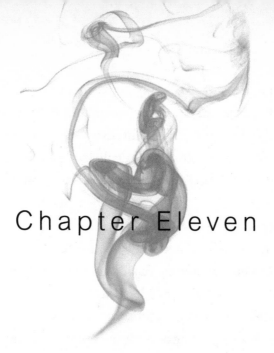

Chapter Eleven

Much later that night, I wake to a *click*.

I ease my eyes open, stifling a yawn. Sleet lashes against the narrow window near our ceiling. I listen to the slushy sound of it hitting the glass for a few long moments before I'm fully awake. I roll onto my side.

The bunk across from me is empty.

My first thought is of Cara. She's somehow managed to sneak out of the dorm, she's wandering through the halls with that pocketknife. But no—Jessica and Cara switched bunks. I blink and lift myself to my elbow to check the rest of the dorm. Jessica's not here.

I kick the blanket from my legs and sit up, sure she's crouching in the corner, hidden by the shadows. But a quick search of our tiny dorm room reveals that I was right the first time. She's gone.

With Issie's snores echoing above me, I ease my feet onto the cold concrete floor. I creep over to the door and lower my hand to the knob. It's warm. Every night at nine o'clock on the dot a dead bolt automatically slides into place, locking us in our dorms till morning. I twist, waiting for the lock to catch, but the knob turns beneath my fingers and creaks open.

What the hell? I poke my head into the hall in time to see Mateo's swinging flashlight beam round the corner into another hallway. I hesitate. I don't know if this is what Dr. Gruen had in mind, but curiosity gnaws at me. Room checks are twenty minutes apart, so I have fifteen minutes before Mateo comes past the dorm again and sees that Jessica and I aren't there. Sucking in a breath, I tiptoe into the hallway.

Brunesfield looks different at night. Deep blue shadows stretch across the hallways, hiding the nicks and scratches that decorate the walls. A rubber SciGirls bracelet lies in the corner, abandoned. The halls themselves feel strange when they aren't crowded with a hundred screaming, swearing girls. They're almost peaceful.

I creep down the hallway, the concrete like ice beneath my toes. Brunesfield is a labyrinth, with halls twisting off in every direction. They call to me as I make my way past, tempting me to explore their darkened corners. But I'm here for Jessica, not myself. I pause at the foot of a staircase. Would Jessica have climbed to the higher floors to watch the cranes again? Or would she have taken the staircase coiling down to the kitchen and the Segregation Block?

A heavy charred smell drifts down the hall before I can decide. I recoil when it reaches my nose. Something's burning.

I follow the smell to my left. It stings my nostrils and makes my eyes water. I'm close. I walk faster.

The girls' bathroom sits at the end of the hall. It's not a nice place during the day, but now it looks horrifying. An open door yawns before me, revealing a perfectly dark, black room. The overhead lights are all on timers so none of them will work for Jessica, even if she did manage to break the lock on our door. I step forward, ignoring the voice in my head that screams for me to run back to my dorm. Icy rain crashes against the windows and echoes off the tiled walls. I squint into the shadows.

Something flickers in the darkness: a tiny orange light.

Fear prickles along the back of my neck, but I step into the bathroom anyway. Strange light dances over the tiled walls, and the floor feels suddenly warm beneath my feet. It's too dark for me to see smoke, but the smell is so strong that I pull my T-shirt over my nose to keep from coughing. Water drips from the broken faucets and the air buzzes like static.

I hesitate at the long tiled wall that separates the showers from the sinks and toilets. I don't want to know what's on the other side of that wall, but I *have* to know, otherwise all

I'll ever have is this theory that seems impossible. I'll always wonder if I guessed right. If magic is real.

I peek around the corner.

Jessica sits cross-legged on the floor, her back to me. Her wild, curly black hair sticks out of her head in crazy corkscrews. Her teddy bear lies on the tile in front of her knees. One black eye hangs by a thread from his face, and his fur is so charred that black ash crumbles onto the tile around him. I slink forward, curiosity curling in my stomach like a cat. Jessica rocks back and forth, back and forth. She hums a tuneless song under her breath.

A blue flame leaps across the bear's fur and climbs his arms and legs. I'm holding my breath, partly because of the smoke and partly because *fire just appeared out of thin air*. The flame crackles up the bear's torso to his face. The bear's remaining eye blackens.

Jessica rocks faster. Her tiny body whips back and forth so quickly that it looks like she might break in half. I watch in horror as the flames climb toward the sunken ceiling, sending flickering shadows over the tile-covered walls. The fire leaps from the bear to a puddle of water on the floor just inches from Jessica's knee. Instead of dying, it flares higher, like the puddle was made of gasoline instead of water.

Jessica stops rocking and pitches forward, holding herself up with shaky arms. Fire licks the ceiling, leaving black scorches on the cracked plaster. Jessica wrenches her head around, staring at the row of showers along the wall. Gurgling echoes through the pipes, and waters spurts out, bubbling and boiling onto the floor. The tiles below my feet burn. I shriek, dancing backward.

Jessica whips her head around. The black has just started to melt from her eyes and I watch in mixed horror and fascination as the oily tendrils crawl back to her pupils, leaving her eyes white again. Normal.

She stares at me, shocked, for what feels like a full minute. Sounds from the outside world rush in to fill the sudden silence. Sleet and rain rattle the windows. Wind howls. The heat fades from the tiles, and I feel cold all the way to my bones.

Jessica grabs the soaked and crumbling teddy bear off the floor.

"Don't tell," she whispers.

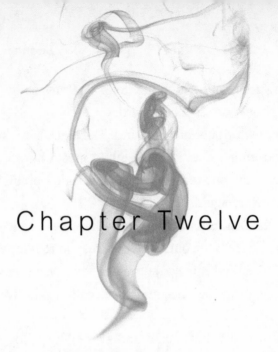

Chapter Twelve

Jessica's eyes are the first things I see when I wake up the next morning. They peer out from the bunk across from me, half-hidden by the thin blanket bunched around her face. God, she's small. Her feet don't even reach the end of the bed.

"Line up!" Officer Crane raps her knuckles against our door. An alarm buzzes down the hall, telling us the doors have been unlocked. Officer Crane pushes our door open.

"Out of bed," she says, knocking on the wall this time. The twisted, red scar pulls at her top lip, making her sneer even more pronounced than usual. "If you're not in the hall in two minutes, you can kiss your shower good-bye."

Cara groans and pulls her blankets up over her head. Issie sits up, sending her bedsprings creaking. Early-morning cold seeps in through the walls, making my fingers feel slow and clumsy. I push my blanket back, reluctantly.

"Shower time," Issie says in a singsong voice, swinging her legs over the side of the bunk. There aren't enough showers in Brunesfield for every girl to bathe every day, so each dorm has an assigned shower time twice a week. Last night's excursion kept me tossing and turning until morning, and I'm so tired that my eyelids feel like lead. But missing your time slot means an extra three days of smelling like feet, so I crawl out of bed and grab my towel and flip-flops.

"Rise and shine," I say, giving Cara's steel-framed bunk a shake.

"Ugh. *Stop*," Cara says, but she crawls to the ladder, her eyes half-closed. Jessica slips out from under the blanket and huddles next to my leg. I drop my hand to her shoulder. It's muscle memory left over from years of being an older sister. As soon as I notice what I'm doing I pull my arm back, my fingers tingling.

"Don't look so nervous, runt." Issie loops her towel around her shoulders and cuffs Jessica on the arm. If Jessica looks terrified of anything, it's Issie. It takes a little while to get used to her massive frame and the colorful tattoos winding up her arms.

"She's cool," I say to Jessica, nodding at Issie. "Don't be scared."

"Damn straight I'm cool." Issie leans against the door. "I'm ice. I'm the tundra."

Cara slams her locker door and Jessica jumps. "Move your asses," Cara says, slipping a pair of bright orange flip-flops onto her feet. "I don't want to miss my shower."

"Someone woke up on the wrong side of the bed," I say, following Issie into the hall, Jessica trailing behind me like a puppy. If I turned too quickly, I'd step on her.

"No, I woke up on the wrong side of the bunk," Cara says. "The *top* bunk."

I roll my eyes to tell her to get over it, then hurry behind the other girls already waiting in the hall. They're lined up at the blue line, their hands forming diamonds on their lower backs.

I glance down at Jessica. "Like this," I whisper, touching the tips of my fingers together to show her what to do. Jessica twists her skinny arms behind her back and something inside my chest pinches. I study the top of her head. I don't think it's an act—she really does look terrified. She flinches at every loud noise and hasn't once met another girl's eyes. She's practically trembling in her too-large scrubs.

If she were anyone else, I'd say she wouldn't last a month. Weakness is preyed on here. Brunesfield is very much a bully-or-be-bullied environment.

But last night I saw Jessica coax flames out of thin air. Soot still coats the bottoms of my feet, proving it wasn't just a dream. She's stronger than anyone here, maybe stronger than anyone I've ever met.

So what's she afraid of?

"Looking good, ladies." Officer Crane's eyes travel over the twenty or so girls lined up in front of their dorms. "Let's get through this quickly."

"Like hell," Issie says. When Crane turns her back, Issie nods at the girls in the line ahead of us.

Peach watches us. "*Dyke*," she taunts. I resist the urge to roll my eyes. I guess she's decided that *slut* and *whore* aren't insulting enough anymore.

"You'd think she'd be bored with us by now," I say. Cara pulls at a thread hanging from her shirt.

"When you only have two brain cells I guess it takes a long time to get bored," she says.

"Ignore her," I whisper.

"Whatever," Cara says. She yanks the thread out of her shirt with more force than necessary.

"No talking when your hands are in diamonds!" Officer Crane shouts. Cara and I fall silent. Crane turns around, and I wiggle my fingers at Peach behind her back. Peach bares her teeth and hisses like a cat.

The line shuffles forward, and Crane makes her way back to the front. Cara waits until she's out of earshot, then picks up a crumpled SciGirls brochure that someone dropped on the floor.

"You heard about this?" she asks, straightening out the brochure.

I shake my head. "No Just what Dr. Gruen told me."

"Aaliyah was talking about it in the activity center. She's all nervous about passing some big test you have to take in order to get in."

"Are you thinking about what Mary Anne said?" I ask, plucking the brochure out of Cara's hands. "That you should sign up?"

"No," Cara answers quickly. She clears her throat. "I mean, it doesn't really seem like *my* kind of science. Dr. Gruen called me into her office to talk about it, but she called Roswell a hoax when I asked about aliens." Cara flicks the edge of the brochure with one figure. "Why, are you signing up?"

"I hadn't thought about it," I say, truthfully. I've been too distracted by Jessica to consider whether or not I want to get involved with SciGirls.

Cara tosses the brochure back onto the floor. "Probably better that you don't," she says. "Just another government official attempting to brainwash us with her crazy propaganda."

"Right," I say.

"Stay on the blue line, ladies," Crane calls out once we've reached the end of the hall. Nobody moves, but as soon as she heads into the bathroom to supervise, we drop our hands from behind our backs and lean against the wall.

"So, what're you in for, runt?" Issie asks. She has this way of talking to everyone like they're her very best friend in the world. It works too. I've seen her make friends with the meanest girls in here. But Jessica just stares at the floor.

"What's wrong? Did the Seg Block get you down?" Issie asks. "Cara was in Seg for a week and she didn't talk for like a month after she got out."

"I didn't talk for *two days*," Cara snaps. Issie shrugs.

"Whatever. I'm just saying it's okay if you're scared." Issie slides a black Sharpie out from the waistband of her pants and weaves it through her fingers. The word on her knuckles still reads "ham!" but she'll have us write something new after her shower washes it away. "I was scared when I first came here. Used to cry myself to sleep every night."

I've been sharing a dorm with Issie since the day we both arrived, and I've never heard her cry herself to sleep, but I keep my mouth shut.

"Anyway, the girls here aren't that bad," Issie continues. "You'll see."

"Don't touch me, you fucking whore!" someone shouts from inside the bathrooms. Officer Crane pulls the nightstick from her belt and raps it against the wall. It makes a deafening *crack* against the concrete.

"Knock it off in there or you lose shower privileges for a week," she yells. The girls in the bathroom fall silent.

"Anyway, you're lucky you ended up with *us*," Issie continues, like the disruption was nothing. "Because Angela and Cara and me are pretty tough. And we got your back."

"God, she doesn't care, Issie," Cara says, examining her cuticles. But Cara's wrong. Jessica's still staring at the floor, but she's tilted her head slightly to the left. She's listening.

"Issie's right," I say. "Your dorm-mates are like your family, okay? So if anyone ever gives you any trouble, you come talk to us."

Jessica looks up to me and opens her mouth like she might say something.

A scream echoes out of the bathroom, cutting her off. Officer Crane swears under her breath and yanks the nightstick out of her belt again. She storms out of the bathroom a moment later, leading Aaliyah and a girl named Carmen out by the arms. Three long red scratches cut across Aaliyah's left arm. Carmen hisses something at her in Spanish.

"Mouths shut, both of you," Crane says. She pauses next to Issie. "I'm taking these two to see Director Wu. Keep the line moving."

"Yes, ma'am," Issie says, and the four of us head into the bathroom. The tiles are a pukey shade of beige in the light of day, and moisture makes the paint droop from the ceiling like stalactites. Black mold reaches out from the corners and stretches across the floor.

All the showers are currently full. Peach stands in front of the last stall in the row, an orange towel draped over her shoulders. She scowls when she sees us. A tiny hand slips into mine. I look down to see Jessica clutching my fingers.

"This is crap," Issie says. I know what she means. Showering at Brunesfield is miserable on the best day. You're only allowed two minutes under the water to clean as much of yourself as you can. Going over means the next person in line gets less time, so there's always someone barging in on you, screaming that your turn is over.

And then there are girls like Peach, who are constantly looking for someone to torture. A cruel smile twists her lips when she sees Jessica shuffle into the bathroom, holding my hand.

"New girlfriend?" she asks.

"Knock it off," Issie says. "She's just a little kid."

"Was I talking to you?" Peach snaps.

Issie lifts a bushy eyebrow. I sometimes forget how scary she is. I've known her for so long that all I see is my friend, the girl who likes origami frogs and stories about running away to live in the woods. But Issie's also the two-hundred-and-fifty-pound little sister of some seriously terrifying gang members.

"Someone should teach you a lesson about calling people names." Issie taps her knuckles together, flexing the muscles in her heavily tattooed arms.

"Issie, *don't*," I say, stealing a glance at Cara. She could still have that knife tucked in her waistband, and I really don't know if she's stupid enough to use it. I step between them and Jessica drops my hand. She rocks back on her feet, staring down at the tile.

"What's the matter, Davis?" Peach says. "Thought I heard you were tough?"

"Give it a rest," Cara hisses.

"Standing up for your girlfriend?" Peach snaps back. She jams her shoulder into my side, sending me stumbling into Issie.

"It's three against one, girl," Issie says. "You really want to do this?"

"Sounds like a party." Peach smiles wide to show off all her teeth. That's the thing about Peach—she doesn't care whether she can win a fight. She just wants to do some damage.

"Guys—" I start, but I'm cut off by a low, tuneless hum. I turn around.

Jessica rocks back and forth, her skinny arms twisted around her chest. She digs her fingernails into her arms and hums steadily under her breath.

Oh, *shit*.

"Is she okay?" Cara asks.

"No." I push past Cara and drop to my knees, grabbing Jessica by the shoulders. "Jessica? Look at me."

Jessica shakes her head and pulls away. She drops her arms. The air around me buzzes.

I think of Jessica making the sink explode, of fire clawing at the ceiling, and of the tiny red burns crawling up my arms. Fear uncurls inside me, and time slows. I need to do something, calm Jessica down or distract her. No, I have to get the other girls out of the bathroom before she hurts someone. I open my mouth to shout at them to run—then Dr. Gruen's voice echoes through my head, warning me not to say a word.

I haven't told anyone what Jessica can do, but I don't think that matters if they see it for themselves. I feel everyone watching us, waiting for an explanation. So I blurt out the first thing I can think of.

"She's having a panic attack. Issie, help me get her into the shower. That's supposed to help."

Issie mans the situation like a linebacker, using her body to separate Jessica from Peach as she ushers her to the shower. Jessica doesn't stop humming until she's safely inside the stall, and I've yanked the flimsy curtain closed. I hold my breath, waiting for flames to shoot out from under the curtain and set the bathroom ablaze.

The shower sputters on.

"You okay, runt?" Issie calls.

For a long moment there's silence. Then a tiny voice squeaks, "Yes."

"You guys are a bunch of freaks," Peach says. She slides the shower curtain aside and slips into the stall next to Jessica's. There's the sound of rustling behind the curtain as she undresses and turns on the shower.

I exhale and collapse against the wall.

Suddenly, Peach screams. A billowing cloud of steam rises from her shower. She yanks the curtain aside and stumbles back out into the bathroom, wrapping her orange towel around her body. Burns cover her arms and shoulders.

Officer Crane races in from the hall. "What is it?" she asks. Peach gasps and points at the shower behind her.

"The water," she says. "It just started boiling."

The shower next to her switches off and Jessica pulls her curtain open. She moves past Issie, her own orange towel wrapped around her shoulders.

Chapter Thirteen

Plumbers arrive the next day. They replace our old rusted showerheads with shiny stainless-steel models that have adjustable water pressure and get hot in ten seconds flat. New sports equipment appears in the rec yard the day after that: soccer balls that are actually filled with air, and nets to kick them into, basketballs, and a hoop. Even the guards suddenly have top-of-the-line walkie-talkies hanging from their hips.

We all know Dr. Gruen is behind the changes. Most of the girls have already been asked into her office to talk about school and volunteer work and their futures. Sci-Girls sign-up sheets show up outside the cafeteria and in the halls. In less than two hours, there's a name scribbled in every single slot. I scan the sheets to see who got talked into signing up.

Halfway down the page, I spot the name Isabella Suarez written in Issie's loopy, girlie cursive.

"Since when are you joining SciGirls?" I ask Issie later that day. We're in the kitchen making lunch. Today's delicacy: chicken potpie.

Issie goes back to cutting the chicken into cubes. "You can't just *join*. You have to be accepted. They only take the best. There's a test and everything."

I pull open the freezer and start rooting around in the back for a bag of frozen peas. "I thought you said all that science stuff was geeky."

"It *is* geeky, but nobody's asking me to join a watching-TV and eating-M&M'S club." Issie shrugs and looks up from the chicken. "And Dr. Gruen said the girls get to go on field trips to, like, museums and stuff."

"Maybe when they're not getting experimented on," Cara calls from the other side of the kitchen. She wrestles a cookie tray out of the cupboard next to the stove and another three clatter to the floor.

"Ignore her," I say. "I think it sounds kind of cool."

Issie brightens. "Really? Because me and Aaliyah and Erin are forming a study group to prepare for the test. You could come."

The kitchen door swings open before I can answer, and Officer Crane walks in.

"Hands in diamonds," she barks. I put down the frozen peas I'd just found and glance at Issie.

"But we have to make lunch," I say.

"*Diamonds*," Crane says, her voice harder this time. I toss the peas back into the freezer and twist my arms behind my back.

Crane holds the kitchen door open for us. "Let's go. Yellow line."

"*Yellow* line?" Cara drops her hands. The yellow line leads to the infirmary on the second floor. "Why are we—"

"Demerit, Miss Walker," Crane says. "You know there's no talking with your hands in diamonds."

"Well, technically they weren't—"

Crane raises an eyebrow. Cara shuts her mouth and winds her arms behind her back, making a diamond with her fingers. Every muscle in her body tightens, giving her the look of a very small prizefighter. Officer Crane brushes a finger against her scar absently.

"To answer your question," she says, "you'll be getting physicals today. Now move along. Yellow line."

"Physicals?" Issie mouths silently behind Crane's back. I shrug. The three of us follow Officer Crane down the hall and up two flights of stairs.

A long line of Brunesfield inmates twists away from the infirmary door, surrounded by unfamiliar girls in crisp white polo T-shirts. The green patches on their sleeves read "SciGirls."

Issie pokes me in the back. "Look," she whispers, nodding.

"Yeah, I see them," I say, careful to keep my voice low. The SciGirls look just as carefully perfect as the photographs in Dr. Gruen's brochure. They're all pretty and healthy, with little bows and headbands perched in their hair, their lips curved in polite smiles. I try to imagine anyone from Brunesfield wearing a SciGirls polo and beaming at a camera, but I can't. We could never look like these girls do.

"This way," Crane says, leading us to the front of the line. "You three will need to get in and out so you have time to prepare lunch."

She ushers us into a long skinny room. Narrow cots line the walls and a single barred window overlooks the snow-covered ground and distant trees. I don't know where they expect us to sit. The room is crowded with people, and nearly every cot is already taken. The SciGirls stop to chat with the inmates as they dart in and out of the infirmary and the rest of the girls seem just as dazzled by them as Issie was. There are bound to be a few new names on Dr. Gruen's sign-up sheets by the end of the day.

We make our way to the back, weaving past nurses and medical equipment. Dr. Gruen and Director Wu chat with Nurse Ramsick in the corner next to her desk, but Dr. Gruen glances up when I walk past.

"Nice to see you again, Angela," she calls.

I nod, giving her an awkward wave.

"Doctor's pet," Cara says.

"Another demerit," Officer Crane snaps. I flinch—I hadn't realized she was still behind us. Cara turns to argue, but I pinch her on the arm.

"Is that necessary, officer?" Dr. Gruen crosses the room and drops a hand on Cara's shoulder. I think it's meant to be comforting, but Cara stiffens. She's not exactly touchy-feely.

"I don't see why the girls need to have their hands in diamonds anymore," Gruen says, flashing Crane a smile made entirely of perfect white teeth. "I think we can handle them."

Officer Crane gives her a curt nod. "Very well."

Dr. Gruen squeezes Cara's shoulder, then ambles back over to where Nurse Ramsick and Director Wu are still standing.

"Now who's the doctor's pet?" I ask.

"Still you," Cara says. She absently touches her shoulder, staring at Dr. Gruen's back. "That woman is creepy."

I frown. "Dr. Gruen? She was being totally nice to you."

"If you say so," Cara says, shaking out her arm. "You know that would have been my fifth demerit this week?"

"You're kidding," Issie says. Aaliyah waves from across the room, then motions to an empty cot next to her. Issie holds up one finger.

"Not kidding," Cara says. "Two more and I'd have to spend the night in the Seg Block."

"Girl, you've got to handle your shit," Issie says. She claps Cara on the back, then heads over to Aaliyah.

"She's not wrong," I say. We've reached the end of the room, and our seating options are limited. "There's an empty one," I say, pointing to a cot.

"You can take it," Cara says. She waves at Mary Anne, who's standing at the other end of the room. Mary Anne turns to wave back at us, and I see Jessica perched on the cot behind her.

"Hey, runt!" I call, crossing over to her. Jessica looks up. A smile flickers over her lips, then disappears so quickly I'm certain I imagined it.

"Can I sit next to you?" I ask. Jessica jerks her shoulders up and down.

"Hi, Angela," Mary Anne says. She's wearing the same polo as all the other girls—crisp white with a green logo on the shoulder. She wraps a blood-pressure cuff around Jessica's arm and pumps the little black ball attached to it.

"Hey," I say, sitting on the empty cot next to Jessica. "Do you know what this is all about?"

"Dr. Gruen set it up," Mary Anne explains. "You have to submit to a physical before you can join SciGirls, but there's been so much interest that she just arranged for all the girls to get them at the same time. She figured it'd be easier."

Mary Anne finishes the blood-pressure test and picks up a tongue depressor. "Say 'Ah.'"

Jessica tilts her head back and opens her mouth. "Ah."

"Is everyone here in SciGirls?" I ask, looking around at the dozens of girls in white shirts in the infirmary. Mary Anne shakes her head.

"About half of them are real nurses," she explains. "The rest of us aren't certified to draw blood or give shots."

"Shots?" Jessica squeaks.

"Don't tell me you're nervous," I say. Jessica crooks her finger, and I lean closer.

"I don't like needles," she whispers.

"It's a little needle," I explain. "You won't even feel it."

"I don't like big needles *or* little needles."

I reach for her hand. Her fingers feel warm. Like she just ran them under hot water. I tell myself there's nothing to worry about, but my heart beats a little faster.

Mary Anne weighs Jessica and takes her temperature, then motions for a tiny nurse with blond hair to come over to us. The nurse starts to set up, and behind her, Mary Anne frowns. I follow her gaze to Cara, who's arguing with the nurse standing beside her cot. The nurse holds up a long needle. Cara shakes her head. She says something that makes the nurse take a step back and lift a hand to her mouth in shock.

Mary Anne sees me watching her. "I'll be back in a moment," she says, hurrying across the room.

I wish Cara would draw less attention to herself. She could end up in the Seg Block again—or worse. I think of her pocketknife and wonder, for the millionth time, where she's hidden it. The Seg Block isn't the only place they could send her.

The nurse beside me pulls a syringe out of a plastic wrapper and flicks the needle. Jessica stiffens. I look away from Cara and reach for the little girl's hand.

"Watch her do me first, okay?" I say. "Then you'll see that it doesn't hurt."

Jessica presses her lips together. She nods. "Okay."

The nurse leans forward. "Ready?" she asks. I nod, and she swabs my arm with alcohol. "Three . . . two . . ."

I feel a pinch, and stick out my tongue, making a face. Jessica giggles.

"All done," the nurse says. She pulls the needle out of my arm and slaps a Band-Aid over the tiny prick in my skin.

"What do you think?" I ask Jessica. "Not that scary, right?"

The nurse picks up another wrapped needle. Jessica reaches for my hand again.

"It was a little scary," she says.

"Where's your teddy bear, hon?" the nurse asks, unwrapping the second needle. Jessica shrugs.

"Don't have it."

Annoyance flashes across the nurse's face, then disappears a second later. "Oh well," she says with a cheery smile, "I guess you'll just have to hold on to your friend, then." She winks at me and douses a cotton swab with alcohol. Jessica watches. The lightbulb above her flickers.

"Jessica . . ." My chest clenches. Jessica grabs my hand. Her fingers feel like lit matches. The air around us grows warmer.

"Ready?" the nurse asks. Jessica starts humming below her breath. Just one note.

"Give me a second?" I ask. The nurse shrugs. I kneel in front of Jessica, making her look me in the eye. Charlie used to hate getting shots. I'd have to pull out every big-sister trick I had just to get him into the doctor's office. But now, crouching in front of this terrifying little girl, my mind goes completely blank.

I clear my throat. "Um . . . why did the cow cross the road?"

Jessica blinks at me. "I don't know."

"To get to the udder side."

There's a beat of silence. Jessica frowns.

"Get it?" I say. "*Udder* side? It's a joke."

Her lip twitches. "It was dumb."

"Are you kidding? Those are the best ones!"

The nurse pricks Jessica's arm with the needle. Black floods Jessica's eyes, and the light switches on and off. I turn on instinct, my mouth already open to shout at the nurse for surprising us. But she isn't looking at me. She's watching Jessica's face. Curious.

She pulls the needle from her arm, and the black fades from Jessica's eyes.

Something slams to the ground behind me. I jump and spin around. Officer Crane is standing between Cara and the nurse she'd been arguing with. A metal table lies on its side on the floor, needles and tongue depressors scattered around it. Mary Anne stands with Dr. Gruen on the other side of the room, her forehead wrinkled in concern.

"That's another demerit, Miss Walker," Crane says.

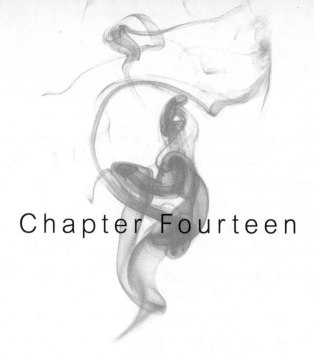

Chapter Fourteen

I slip Cara a note in the middle of math class.

What the hell happened in the infirmary?

I tried to talk to her during lunch, but she decided today was the perfect day to scrape all the gum off the tables in the cafeteria, leaving Issie and me to prepare the meal alone. She reads my note under the table, then glances at me and shakes her head, pretending to be distracted by the video playing on the ancient television at the front of class.

I glance at Brody, who's collapsed behind a giant steel desk, his head resting against the chalkboard. Aaliyah snuck out of her seat the second he started snoring and drew a pair of twisting devil horns behind his head. We don't normally have chalk, but this morning a brand-new box appeared in every classroom, courtesy of Dr. Gruen. Girls have been drawing things on the blackboards ever since.

Jessica sits in the seat next to me, sucking on the end of her braid and doodling on her own knuckles. Issie let her borrow her Sharpie, and she's started sketching tiny pictures on her fingers. A sun. A moon. A heart. The rest of the class huddles around a desk at the back of the room, trying to figure out what will be on the SciGirls test.

"Cara," I whisper, shooting an anxious look at the front of the room. Brody releases a guttural snore and shifts in his seat. If he wakes up now he'll be pissed and probably spend the rest of the period quizzing us on how to multiply fractions (always doubly hard because he doesn't know how to do it himself and tends to make up the answers). A crumpled-up paper ball sails over my head and lands on the floor just inches away from his heavy black boot. It's another one of Dr. Gruen's brochures; I can tell from the thick, glossy paper. They've been everywhere lately.

I spin around in my chair, shooting Issie a look.

"Sorry! That was meant for Cara," she whispers. Cara glances over her shoulder.

"What?"

"Do you think we'll need to know the equation for calculating velocity?"

"Why would you need to know that?"

"For the SciGirls test, Issie says, like this should be obvious.

"It's a stupid volunteer program," Cara says. "Why do you even want to join?"

She turns around again, and Issie shakes a fist at her back. Today her fingers read "hell."

I glance back to Cara. She's still intently watching the video, which is ridiculous because (a) the video is about subtraction, which even the most undereducated girls in lock-up actually know how to do, and (b) we've already seen it three times this month.

"Are you really going to ignore me?" I whisper. Her jaw tightens and she shrugs.

"They wanted to give me a flu shot, okay?" she says.

"That's why you pushed over a *table*?"

"I didn't *want* a flu shot. Who knows what they put in those things?"

I close my eyes, so frustrated I can hardly speak. I shouldn't be surprised. Cara has always had trouble with authority. But I keep thinking of Mary Anne studying her from across the infirmary, that disapproving wrinkle between her eyes.

"Did you ever think of just telling them no?" I ask. Before Cara can answer, the classroom door opens and Officer Mateo steps in. Carmen releases a loud catcall and Brody, giving one final snort-snore, wakes up. Jessica wrinkles her nose at him. It makes her look like an angry kitten.

"Can I help you, officer?" Brody asks, trying to nonchalantly wipe the drool from his chin. Mateo clears his throat, pretending not to notice.

"I need to borrow Miss Davis for a moment," he says. I sit up a little straighter.

"Angela, on your feet!" Brody barks, and even Mateo shakes his head in disbelief. I slip out of my desk, casting one last glance at Cara.

"We can talk more later."

She rolls her eyes. "Goody."

A few girls whistle as Mateo leads me out of the room. A smile curls the corners of his lips.

"Dr. Gruen's asked to see you again," he says once the door swings shut behind me. "Seems like she likes you."

"Yeah?" I say. There's a tiny blob of shaving cream on Mateo's neck, just below his jaw. I want to wipe it away but, instead, I cross my hands over my chest. God, this feels weird. What do I usually do with my hands?

"Did you ever listen to that book?" he asks. When I don't answer, he frowns and wipes his lower lip with the back of his hand. "What is it?"

I blush. *Stop staring like a freak, Angela.* "Um, shaving cream? Right there."

He turns his head at the exact moment that I point and my finger grazes his jaw. It's rough, like sandpaper. My ex-boyfriend Jake had little-boy skin, even though he was two years older than me. He could barely grow a wispy mustache. Mateo has actual *stubble.*

I drop my hand, but Mateo just laughs. He stops walking and pulls his shirt up to wipe the shaving cream from his face. The bottom comes untucked, and I catch the slightest glimpse of skin just above his belt.

I swear to God I almost stop breathing. I haven't seen this much of the opposite sex in nearly two years. It feels borderline pornographic.

"What would I do without you?" Mateo says, clumsily tucking his shirt back in.

"I'm sure you'd get by," I say.

For a few minutes the only sounds in the hallway are our shoes thumping against the floor. Mateo clears his throat.

"You didn't answer my question," he says. "That book? *Tuck* something? Did you listen to it?"

"Oh yeah," I say, grateful for the change of topic. I usually listen to the tapes while I'm doing the dishes after meals, but I've been so focused on Jessica for the past few days that I keep forgetting to stick them in the cassette player. "Just once, though. Been busy."

"Just once?" Mateo asks. "Do you usually listen to them more than that?"

He holds the door for me and I shuffle into the next hallway. "There are only six audiobooks in our entire library," I explain. "I've heard them all at least five times."

"Wait, really? That sucks."

"I can't even tell you. Do you know we have copies of the first two His Dark Materials books, but not the last one? I've spent a year and a half wondering what happened to Lyra."

"You're *kidding*." Mateo laughs. It's a big, booming noise that echoes of the walls around us. I so rarely hear laughter in these halls. It makes them feel different, somehow. Warmer. "That's torture."

"Tell me about it. The first thing I'm going to do when I get out of here is buy that freaking book and see how the series ends."

We turn down the hallway that leads to Dr. Gruen's office. Mary Anne sits at a small desk just outside Dr. Gruen's door, like a secretary. She looks up as we approach.

"Angela Davis," she murmurs, studying a chart attached to the front of her binder. "There you are—three thirty. You can go right in."

"Thanks," I say, reaching for the door.

"See you around," Mateo says. He winks at me and, once again, all the air whooshes out of the room. *He's a guard*, I tell myself. *He's a guard he's a guard he's a guard.*

I slip into Dr. Gruen's office without a word. Wet, sticky snow falls outside the window next to her desk. It clings to the tree branches and creates gray slush on the fields surrounding us. I think of the thin sweatshirt I left crumpled in a ball on my bunk, and I shiver.

Dr. Gruen doesn't look up from the folder she's examining. It isn't mine, I can tell by the unfamiliar photographs clipped to the inside cover.

"Miss Davis." She closes the folder and places her hands on top of it. "Thank you so much for seeing me again."

"Sure." I settle myself in the leather chair across from her desk.

"How are things with Jessica?"

"Good," I say. "I think she's starting to feel a little more comfortable here."

Interest flickers across Dr. Gruen's face. She clasps her hands together.

"That's fantastic," she says, leaning forward. "So, she's spoken to you?"

I shrug. "A little."

"Has she told you anything interesting?"

I think of the monster trucks and how nervous Jessica sounded when she told me how her father used to teach her about cars. But that story isn't mine to share.

Dr. Gruen closes her eyes, shaking her head. "I apologize. How inappropriate of me. Of course you shouldn't reveal anything Jessica told you in confidence."

She flashes me a smile. I release a breath I didn't realize I'd been holding.

"That's okay," I say.

"Good." Her hand hovers above her desk for a split second before she lowers her palm to the folder. "Do you know what this is?" she asks. I shake my head. "This is Jessica's file. I thought you should know a little more about why she was sent here since you'll be spending so much time with her."

Aaliyah's voice echoes in my ear. *She killed her whole family*. Nerves crawl over my skin, and I find myself sitting up a little taller in my chair. I'm not sure I want to know what Jessica did, but Dr. Gruen doesn't wait for me to protest. She flips the folder open and slides it around so I can see the photographs.

Jessica stands in front of a white man and woman with dull blond hair and slumping shoulders. A little boy crouches next to her. His shaggy brown hair hangs over thick glasses that take up most of his face. A run-down house towers over them, surrounded by a field filled with dead grass and skeletal trees. The scene belongs in a slasher film. All that's missing is a man wearing a creepy mask and holding a bloody ax.

"This is Jessica's foster family." Dr. Gruen tugs the paper clip off with a manicured fingernail and fans the photographs over her desk. "Family" isn't the word I'd use to describe these four people. They look more like strangers asked to stand next to one another in line. The man and woman don't touch or even *look at* Jessica and the little boy. Instead they glower at the camera, arms stiff.

One photograph hides behind the others, only the corner visible beneath the stack. I lean forward.

"Can I?" I ask.

"By all means."

I tug the bottom photo out from under the stack. It shows Jessica and the little boy kneeling next to the front porch, tracing pictures in the dirt with a twig. The corner of her mouth slants upward, like she's thinking of smiling but hasn't decided yet. I grin at the photograph before sliding it back beneath the others. I've seen that look before.

"Has she mentioned them to you?" Dr. Gruen asks.

"No. I didn't know she was in foster care."

"I see." Dr. Gruen taps the photographs into a neat stack and paper clips them together. "Prepare yourself. These next photos are a bit shocking."

She flips a page in the folder before I can respond. A new photograph stares up at me: fire eating away at the run-down house and racing over the field. Smoke billowing into the sky, obscuring everything but the angry orange flames.

I don't realize I'm digging my fingers into my legs until I feel a prick of pain on my thighs.

"She didn't tell me," I say, flexing my fingers. Dr. Gruen nods and turns the page. There's another photo, this one of the little boy with the floppy brown hair lying in a hospital bed. Tubes wind out of his nose and around his head. His glasses sit on the table next to him, cracks splintering the lenses.

"Her foster father was killed in the fire," Dr. Gruen explains. "And her little brother is still in the hospital. They don't know if he'll ever wake up."

"*Jessica* did that?" I ask.

"We believe so. She's awaiting trial for arson and man-slaughter. The State of New York wants to try her as an adult."

I stare at the little boy lying in that bed and imagine Charlie. Charlie with tubes coming out of his mouth. Charlie unable to open his eyes. Acid stings the back of my throat, and for a second, I think I might throw up.

"Why are you telling me this?" I ask.

"You and I both know that Jessica didn't set this fire intending to hurt her family. What happened was an accident, the unfortunate side effect of something she can't control. But the police didn't see it that way. A judge certainly won't. Angela, I came here hoping that I could keep Jessica from life in prison. But since you're spending so much time with her, I thought you needed to know the truth. The whole truth."

I close my eyes, trying to sort out this conversation in my head. But it's hard enough for me to make sense of words written down on a page in front of me, and this sounds like one of my dad's scary stories.

"What about SciGirls?" I ask, finally. "Everyone's signing up for that test. Are you planning on accepting any of them? Or are you just here for Jessica?"

Silence stretches between us. It feels *weighty*, somehow. Like it's filled with more mysterious, creepy things.

"There's a little more to SciGirls than what's in those brochures." Dr. Gruen glances over her shoulder, at the photograph of the girls in lab coats. "When I started my career as a caseworker, it was my job to keep kids like you from falling through the cracks. But kids like Jessica don't have anyone to protect them. No one understands their unique abilities and challenges. No one believes them when they say it wasn't their fault. That's where SciGirls comes in."

A chill spreads through my body. "I don't understand. Kids *like* Jessica? There are others?"

"Oh yes. And when they get in trouble or make something strange happen, it's my job to evaluate them and make a case to have them sent to our facilities, where we can help them. But I never forgot about all the other children I met back when I was a caseworker. There's a place for them at our program as well."

"I don't understand. What kind of place?"

Dr. Gruen taps an ink-stained finger against the folder. "SciGirls focuses on helping children who've developed unusual abilities, but we also employ scientists and researchers and doctors. We reach out to girls who might never have pursued a career in science and help them explore those roles in our labs and hospitals. They start as assistants, of course, but over the years, many of our girls have gone on to study science and medicine at a college level. Like I mentioned before, it's a very prestigious program. I'm not just here for Jessica. I'm here for all of you."

College. I've never even considered college before, but now an image rises in the back of my head: perfect imaginary Stacy with her shiny hair and crisp white lab coat. Then the picture shifts, and it's not Stacy wearing the lab coat anymore. It's me. Mateo stands beside me, holding my hand. He leans over and kisses—

I close my eyes and shake the image out of my head. Kids like me don't go to college. "How can I help?"

Dr. Gruen opens the folder again and checks a Post-it on the inside cover. "Jessica's trial is scheduled for two weeks from today. I mostly need you to keep doing what you've been doing. Be her friend. Get her to open up to you. If she says anything . . . notable, it'd be best if you told me directly."

Nerves buzz up my skin, though I can't quite place why. It's like feeling a prick of water on your arm when it looks like rain, only a second later you can't remember if you felt it or imagined it. "You want me to spy on her?"

"I want you to *help* her," Dr. Gruen amends smoothly. "You might have seen Jessica carrying around a stuffed animal."

"Yeah," I say. "A teddy bear, right?"

"Right. I gave her that bear when she first arrived. It was a kind of experiment, you see. It's common for pyretics to—"

"Pyretics?" I interrupt.

"It's a technical term," Dr. Gruen explains. "We use it to describe children who can start fires with their mind. As I was saying, pyretics often direct their abilities on specific objects. We believe the objects help them to focus their power. Like a token, or a good-luck charm."

I think of blue flames eating at charred fur. "The other kids also set teddy bears on fire?"

"Or dolls or action figures," Dr. Gruen says. "I wasn't certain of Jessica's abilities when I first met her, so I gave her the bear as a test. I know it sounds strange, but the behavior is quite helpful to us. When Jessica burns something, it leaves behind a trace signature. Like a fingerprint. We learn all sorts of things by studying them. Where she got her powers from, for instance, and how developed they are. Pyretic abilities aren't passed genetically, so this information is essential for our research."

Something suddenly clicks into place. "That's why you took my sink," I say. Dr. Gruen nods.

"Exactly. Unfortunately the fingerprint Jessica left on your sink wasn't strong enough to give us the information we need. We'll need to take a look at her bear to gain a full understanding of her abilities. For reasons we don't quite understand, pyretics tend to bond with a single object. The fingerprints they leave elsewhere are never quite as strong." Dr. Gruen pauses, studying me. "We didn't anticipate her *hiding* the bear. Do you think you might be able to bring it to me?"

There it is again—that nervous feeling. Like a tiny prick of water. I wrap my fingers around my arms, trying to ignore it. I don't love the idea of spying or stealing Jessica's things. But then I think of that burning house and the little boy with the tubes running up his nose. Dr. Gruen's right—Jessica didn't set that fire on purpose. She doesn't belong in prison. But she needs help.

If SciGirls can help her, that's where she should be.

I nod. "I can get it."

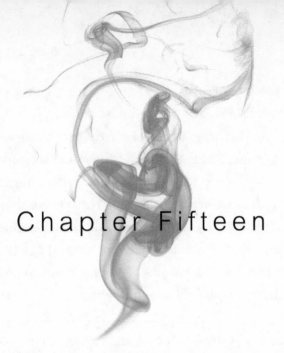

Chapter Fifteen

I lie awake in bed that night, my eyes pressed shut so it looks like I'm sleeping. It feels like hours pass before I hear blankets rustle in the bunk next to mine. I wait. The mattress moans. Our door creaks open.

One second. Two seconds. I hold my breath until I start to feel dizzy. The door clicks shut again. I exhale and open my eyes, pushing the blanket off my legs.

I wait until Mateo's flashlight disappears around the corner, and then I creep through the door. Brunesfield yawns before me, dark and threatening. I shiver. Fifteen minutes until he passes this way again.

Jessica drifts down the hall, the charred teddy bear dangling from her hand. Ashy fur flakes away and flutters across the floor. Silvery light pours in from the windows at the ceiling, illuminating her like a ghost.

She goes to the same bathroom. I hide at the end of the hall. Wind presses against the windows. The walls creak. I wait until the smell of burning fabric reaches my nose. Then I follow her.

Cold spreads from the concrete floor to my toes and up the back of my legs, like Brunesfield itself is reaching through my skin and wrapping its fingers around my bones. I wish I could turn around and hurry back to my dorm. But then I think of Dr. Gruen tapping her ink-stained fingers against Jessica's file, and I force myself into the bathroom.

Orange light dances across the moldy tile. A faucet drips, and the sound bounces off the walls. Jessica sits cross-legged at the same spot on the damp floor. Her teddy bear lies in front of her, flames flickering over its ruined fur. She stares at the bear, and when the fire grows too high, she jerks around to face the sinks on the right wall. Water gurgles in the pipes and pours from the faucets, boiling. It bubbles as it splashes across the tile.

She's practicing, I realize. She's pushing her powers as far as they can go, then looking at the water to calm herself down. Jessica's shoulders quake. She lowers her hands to the floor, and rocks back and forth.

I step forward, and water gathers beneath my toes. Dr. Gruen said that a lot of the kids she works with do this, but all at once I put together why: the humming, the rocking, the way Jessica refuses to talk or look people in the eyes.

"You're scared," I say.

Jessica flinches, then turns so quickly that I duck behind a wall. I imagine flames eating away my skin, smoke choking my lungs. My heart beats so fast and hard that it makes my chest ache. But nothing happens. I inhale, then peek around the corner again.

Jessica stares at me with those black eyes, digging her fingers into the spaces between the tiles. I'm suddenly aware of the empty hallways twisting around us, the girls fast asleep in their locked dorms, and Mateo wandering around on the other side of the building. I'm alone. Completely, perfectly alone.

"I'm not going to hurt you." I step into the bathroom, holding my hands in front of me. She cocks her head, like a bird.

"Stop." Her voice comes out sounding raspy and thin. It raises the hair on the back of my neck, like fingernails on a chalkboard. I stop where I am, though I feel like I should be running.

Ragged breathing shakes Jessica's chest. The black fades back into her pupils, and she's normal again. She could be a girl at Charlie's school. The next-door neighbor's daughter. She shuts her eyes, and relief floods her face. Something inside me twists.

"Are you okay?" I lower myself to the floor and pull my knees to my chest.

"I almost hurt you."

"But you didn't," I say. "You stopped it."

"This time," she whispers.

I think of the photographs Dr. Gruen showed me: the boy in the hospital with tubes running up his nose, a little gray house being devoured by fire. "Is that why you don't talk to anyone?" I ask. "You're afraid of hurting them?"

A minute passes. Jessica presses a drop of water into the floor. Wind howls through the distant trees, and I swear I can hear the shaking branches even though they're miles away.

"You can tell me," I say. Jessica swallows.

"I've hurt people before," she says in a small voice. "My foster brother. He's in the hospital."

"And you think it's your fault?"

"It *is* my fault."

"Why?"

Jessica doesn't answer. Her teddy bear lies in front of her on the tile. Forgotten. I could grab it now, take it directly to Dr. Gruen and be done with this whole night. But something stops me.

I clear my throat. "Did I ever tell you why I'm here?" I ask. Jessica shakes her head. "Uh, so I was dating this guy, Jake. He was really cute, you know? Best-looking guy at my school."

I pause, remembering Jake's face. He had a gap between his two front teeth, and a dimple in his left cheek. He wore his hair long, so it flopped over his pale blue eyes. I used to run my hands through it and tuck it behind his ears. Afterward, my fingers always smelled like pine needles, and like the clove cigarettes he smoked.

"I knew he was bad for me," I continue. "But I pretended I didn't."

"Because he was cute?" Jessica's voice is barely a whisper.

I roll my eyes. "Right. Because he was cute."

The corner of her mouth twists into an almost-smile.

"It was more than that, though," I continue. "He looked at me. *Really* looked at me, you know? Everyone else thought I was just some rotten kid, but with Jake . . . well he didn't even *care*. Like, maybe, that's kind of why he liked me. So when he started breaking into apartments, I helped."

Jessica traces her finger over the tile. "That's why you're here? Because you robbed someone's apartment?"

I open my mouth, but my voice catches in my throat. I never really learned how to tell this story. I stumble over details and misremember the exact chain of events. How do you talk about the worst thing you've ever done? How do you describe the way the floor falls out from under your feet? How you drop down to a place you can never crawl back out of?

I swallow and force myself to keep talking. "Someone got hurt at the last place we broke into. The woman who lived there heard us and came into the hallway to see what was going on. Jake and I tried to run past her and she lost her balance. Fell down the stairs."

I remember that moment like it just happened. We'd already finished getting the good stuff: the computers and electronics were in the car, and I'd stuffed all the cash from her purse into my back pocket. We were just taking one last sweep of the place to see if we missed anything when I heard a door rattle and a woman's voice ask, "Who's there?"

Jake took off. He was down the hall and out the door before the woman knew what was going on. I'm the one who messed up. She grabbed for me as I ran past, caught me by the wrist. I tried to pull my arm loose, and she lost her balance and fell.

I shiver and pull my sweatshirt sleeves down over my hands. She didn't even scream, but the sound her body made as it rolled down the steps was worse than anything I'd ever heard.

Jessica stops tracing the tile. She watches me from the corner of her eye.

"I'm telling you this because you should know that *I* deserve to be here." I inhale, and the raspy sound of my breathing echoes off the walls. "I did something bad even though I knew it was bad, and a woman got hurt. Because of me."

"But you didn't mean to," Jessica says.

"Did *you* mean to?"

"Yes." Jessica touches her teddy bear, and a flake of black fur crumbles onto the tile. "I wanted to hurt him."

I think of the photograph of Jessica crouching next to that little boy drawing pictures in the dirt. "You wanted to hurt your foster brother?"

"No."

"Then who?"

Black tendrils race across Jessica's eyes like clouds in a storm. The tenderness I'd started to feel toward her snaps right off. I scramble to my feet, fear raising the hair on the back of my neck.

"Holy—" I murmur, covering my mouth with my hands. Jessica rocks forward, pressing her hands flat against the floor. I want to run, but I picture flames chasing me across the bathroom, fire eating into my skin. The floor grows hot. The bottoms of my feet blister against the scorching tile, and tears prick the corners of my eyes. The air around Jessica hums. Like the air around power lines.

"Jessica," I whisper. I can suddenly feel each inch of space between me and every other person in this building. There's no one to help. No one to come if I scream. "Jessica, calm down. *Please.*"

"It was my foster dad," she whispers in that too-high, nails-on-the-chalkboard voice. "He was the one I wanted to hurt."

"He's not here," I say, but Jessica doesn't seem to hear me. She rocks back and forth, her eyes oily and dark. The light above us flicks on and then off again.

"He was mean to us," she says.

"You're safe now."

"He called me a monster."

The teddy bear sparks. Crackling red and orange flames explode from its fur. Smoke curls around my arms and legs and singes the skin inside my nose. I leap backward, banging my hip against one of the cracked porcelain sinks. Pain spreads up my back and through my pelvis. I bite my lip to keep from crying out.

"I don't want to be a monster," Jessica says.

For a moment I'm too terrified to do anything but watch the stuffed bear burn. But that word, "monster," cuts into me, touching something deep and hidden. I know about monsters. They're dark, beautiful things, just like in my dad's stories. They're as familiar to me as his deep voice and the spicy smell of his cologne. There's no reason to be afraid.

I lower myself to my knees, careful not to touch the burning bear. Firelight dances in Jessica's eyes. Hands shaking, I reach for her shoulder. Her skin burns hot beneath her T-shirt.

The words come to me, and it's like they were always there. Like I always knew what I was going to say.

"Monsters are more interesting."

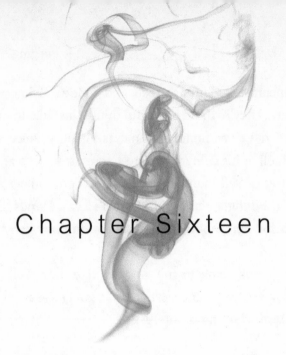

Chapter Sixteen

Jessica lurches forward, like she might vomit. The flames on the floor burn down to embers.

"Are you okay?" I ask.

Jessica's eyes clear, the black fading back to brown and white. She nods, and the heat drains from her skin, leaving her arm cold beneath my fingers. The last embers go dark, and thin ribbons of smoke twist toward the ceiling. The smell of burned teddy bear stings my nose.

"I'm sorry," she whispers.

"That's okay." My voice comes out fast and high. I clear my throat. "We should get back to the dorms."

Jessica frowns, and a crease appears between her eyebrows. I see an echo of my brother in her expression. He always got the same look on his face when he was working on a math problem or trying to beat a new level in a video game. Even when he was little, he was always serious. Determined.

"Come on." I drop my hand on Jessica's shoulder.

She picks up her bear, and we creep across the bathroom. The floor has cooled again, and the damp tile chills the bottoms of my feet. Smoke clogs the air, making my eyes water. I pull my shirt over my nose to keep from coughing.

Jessica drifts along beside me like a shadow. The snow piled beside Brunesfield's walls muffles the outside noise, so all we hear are our own footsteps and the distant sounds of inmates talking in their sleep. I don't think fifteen minutes have passed since I followed Jessica out of our dorm, so the coast should be clear. Still, nerves climb my skin. Getting caught by the night guard is the best way I can think of to completely screw myself over.

I hesitate at the end of the hall and motion for Jessica to stop walking. I don't hear anything, but the rubber-soled boots the guards wear don't make much sound on the concrete. After a moment, I risk poking my head around the wall to look.

The hall stretches before me, dark and empty. I exhale a breath I didn't realize I was holding and gesture for Jessica to move closer.

A narrow beam sweeps across the floor: flashlight. *Shit.*

I push Jessica back and ease my body behind the wall. I wait for Mateo to come bounding down the stairs but the man who appears is taller, thinner.

Brody.

No. I mouth the word without making a sound and duck back behind the corner, praying Brody doesn't come this way. This doesn't make sense. Mateo's shift doesn't end until midnight, and there's never more than one night guard on duty. They'd only call Brody if someone thought there was trouble.

Something cold hits the back of my throat. *Trouble.* Of course. They know we snuck out.

I press my lips together, trying to ignore the alarm bells sounding in my ears. This can't be right. If they knew we snuck out, it wouldn't be two guards patrolling the halls in the dark with flashlights. It would be a team, and there'd be sirens blaring. Officer Crane would be lining everyone up with their hands in diamonds.

So they can't *know*; they must suspect. Which means we can still make it back to our dorm without getting caught. I suck a breath in through my teeth. Brody's blocking the quickest route, but if we circle around and head down the east hall, we could still make it to our beds before anyone discovers us missing. I wrap my hand around Jessica's, and her fingers feel sweaty in my palm.

"This way," I whisper. She nods.

Moonlight pours in through the windows in the hallway, painting the floor black and silver. I hold my breath and roll my weight to my toes to soften my footsteps. Jessica and I retrace our steps to the bathroom and then creep down toward the east hall that curves back around to our dorm. I listen for the sound of boots, but Brunesfield is eerily silent. The quiet magnifies every noise I make, until each heartbeat and footstep booms in my ears.

I pause at the corner leading to our dorm and peer around the wall.

Officer Mateo stands less than a foot away, close enough that I could run a finger along the back of his stiff shirt. Blood pounds in my ears. I try to duck back behind the wall, but he turns, catching me full in the face with a white beam of light.

"Angela?" Mateo angles the flashlight away from me, illuminating his face from below, casting strange shadows over his chin and nose. The muscles along his jaw tighten. He grabs my arm and pulls me closer.

"What the hell are you doing out here?" he snaps. He glances over his shoulder. He's worried Brody will see us.

"I'm sorry," I whisper, racking my brain for a good excuse. "I . . . I thought I heard something, and I came to see what it—"

"Don't lie to me, Davis!"

I flinch. He's never called me by my last name before. I've always been Angela. Like I'm a friend.

"I . . ." I try to come up with an explanation for why we're out, but nothing could explain how we got through the locked door.

I glance at Jessica. She's standing on the other side of the wall, where Mateo can't see her, hugging her teddy bear to her chest. She'll be sent back to Seg if anyone finds out she broke out of our dorm. She watches me, eyes wide. Trusting.

Mateo rakes his fingers through his hair. A stray lock falls over his forehead. It looks almost black in the darkness, and I have a sudden, fierce desire to brush it off his face.

"How'd you get out of your dorm?" Mateo asks, pulling me out of my daydream.

"The door wasn't locked."

"You're lying."

"It *wasn't*," I insist. My cheeks burn. I hate that he's the one who found me. His disappointment feels like a slap across the face. "What do you want me to say?"

"What do I want you to say? It's the middle of the night, and you're out of bounds. Do you have any idea how much trouble you could get in?" He steps closer and lowers his voice. "Haven't you been paying attention to what's happening around here?"

Something rises in my chest—this feeling of having missed the last step on a staircase. "What are you talking about?"

Mateo cocks an eyebrow. "You haven't noticed?"

"I thought things were getting better. The showers and the physicals . . ."

"Punishments are getting harsher. Yesterday, Officer Sterling gave Ellen a demerit for *coughing* while her hands were in diamonds." Mateo leans in closer. "Sneaking out at night could get you a night in Seg. Girls have already been sent down for less."

Seg. A shiver crawls up the backs of my legs. "I didn't know that."

"Well, now you do. Dammit, Angela. This isn't the time to get in trouble!" Mateo looks so much like a guard right now, more than he ever did when he was crouched over a crossword puzzle in the Seg Block. He glances over his shoulder again, then leans in closer. The hard line of his jaw softens. "Tell me what's going on. Really."

I swallow. Mateo's standing so close that I smell the soap-and-coffee scent of his skin. I see the tiny nick on his neck where he cut himself shaving. It's dark enough that I can almost pretend he's not a guard and I'm not just some juvie girl. We're just two teenagers in a club somewhere and Mateo—*Ben*—is asking me to tell him my problems.

Then I see Jessica's thin body out of the corner of my eye and it's like a cold hand clamps down on my neck.

I didn't tell her the whole story back in the bathroom. It's true that I robbed a house, and it's true that, because of me, someone got hurt. But after I was arrested, the cops offered me a plea bargain. If I gave them Jake's name, they promised to let me walk. Aside from the assault charge, my record was mostly petty theft, but Jake had graduated to armed robbery. And, at the ripe old age of eighteen and six months, he could be tried as an adult.

Charlie once asked me why I didn't take it. "Juvie only lasts two years," I told him. "You betray someone, and you have to live with it for the rest of your life."

I think of that now, as I stare at the charred teddy bear hanging from Jessica's hand. I followed her because Dr. Gruen asked me to bring her that bear, didn't I? So what am I waiting for? I could ask Mateo to take me to the doctor right now. I could hand over the bear, tell her what I saw, and make this entire thing disappear.

Just as I'm about to open my mouth and do exactly that, I feel it again—that sudden jolt in my gut telling me I've missed something big. This entire night feels wrong. I wish, for the millionth time, that I were just a little bit smarter. That I could work it out on my own.

Jessica frowns. She looks so much like Charlie. They could have been classmates. Friends.

"Nothing's wrong," I say, turning back to Mateo. "I scored a cigarette, and I know there's a broken smoke detector in the bathroom, so I snuck out to light up."

Mateo studies me for a long moment, like I'm one of his stupid crossword puzzles and he can't figure out the clue. I'm used to disappointing people. But this time it feels fresh, like someone cutting open a wound that's long healed.

"You know I have to report this, right?" he says.

"I know."

"And you're sure you want to stick with that story?"

I stare at the nick on his neck so I don't have to meet his eyes. "Yes, sir," I say.

"Heya Ben, you there?" Brody's voice comes out of nowhere. Every muscle in my body tenses, but then I hear the crackle of static and realize it's just Mateo's walkie-talkie. Mateo unclips it from his belt and raises it to his mouth.

"I'm here," he says. "Find anything?"

"Negative. You?"

Mateo hesitates. I feel his eyes on me, but I can't bring myself to look at him. Not when he's about to give me up to Brody. I swallow and stare down at my feet, bracing myself.

"No," Mateo says. "There's no one here."

"Dammit. One more lap, then we call it?"

"Sounds good," Mateo says. I wait until he clips the walkie-talkie back to his belt before looking up.

"You didn't turn me in," I say.

Mateo switches his flashlight off. Darkness rushes in around us.

"I'm finishing my rounds," he says. "You *will* be in your bunk by the time I make it past your dorm, or my first stop tomorrow morning is Director Wu's office. You understand that, Davis?"

"Yes, sir," I say. For a moment there's silence. Then Mateo nods, and without another word, he turns and stalks down the hall in the opposite direction.

Chapter Seventeen

I replay those last few moments with Mateo as Jessica and I sneak back to our dorm. I picture the downward tilt of his mouth and the way his forehead furrowed with disappointment. I think of how every muscle in my body went rigid when he turned off his flashlight.

Haven't you been paying attention?

It's true, punishments have gotten harsher. Issie even mentioned that she had more demerits than ever. But so many other things are better—the new equipment and flu shots and SciGirls.

Once again, I picture myself in the SciGirls lab coat, Mateo standing beside me. Shame warms my face. I shake my head, trying to force the fantasy away.

"Stupid," I say under my breath. This crush is getting out of control. Confusing. In fact, it's a *good* thing Mateo found me. Now I can squash this thing once and for all.

Jessica and I turn onto our hallway and relief rushes through me. No Brody, no Mateo. The route to our dorm is all clear. I start forward, but Jessica hesitates.

"What's wrong?" I whisper. Something flickers at the corner of my eye, and I flinch, whipping around. But there's nothing there.

"Don't let them take me away," Jessica says, her voice barely a whisper. "Promise."

I swallow. My throat feels cottony dry.

"You mean for your trial?" I ask. "You don't want to go to prison."

Jessica shifts her eyes up, considering me. It feels like she can see through my skin, all the way down to the squishy, ugly parts I don't want anyone to know about.

"Jessica," I try again. "Where do you think they're going to take you?"

A footstep echoes down the hall, cutting us off. I pull the door open, ushering Jessica inside.

"How *did* you get the lock open?" I ask as I push the door closed behind us. The hall outside our door is empty but I still shiver, imagining Brody stepping out of the shadows. I hold the doorknob still until I'm sure it's closed. Only then do I release the latch.

"I didn't," Jessica whispers. She creeps across the room and slips into her bunk, pulling the scratchy blanket up to her chin.

"What do you mean you didn't?"

"It's always unlocked," she says. I frown. That's impossible. The doors lock automatically.

"It morning already?" Issie murmurs, rolling over on the top bunk. The bunk bed's metal frame shifts as she moves. The sound makes me cringe.

"It's still nighttime, Is," I say, crawling into bed. "Go to sleep."

"I *was* asleep." She yawns. Loudly. "Tell me a story."

"It's too late for that." I punch my pillow and fold it in half, but it's still too thin. I groan and shove my arm beneath the pillow to prop it up.

"Please? Tell the story of us."

I sigh and drop my head onto the flat, lumpy pillow. Moonlight reflects off Jessica's black eyes. She hugs the teddy bear to her chest.

"It's not a story," I say. "It's what's going to happen."

My eyes droop, already heavy with sleep. When I open them again, Jessica's no longer holding her teddy bear. She's wrapped her arms around her pillow, and her eyes are shut.

She hid it, I realize sleepily. *Why would she do that?*

"Angie," Issie urges. I yawn.

"One day, we're all breaking out of this place," I murmur. The story flickers through my brain, but it's not me and Issie racing through the woods. It's me and Charlie. We're running and running, but the wolves are right at our heels.

"One day we're going far, far away."

Loud pounding echoes through our dorm room the next morning. I groan and rub my eyes as the door swings open and Officer Crane steps into the room. The early-morning sun hits her scar, making it look even shinier and more twisted than usual. It's like an oily rope coiling across her face.

"Out of bed, ladies," she barks, rapping her nightstick against the wall.

"The hell?" Cara mutters. She pushes herself onto one elbow and wipes the sleep from her eyes with the palm of her hand. "It's early."

Two more guards follow Crane into our dorm. I recognize Officer Sterling, but the other—a thin Latina woman with heavy eyebrows and a man's haircut—is new. Issie swears from the bunk above me. Her feet swing over the side a second later. At the sight of the guards, even Cara manages to wake herself up and scramble down the rickety metal ladder.

I force myself out of bed and shuffle to Issie's side. Jessica stands directly across from me, her skinny arms wrapped around her chest. She glances at me, her eyes wide with fear. I wink, and some of the tension drains from her shoulders.

"What—" I start, but Crane silences me with a look. Her mouth is a thin hard line.

"Random search," she says, touching a finger to her scar. "Authorized this morning."

Our dorm's only been "randomly searched" once before, and that was after some new girl stole a fork from the caf. Mateo's voice echoes through my head. *My first stop tomorrow morning is Director Wu's office.* I tighten my hands into fists and pretend the pain I feel is from my fingernails digging into my palms.

God, I'm an idiot. I really thought he wasn't going to rat me out.

The guards push past us. They rip the sheets and blankets off our beds. Officer Crane sweeps Cara's conspiracy books off her locker with her nightstick. The books slam into the floor, and Cara flinches. But she doesn't say a word.

"This your bunk?" Officer Sterling points to the bed directly behind me. I nod and step aside to let her search. Across from me, Officer Crane climbs the ladder to Cara's bunk. Cara's shoulders stiffen and my mouth goes dry.

Holy shit—the knife.

I'd been so convinced this was about me sneaking out that I hadn't even considered the knife. Peach could have told someone. Or maybe Mary Anne spotted it while she was here and just now realized how bad it was. I try to catch Cara's eye, but she stares at the wall behind my head, refusing to look at me. A buzzing, restless feeling seeps into my bones.

Officer Crane yanks back Cara's sheets. She pats down her pillow. I knot my hands together to keep them still. Crane climbs another rung and lifts the corner of Cara's mattress. The metal bunk creaks beneath her weight.

I dig my fingernails into my palms, but this time I don't notice the sharp bite of pain. I can't remember how to breathe. I glance at Cara again and her eyes finally flick over to mine. She moves her head a hair to the left, and then to the right.

Oh God. It's not there.

I exhale, and my shoulders slump. Officer Sterling looks up at the sound.

"Something to say, Miss Davis?"

"No ma'am," I say. Behind her, I see that the new officer has completely dismantled Jessica's bed. Her mattress leans against one wall, and her sheets and pillow lie crumpled in a ball on the floor.

"Nothing here," she says.

Officer Crane levels her eyes at me. She purses her lips. I stare back, confused. I feel like I'm listening to a book on tape, only I picked up the wrong cassette and accidentally skipped ahead a chapter. Why are they here? What are they looking for?

Two more guards I don't recognize race past my door. Cara and I share a look. What the *hell*?

Officer Crane starts stripping the sheets off my bunk. I inch closer to the door and peer into the hall. It takes me a second to make sense of what I'm seeing.

Guards are everywhere. They file in and out of dorm rooms, stripping beds and searching lockers. A line of girls stretches down the hall, their arms twisted behind their backs. Real handcuffs glitter from their wrists.

This isn't a random search. It's an all-out raid.

"Davis!" Crane barks. I jerk backward, my shoulders rigid with fear. Officer Crane considers me for a moment, and only then do I notice where she is—and what she's about to do.

"Don't—" I start, but I'm too late. Officer Crane pushes my mattress off its steel frame. Dozens of unopened letters flutter to the floor. My mother's name stares out from each one.

Patricia Parks. Patricia Parks. Patricia Parks.

"What on earth?" Officer Sterling crouches beside the pile of envelopes. She picks one up and flips it over, reading the name printed on the front. "Care to explain what these are, Davis?"

Heat rises in my cheeks. "They're mine," I say, and at least my voice doesn't betray how raw I feel. "They're just letters. From my mother."

Cara tries to catch my eye. I avoid looking at her this time. Officer Crane climbs down from the ladder, and Sterling hands her a letter. She turns the envelope over in her hand and squints down at my mother's tiny, even handwriting. I knit my fingers together to keep from ripping it out of her hands.

That doesn't belong to you, I think.

"They're all addressed to her," Officer Sterling says, dropping another envelope back onto the pile. "I don't think she stole them."

Officer Crane sniffs. "Take this," she says, handing the letter back to Sterling. "And those items, as well."

She points to a small pile of things we're technically not allowed to have: the pictures Cara tore out of library books, a book on tape I never returned, half a crumpled bag of M&M'S Issie's brothers snuck in for her.

"And you," Officer Crane says, fixing us with her steely eyes. "Start getting ready. You'll be expected for morning chores at 8 a.m. sharp." She strides back into the hall, the other two officers at her heels.

"What the hell was that about?" Issie says when the sound of the officers' footsteps has faded.

I barely hear her over the *thud* of my heart beating in my ears. I kneel next to my bed, grunting as I push my mattress back into its frame. I gather my mother's letters, but my hands tremble so badly that an envelope flutters from my fingers and drifts to the floor. Jessica kneels beside me.

"I'll help." She picks up a letter and holds it out to me. I hesitate, staring at her ragged thumbnail.

"I have to go." I rip my mother's letter from her hand and stumble out of the dorm. Cara shouts my name, but I don't turn back around.

My shift in Seg doesn't start until after breakfast, but I head for the staircase anyway. My head feels balloon-light and tears threaten my eyes. Juvie girls don't cry. Tears are targets, and I'm too smart for that shit. But some wounds are always tender. I've barely made it to the landing when a sob bubbles up in my throat and I know there's no use fighting anymore. I press my body into the corner and I breathe and I don't bother swiping at the trails of tears rolling down my cheeks.

My mother is acrylic nails and red push-up bras with underwire poking through the lace. She's lipstick prints on cigarettes and high, sharp laughter in the middle of the night, followed by deep, strange voices in the living room. I never particularly liked living with her but I always took it for granted that I *could*, that she'd take me in. That she had to.

I glance down at the letter in my fist. My mother's name stares out from between my fingers. She started writing two months ago, right after my release was approved. Her handwriting is small and cramped and slanted. It took me more than an hour to figure out what the first letter said, but she always writes the same thing. I slip my finger into the envelope and tear it open, dumping the letter into my hand. I unfold the paper and stare down at the angry, hateful words that I've long since memorized.

Don't ever come back here.
You are not welcome.
Leave your brother alone.

Chapter Eighteen

I stay crouched in that corner until my breathing returns to normal and my tears have hardened into salt-crusted lines on my cheeks. I fold my mother's letter and slip it back into the envelope.

You can't leave juvie unless you have someone to vouch for you—someone who can pick you up and sign all the forms and promise you'll go to school and eat your vegetables and stay out of trouble. Without that, the system keeps you until you turn eighteen and can officially take care of yourself. I don't turn eighteen for another nine months.

I had a plan, though. Ex-boyfriend Jake has this older sister who could sort of pass for my mother if she wore sunglasses and left her hair down. He was going to steal my mom's wallet (wouldn't be the first time) and get me as far as Brooklyn. After that, I'd stay with some old friends and lay low until I turned eighteen and could get a place on my own. Jake even mentioned a friend who made fake IDs, but I wasn't sure about breaking the law again.

I close my eyes. Those letters contain my biggest, most painful secret. They can ruin everything. And now the guards have one of them.

"Davis!"

My eyes pop open, and I scramble to my feet. Officer Sterling hurries down the stairs. She's gritting her teeth, trying to make her Cabbage Patch face look hard, but her expression softens when she sees me. I swipe at my cheeks, but my palms come away dry. My puffy eyes must've given me away.

"Where are you supposed to be?" she asks.

"On my way to Seg, ma'am," I say. She must know that I'm lying, that breakfast hasn't even started yet. She glances behind her, like she's worried someone's watching. Then she nods.

"I'll take you."

I shuffle down the last few steps, moving so slowly that it's almost a surprise when I find myself at the end of the hall, standing in front of the Seg Block door. Mateo crouches over his crossword puzzle. His uniform's more wrinkled than usual, like maybe he dug it out of a pile on the floor. Hair falls over his forehead, hiding his expression.

I stare at the toes of my shoes. He's the last person I want to see right now, with my cheeks all red and puffy and my chest heavy from the weight of my mother's words. But

Sterling stands behind me, blocking any chance of escape, and teleportation hasn't been invented yet. So.

Mateo hooks his pen onto his folded newspaper. "I'll take it from here, officer," he says, looking at Sterling instead of at me. If he's surprised that I'm here early, he doesn't show it.

"Very well," Sterling says. Her boots thump against the concrete as she walks back to the stairs.

I study the blackened rubber soles of my slip-ons. A small part of me thought he wouldn't act all weird about what happened last night. But old Mateo never said "officer" and he always smiled when I came down the steps and his voice didn't sound robot-stiff.

New Mateo acts like all the other guards in this hellhole.

He leans over and jabs the security-door button with his thumb. A loud, irritating buzz echoes down the hall.

"Thanks," I say. He nods. It's one of those curt nods where you lift your chin a little instead of moving your entire head. This infuriates me for some reason. I want to slap him, just to get him to make an expression. How can he be this mad at me for breaking the rules? He breaks the rules all the time. I don't even think he *knows* the rules.

I swear under my breath as I shuffle past him. He sits up straighter on his stool.

"What was that, Davis?"

So I'm Davis again. Wonderful.

"Nothing. *Sir*."

I let the security door slam shut behind me. The hall smells foul today, like some small animal crawled into a hole in the walls and died. Bea presses her face against the glass wall of her dorm, whispering to me. I ignore her and pull my mop out of the bucket of greasy water and slop it onto the floor.

The security door opens behind me. Metal screeches against concrete as Mateo pulls his stool into the hall. I tighten my grip on my mop.

"What are you doing?" I ask without looking up.

"Guarding," he says. I can see him out of the corner of my eye. He straightens his newspaper and squints down at the tiny black print.

I dig my teeth into my lower lip and push the mop in small, tight circles. The silence between us feels like another person. I hate it, but I also don't want to be the one to talk first.

Don't talk first, I tell myself. Bea slaps the glass wall of her cell, leaving greasy handprints behind. I stare at the wooden grooves in the mop handle. *Don't talk first. Don't talk—*

"I thought you were all about the rules now," I say. Dammit.

Mateo glances up at me from beneath the hood of his dark brows. "*Some* rules," he says. "Sometimes they're important."

"And you get to decide when they're important and when they aren't?"

Mateo hesitates. "Well, yeah. I'm a guard."

"No shit." I slam my mop back into the bucket and a river of sludgy water leaks onto the concrete. Bea giggles, distracted by her own shadow. A new scar stretches over half of her face. It's left's her skin all red and puckered, like a burn. I grimace and look away.

More silence. Mateo moves, and the stool creaks beneath him. He writes something on the crossword, the newspaper crinkling beneath the weight of his hand.

Finally, he looks up. "You don't smoke."

I pause, leaking greasy mop water onto my shoes. "What?"

"You don't smoke," he says again. "You said you left your dorm last night to have a cigarette."

"We all smoke."

"No." Mateo stands, placing the folded crossword puzzle on his stool. "Not you. You said your grandmother died of lung cancer and that no one would ever smoke if they had to see someone they loved hooked up to a hose to breathe."

I stare at Mateo. I feel like someone's grabbed me by the shoulders and spun me around in a circle until the walls all switched places. I did say that—but not to him. I was in the kitchen with Issie. She was bitching about how badly she wanted a cigarette so I told her the story of how my favorite grandmother got lung cancer when she was only forty-seven.

"You weren't even there," I say, slowly.

"Sterling got called to Director Wu's office, so she asked me to stand in for her." Mateo loops his thumbs through his belt buckles. "I was right outside the door."

Nope. This still doesn't add up. "I said that like two months ago. How do you remember . . . ?"

"Who cares how I remember? You lied to me about why you were out of your dorm last night."

"You're mad because I *lied* to you?"

"I'm mad because you're smarter than this, Davis!"

Again with calling me Davis. Anger flares inside me. "Look at where we are," I snap, motioning to the Seg Block with the handle of my broom. "This is where they put stupid girls who smoke cigarettes and sneak out of their dorms and fuck up their lives. What the hell makes you think I'm *smart*?"

"Because you *are* smart! Dammit. Why are you even here?"

He stares at me, wrinkles creasing the skin on his forehead. When I don't answer, he takes a step closer. "Well?" he asks. "Why are you here?"

Sweat gathers between my fingers and the mop handle. I'm here because a woman fell down the stairs and broke her collarbone in three places. I'm here because I trusted a mean boy with a nice smile.

But I will never tell him that. Never.

I dig my thumbnail into the wooden handle. "I don't know what you want me to say."

"You should be in school." His eyebrows hitch in the middle. "All I can figure is that somewhere along the line someone convinced you that you were a bad person."

Monsters are more interesting than heroes.

"You don't know shit about my life." I lean my mop against the wall but it wobbles and crashes to the ground. "You have your crosswords and your detective grandfather and your perfect girlfriend."

Mateo parts his lips, like he's going to say something.

"You don't know what it's like to be . . ." I stop talking, not sure how I planned to finish that sentence. He doesn't know what it's like to be stupid? Bad? Unwanted?

Mateo takes another step closer. I smell the soap on his skin and the cottony detergent he uses on his uniform. It does something to me, softens something I didn't know could be softened.

I stand up straighter and thrust the mop between us. Juvie girls can't get soft. It's suicide.

"What do you think my life's going to be like when I leave here?" Anger gives my words sharp edges. "You think I'm going to go to college? You think I'm going to get a nice little job?"

"Why not?"

"That's not how things work."

"It could be. You could *try*."

"Try to what? Get my degree?" My short, bitter laugh bounces off the pink walls. "Become a veterinarian?"

The word slips out on its own, and it's only because I was thinking about perfect, beautiful Stacy. I'm always thinking about perfect, beautiful Stacy.

"That's the second time you brought her up," Mateo says in a low voice.

Heat climbs my neck and flares through my cheeks. "I should go," I say.

"Wait." Mateo grabs my arm. I jerk back, and my mother's letter rustles against my waistband. It seems to burn through the fabric of my scrubs, her hateful words searing themselves into my skin. *Don't ever come back here.*

I think of my sad, small future, and suddenly I want to scream. Something ugly flashes through me. All at once I understand why the girls in here claw at the walls and peel the skin away from their fingernails. I want to punch something, just to watch my knuckles bleed. I want to hurt Mateo like I hurt.

"You're just like the rest of them," I say. "You're just another guard."

"Angela." His voice is barely a whisper. "Stop, please."

"Is that an order?" I ask. "Sir?"

Mateo hesitates, then moves out of my way. "No," he says.

For a second I want to know what he was going to say, but more than that, I want to be far, far away from here. I push through the security door and hurry back up the stairs to my dorm.

Mateo doesn't call after me again.

Chapter Nineteen

I take the steps to the first floor two at a time. This is Dr. Gruen's fault. I wouldn't be in this stupid fight with Mateo if I hadn't been wandering around at night playing superspy. Dr. Gruen told me to watch Jessica, she convinced me we were helping her. But Jessica begged me not to let them take her, and she hid the damn bear Dr. Gruen wanted me to bring her anyway. She doesn't want our help.

So I'm done. If that means spending a few more months in this place—fine. It's not like there's anything waiting for me on the other side.

I stop in front of Dr. Gruen's office door. Mary Anne's chair is empty, so I knock, banging so hard my knuckles hurt.

"Come in." I barely hear her voice through the thick wood. I push the door open and step into the office.

Dr. Gruen's eyes widen when she sees me. "Why, Angela," she says. "This is a surprise."

I hesitate for a second and try to steady my breathing. I'd forgotten how clean Dr. Gruen keeps her office. The surfaces all shine in the way that only very expensive furniture shines. Everything I'd been about to say seems stupid now that I'm standing here. Dr. Gruen never told me to sneak out. All she's ever done was try to help.

"I'm sorry," I say. "I didn't mean to barge in."

Dr. Gruen raises a hand to stop me. "Please, don't apologize. Take a seat. Mary Anne, will you excuse us for a moment?"

I look over my shoulder. I hadn't noticed Mary Anne when I came in, but now I see her perched on a chair in the corner of the room. She looks more like a shadow than a person. She stands and slips through the door without a word.

I slide into a leather chair.

"What's on your mind?" Dr. Gruen asks.

"It's about Jessica's bear," I say. Dr. Gruen tilts her head to the side, studying me with those clear, beautiful eyes.

"Are you having trouble finding it?" she asks. I nod. It's not even a lie, really. I don't know where Jessica hid it.

"I'll keep looking," I say. "But it's not in our dorm, and I haven't seen her carrying it around. Maybe she lost it?"

Dr. Gruen purses her lips. "Maybe," she says, but her voice turns the word into something sharp. A cold feeling fills my chest.

"I'll make sure to let you know if I see anything," I say, rising halfway out of my chair.

Dr. Gruen considers me, one finger tapping her chin. I realize, for the first time, how cruel she looks when she doesn't smile. All the shapes that make up her face seem harder, sharper.

"Sit down, Miss Davis."

The cold feeling moves into my lungs. I sit, suddenly aware of just how stiff the leather chair is. Like Dr. Gruen wants her visitors to be uncomfortable.

"Perhaps I didn't make myself clear," she says. Even her voice sounds different—lower, harder. She removes something from the top drawer of her desk. "I'm not the kind of person who entertains incompetence."

She holds up a white envelope. I immediately recognize the small, even letters of my mother's name. I can't breathe. Can't speak.

Dr. Gruen opens the envelope and pulls out a folded slip of paper.

"*Dear Angela*," she reads.

"Don't," I say. Dr. Gruen's eyes flick from the letter to my face. She smiles, but this smile is a different species from her warm, comforting one. This smile is a weapon.

"Does it hurt?" She folds my letter, making a sharp crease with her perfectly manicured nails. "Knowing that your mother doesn't want you."

"You were behind the raid this morning, weren't you?" I say in a low voice. "You were looking for Jessica's bear."

Dr. Gruen slides the letter back into its envelope. "If you refuse to cooperate, then I'll be forced to hand this letter over to Director Wu," she says. "And you'll stay here until your eighteenth birthday. What would happen to your poor little brother then?"

"Stay away from him." Even as I say the words I realize how meaningless they sound. I'm in no position to make a threat.

Dr. Gruen steeples her fingers below her chin. "Then bring me what I want," she says.

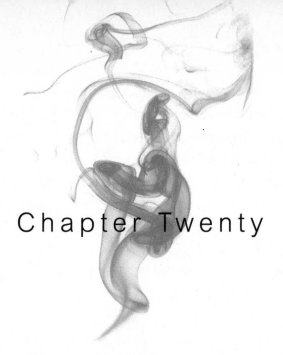

Chapter Twenty

I head straight for our dorm. Girls' voices echo down the hall after me. I'm used to hearing laugher during free periods, but today everyone seems to be arguing. A few girls glare at me as I hurry past. Twice, I see people crying.

They're all upset about the raid, I realize. I wonder, dimly, if Dr. Gruen found things to threaten them with too. I walk a little faster, suddenly uneasy. Issie and Cara will only be at morning chores for another ten minutes, tops. This might be the only time I have the room to myself.

I glance over my shoulder to make sure I'm alone, then ease the door open. It swings in without creaking. I step inside, holding my breath even though I know the room is empty. Jessica's tucked away in the basement right now, poring over stacks of library books on rickety tables.

Still, I check over my shoulder before moving inside, half-afraid I'll see the little girl hovering at the end of the hallway, her eyes slowly turning black.

I close the door behind me with a soft *click*. Technically we're not allowed to close our doors except for at night, but I don't want anyone to wander past and wonder what I'm doing. Ten minutes isn't a very long time, so I get to work. Officer Crane and the others did a pretty thorough job of checking our room, but I've lived in this eight-by-eight-foot space for almost two years. I know every inch of concrete by heart.

I crouch next to Jessica's bed and peer into the shadowy darkness below. About a year ago, Cara got it into her head that she could roll makeshift cigarettes using old math worksheets and chamomile from torn-open tea bags. She hid them in the wire frame beneath her mattress. They burned too quickly and tasted like chamomile-flavored ass, though, so she gave up and threw them out.

Now there's nothing under the bed but dust bunnies and an old gray sock with a hole in its toe. I dig my teeth into my lower lip, thinking. I scramble to my feet and head over to Issie's locker. There's a gap between the wall and the locker itself where we usually hide the cookies and tiny bottles of tequila Issie's brothers sometimes sneak in. I swipe my hands over the cold, crumbly concrete. Nothing.

I lean against my bunk, pulling my knees up to my chest. I run my hands over my short, curly hair, then lower them to my eyes. This room is the size of a closet. There aren't many places to hide a stuffed bear.

I stare through my fingers at the bed across from me. Jessica's bunk. Her thin blanket stretches tight across the mattress, and she's tucked her lumpy pillow neatly on one end. She was lying there when she hid that damn bear. I remember how the moonlight bounced off her eyes as she hugged it to her chest. A second later, it was gone.

I kneel, then crawl over to the bunk, checking the metal frame. I look for holes along the mattress edges and pillow seams. Nothing. *Damn.*

Frustrated, I fall back on Jessica's bed. One of Cara's conspiracy-theory posters still stretches across the wall, held in place with yellowing Scotch tape. I stare at it for a moment, then carefully peel the tape away from the wall, revealing a small hole in the drywall.

"Jesus," I whisper. My heart beats so hard that I can feel my pulse in the veins running down my arms. The hole is small, barely large enough for me to shove my hand through. I hold my breath and reach inside. My fingers brush against dry, ashy fur.

If I were a spy in a crappy mystery novel, this would be the moment I got caught. My palms start to sweat. The back of my neck tingles. I'm suddenly certain there's someone behind me. Watching. I spin around, nearly falling off the bed.

There's no one there.

"Chill," I whisper to myself. Dr. Gruen's in her office. She didn't follow me here. I exhale and pull the teddy bear out of the hole and onto my lap.

It looks worse in the daylight. Bits of snowy fluff spill into my hands, and the bear's glassy eye hangs from its face by a long thread. Jessica's burned this thing clear through. Every inch of fur is black and crusty.

Seeing the tattered, burned bear in my lap rattles something deep inside my chest. I picture Jessica standing in the hallway, clutching the bear in one hand. *Don't let them take me.*

I pinch the glass eye between two fingers, tempted to tug it clean off. Nerves prickle up my arms. What am I doing? Jessica trusted me. Am I really going to hand her over, just like that?

I have no choice. I'm screwed if I don't cooperate with Dr. Gruen.

But I shove the tattered bear back into its hole anyway, and I tape the poster in place over it. Then I lie back on Jessica's bed and spend a long time thinking about absolutely nothing.

The mood inside Brunesfield changes after the raid. Everyone knows at least one girl who's been sent to Seg, either because of something found during the raid, or for walking too quickly in the halls, or for forgetting to say "officer" when addressing a guard. The girls are silent in the corridors, whether their hands are in diamonds or not, and even the nicest guards have stopped joking around with us. Even Mateo seems stiffer with us than usual, like someone warned him to stop being so friendly. If we aren't being punished, it's like we don't exist.

This isn't the time to get in trouble, Mateo said. But it's practically impossible not to.

It seems obvious that Dr. Gruen is behind the changes, but I can't figure out *why*. What can she gain from making the rest of us miserable? She's supposed to be here to help.

I lower my head to the sticky breakfast table, doubt and curiosity gnawing at me. It's been two days since the dorm raid and we're all huddled together in the caf. Something smacks against the table behind me and I jerk around. But Ellen just knocked over a glass of water.

"Jumpy much?" Cara asks.

"Just tired, I guess," I lie. Most of the other girls have already finished their breakfast but they're all still here, poring over the twenty-year-old science textbooks they found in the library. Every few minutes, I hear someone snap at someone else to stop chewing so loudly, or to quit tapping her pen against the desk. Even Issie has a ratty biology book propped in front of her.

"Did you know the Atlantic puffin can swim underwater?" Jessica says this with her mouth full, and when she gets to the word "water," a Cheerio flies across the table and lands next to Cara's thumb.

"Oops," Jessica says. Cara flicks the Cheerio away.

"I think you broke her," Cara says to me. Jessica hasn't stopped talking all morning. It's been a nonstop barrage of questions about our lives, mixed in with obscure animal facts. Ellen has already shushed us twice.

"I guess." I hunch back over the table, my head resting on my folded hands. It's Visitors' Day, and family members will be here in less than an hour, but the girls in the caf make no moves to return to their dorms. Issie, Cara, and I have to stay behind until everyone leaves so we can gather dirty trays and wipe down countertops.

Cara pokes me on the arm. "You okay?"

"Fabulous," I deadpan.

"Forget I asked," Cara mutters. I open my mouth to apologize, then close it again. I've been pissy and anxious for the past two days, but I can't tell my friends about Dr. Gruen's threat without explaining my mother's horrible letters and Jessica the pyretic.

I glance at the cafeteria door. I keep expecting Dr. Gruen to walk in. She knows that I know where Jessica's bear is hidden. Any second she's going to drag me to my room and make me tell her everything. Twice now, I've hung behind as the others filed out of our dorm, and twice I've stared at the poster above Jessica's bed, willing myself to just grab the damn bear and get this over with. But something always holds me back. If I believed in things like a sixth sense and intuition, I'd say it was that. Dr. Gruen can't be trusted, no matter what she threatens me with.

But Dr. Gruen doesn't come into the cafeteria. No one does. Mateo's the only guard on duty right now. He leans against the wall, eyes trained on the fly lazily circling his head. We haven't spoken since our fight in the Seg Block. So there's another thing to feel crappy about.

"Why do you write those words on your fingers?" Jessica asks, poking Issie's hand. Issie looks up from her textbook.

"I've got to study, girl," she says, but she makes a fist. Faded Sharpie letters dance across her knuckles, spelling out the word "hurl." Jessica squints to read it, then snorts with laughter. This time she covers her mouth with her hand so she doesn't spit cereal across the table.

"Be *quiet!*" Ellen snaps. Jessica's face turns red.

"Why did you make it say that?" She presses her hand against her mouth, and it muffles her voice. "Why not write something pretty?"

"Like what?" Issie asks.

"What about 'happy'?" Jessica says. Issie frowns and counts her fingers. Mateo catches my eye over her shoulder, then quickly looks away. My cheeks flare. I stare down at the table, pretending it doesn't bother me.

"Nah, that has too many letters," Issie says. "You don't want to use the thumb because then you can't read the word. See?"

Jessica screws up her face like she's trying to think of a good word. I trace a water ring with my index finger.

"You could write 'home,'" Jessica says, taking Issie's hand. She counts off a letter on each finger. "*H-o-m—*"

A scream echoes through the caf, cutting her off. I stand so quickly I bang my elbow on the edge of the table. Aaliyah leaps out of her folding chair, accidentally knocking it to the ground. Metal slaps against the concrete and echoes off the walls.

"The *hell*?" Cara says, swiveling in her chair. Mateo pushes away from the wall, a hand resting on his nightstick.

"All good, ladies?" he calls, ambling over to Aaliyah's table. Aaliyah shakes her head, pointing to the floor.

Something squeaks. A spot of brown weaves between the table legs.

"Mouse!" I say, half in relief, half in disgust. I crawl onto my chair, hugging my knees to my chest. Cara squeals and crawls onto the table.

"Ew," she shrieks, peering over the side. The mouse darts beneath the table, whiskers twitching.

"It's just a mouse," Issie says, but she scoots her chair back and lifts her feet off the ground. Mateo stops next to our table and kneels.

"Why don't you girls move so I can chase it out from under there," he says.

"No way." I shake my head. It was bad enough when the mouse was trapped in a drawer in the library. Now I imagine that tiny, furry little creature climbing up my pant leg, whiskers scratching my skin. The thought makes me want to puke.

Mateo glares at me and yanks his nightstick out of his belt. He must still be stung from our fight because he doesn't order me to get down. He taps his nightstick against the ground, making kissy noises.

"Come on, little guy," he murmurs. The mouse twitches its nose, watching Mateo with glassy black eyes.

"You're scaring him," Jessica says. She crawls out of her own chair and crouches on the ground next to Mateo. "Mice have emotions just like people. They're very empathetic."

"Jessica, don't," I hiss. She ignores me and stretches out a hand, her fingers inches from the mouse's tiny pink nose.

"Hello, Sir," she whispers, like it's a lost pet that got out of its cage.

"Did you just call him sir?" Mateo asks.

"That's what Ellen calls him," Jessica explains. "He must've gotten out of his drawer."

The mouse creeps closer. Its pink feet look like little hands.

"Don't touch it," I say. Jessica crawls under the table. She pulls a Tootsie Roll out of her pocket.

"It's just a field mouse," she says, unwrapping the Tootsie Roll. "We had them where I used to live."

I press my lips together, thinking of the depressing gray house where Jessica grew up. I picture her and her foster brother kneeling on the ground, tracing pictures in the dirt with twigs. I bet they caught mice and tried to keep them as pets.

"This one probably has all sorts of weird juvie diseases," Cara says, as she curls her fingers around the side of the table and leans over, watching. Jessica holds out the Tootsie Roll. The mouse creeps closer, sniffing.

"Ellen feeds him these," Jessica whispers. "She lets me help sometimes."

Mateo shifts his eyes over to Jessica and then back to the mouse. I hold my breath as he edges forward, lifting the nightstick. The movement makes Jessica flinch.

"No!" she yells. The mouse darts away before Mateo swings the nightstick. It disappears into a hole in the wall, its pink tail swishing behind it. Great. One more creature to hide in the pipes while I shower.

"Dammit, Jessica!" Mateo lowers the nightstick, dejected. "We can't have a mouse running around here. Cara's right, it could have rabies."

"You can't kill Sir," she says, popping the Tootsie Roll into her mouth. She scurries over to the wall to examine the mousehole. Or try to coax it out with another Tootsie Roll, I think, grimacing.

"You're such a bully," I say, hopping off my chair. Mateo's lips hitch up at the corner—an almost-smile. He shoves his hands into his pockets.

"You would have tried to kill it too," he mutters.

Chapter Twenty-One

"You gonna tell us what crawled up your butt and died?" Issie asks once we get back to our dorm. I try not to grimace at that delightful visual.

"Nothing." I plop onto my bunk and throw an arm over my face. Jessica's already down in the library, probably explaining to Ellen that her mouse is hiding inside the cafeteria walls. It's just the three of us.

"Wrong answer," Issie says, tossing her textbook onto her bunk. "You've been pouting for, like, three days."

"Seriously, nothing—" I start.

"Come on, Issie. You know Angela's always an überbitch on Visitors' Day," Cara says, shoving her feet into her slip-ons. She catches my eye and winks. I feel a fierce stab of gratitude. She's covering for me and doesn't even know why.

"Are you leaving too?" I ask. I don't feel like being alone right now, and Cara and I usually spend Visitors' Day together.

We play cards and read while Issie greets her legions of admirers. She has this huge extended family, and someone new visits every week, bringing chocolate and presents and telling crazy stories of the outside world.

I only have Charlie, and he's too young to visit without an adult chaperone. Cara doesn't have anyone.

Cara pauses at the scratched mirror hanging on the wall above our newly reinstalled sink. "I've got a meeting with Dr. Gruen." She leans in closer and swipes a finger over a nonexistent spot on her front teeth.

Just that name—*Gruen*—sets my teeth on edge. "What? Why?"

"Uh, because she's gotten about a million demerits in the past week and they're going to make her spend the night in Seg," Issie explains.

I don't know whether I'm more freaked out by the idea of Cara spending a night in Seg, or asking Dr. Gruen for help. "But why do you have to go to *her*?"

Cara frowns at her flawless complexion and pushes her bushy hair behind her ears. "She said we could discuss my options."

"But Cara—"

"Why do you sound so scandalized?" Cara catches my eye in the cloudy reflection of the mirror. "I thought you liked her. And Mary Anne says she helps a lot of girls."

I hug my knees to my chest, trying not to glance at the poster on the wall across from me. I'm starting to realize that Dr. Gruen's definition of "help" is not the same as mine. Cara was the last person I expected to fall for her act. I want to tell both her and Issie what she's really like, but I can't make myself say the words. I have this horrible suspicion that Dr. Gruen herself is waiting just outside our door. That she'll appear the second I say a word against her, my mother's letter pinched between her long, thin fingers.

"Just be careful," I say, finally. "She's . . . different than she seems."

Cara holds my gaze for another beat. It looks like she might say something else, but then Issie pushes past her to get to the mirror, and the moment passes.

"My brother promised to bring me some M&M'S," Issie says, smoothing her thick braid over one shoulder. "The peanut ones. You want me to bring you two some M&M'S? I think you could use them."

She turns around and cocks her head, looking at me like I've just told her my kitten is dying of cancer.

"No, I'm fine," I say, distracted. "Go see your family."

Issie wrinkles her nose. I swear, she's a ninety-year-old grandmother in a tattooed sixteen-year-old body.

"I'll bring you an M&M," she says, squeezing my shoulder. "One of the blue ones. They're the best."

Cara tightens her ponytail and follows Issie into the hall.

I stare after them for a long moment, guilt twisting my chest. I should have warned them about Dr. Gruen, but I'm not sure how I could have. Even now a guard paces up and down the corridor outside my door, reminding me that I'm never really alone. Someone's always watching. Always listening.

I sigh and lean back in bed. I don't look at the poster above Jessica's bunk, even though the spot draws my eye like a magnet. I walk my bare feet up the side of the wall. The cold cinder blocks tickle my toes. I picture Cara perched on a leather chair in front of Dr. Gruen's desk, Dr. Gruen leaning forward to offer her something that sounds too good to be true.

The image changes. Now it's not Cara sitting in that leather chair—it's me. Dr. Gruen's reading my mother's terrible letter out loud and I'm trying not to scream.

I roll over and bury my face in my pillow. I can't lie here obsessing over this. I need a distraction.

I could listen to *Tuck Everlasting* again.

Or try to find Cara's deck of cards.

Or write a letter to Charlie.

The last option is the only one that doesn't involve moving, so I close my eyes.

Dear Charlie, I think. *I've screwed up my last chance of getting out of here, and now I won't see you for practically a whole year. Send cookies.*

I sigh and turn onto my back again. That won't work. I stare at the insides of my eyelids and wait for better words to come to me.

Nothing.

More nothing. I tap my feet against the wall.

Then, "Hi."

Fear shoots through me, and I sit up so quickly that I bang my head on the bunk above me.

"Jesus." Mateo takes a step into my dorm, then freezes. The male officers aren't allowed inside our rooms. Obviously.

I rub the lump on my head. "Sorry," I say. "I've been kind of jumpy lately."

Some of the tightness leaves Mateo's face. I didn't even know it was there until it's gone. He checks over his shoulder, then steps into my room.

"Let me see," he says, perching at the edge of my bed. I lower my hand and tilt my head toward him.

"See any brain?" I ask.

"Nope. No brain at all."

I punch him on the leg, and he snickers under his breath. He leans in closer, and then I feel his fingers on my head. He presses lightly into my skin, tracing the edge of the lump forming on my skull.

"Does that hurt?" His voice sounds quiet. I shake my head. I realize I'm holding my breath and clear my throat.

"No," I say.

"Good," he says, louder this time. He moves his hand down the back of my head and neck before finally letting it rest on my shoulder. My skin tingles everywhere he's touched me, and it tingles everywhere he hasn't. I hold completely still, terrified that any movement will break the spell.

"Angela?" Mateo says. "Look at me."

I tilt my chin up. I don't think I've ever looked him fully in the face like this. Usually I'm only able to catch a quick glance while he's turned away. But now I'm looking at him and he's looking at me and the entire moment is . . . surreal. His eyes aren't really blue. They're gray, with gold flecks near the pupil. He has three freckles on the bridge of his nose. He narrows his eyes and I blush, wondering if he's studying me too.

"Can you touch your nose with your index finger?" he says.

I blink. "What?"

"Like this." He touches his nose with one finger. "Your eyes seem a little blurry. I want to make sure you don't have a concussion."

Oh my God. He was checking to see if I have a *concussion*, not gazing deeply into my eyes. I want to die. I want to sink into the floor and disappear forever.

I clumsily thrust my index finger at my face, and it must brush against my nose, because Mateo leans away from me, satisfied.

"So," he asks. "Why aren't you in the lounge with the others?"

His voice sounds forced-casual. Like he's trying to make up for our awkward fight by pretending nothing happened. I stare at my knees and try to come up with something clever to say. But I can't think of anything, so I settle for honest instead.

"Today's for people with families. Lucky people."

Mateo frowns. "You have a family. What about that kid who's always writing to you?"

"That's Charlie. My brother," I tell him. "Charlie's . . . not allowed to see me anymore." I say each word slowly. Hating them. "I'm a bad influence."

"Who made that decision?"

"My mother."

"I see." He nods. "And she doesn't visit either?"

"She works." I'm not actually sure she does, but it sounds better than the truth, which is that she doesn't care. "Single mom, you know."

"Yeah." I can't tell if he means that like, "Yeah, I know what it's like to have a single mom," or if he's just being polite. He drums his hands against his knees. I'm afraid to look at him again, so instead I focus on the bit of mattress between our legs. There's not even six inches between us.

I have the sudden urge to set my hand down in that space, like I'm on a date at a movie theater in junior high. I wonder if he'd notice. I wonder if he'd weave his fingers through mine.

I twist my hands together and place them on my lap to resist the temptation.

"I have a sister," Mateo says, out of nowhere.

"Yeah?"

"Yup. Julie."

"Pretty name." I knot my fingers and try to focus on Mateo's story instead of my completely immature seduction plan. The empty space between us seems to pulse.

"She's such a brat," Mateo says. He smiles a teasing, little-kid smile. I can suddenly picture him as a boy with floppy hair and big feet and a charming smile that always got him out of trouble.

"She's five years older," Mateo continues. "Growing up, she was always playing these really mean pranks."

"What kind of pranks?"

Mateo hesitates, but I see the story forming behind his eyes. He glances at the door.

"Okay," he says, turning back around. "So I went out trick-or-treating this one year when I was younger, right? Like, maybe seven or eight. And we got these huge Pixy Stix. Must've been this big." Mateo holds his hands about a foot and a half apart. "I was so excited to eat that thing. I saved mine for weeks, until all my other candy was gone, and then I cut off one end and poured half of it down my throat."

His face twists in disgust at the memory. "It was *salt*. Julie ate the sugar out of it a few days before and refilled the thing with salt. She glued it back together so I wouldn't know the difference."

I laugh. "Poor baby Ben!"

Mateo flinches at the sound of his first name. Heat rises in my face. I've never called him Ben before. Not out loud, at least.

He moves, and the entire mattress shifts beneath us. "That's not all," he continues, like nothing weird happened. "She used to replace my Dr Pepper with cold coffee and stick the bottle back in the fridge. I still can't drink soda."

"How awful for you."

"Oh yeah. Worst sister ever." Ben says this with a grin.

"Right," I say, but I'm not listening anymore. He's placed his hand on the mattress between us. It's just *sitting* there, palm up. If I moved an inch to the left, his thumb would brush against my thigh.

He's still talking, but his words sound like static. I imagine laying my hand on his. His skin looks soft and warm. I picture our fingers lacing together, our hands pressed palm to palm.

Something flashes in the corner of my eye—a quick red blink of light. I flinch.

"Angela?" Ben frowns. "Hey, are you okay?"

"Yeah—" The light flashes again, so quickly I almost miss it. I push myself off my bunk and walk over to the door. An oversize, wire-caged clock hangs in the hallway. I wait for the light to flash again, but nothing happens. The clock must be blocking it from view.

I take a step backward.

There it is—a quick red blink. I recognize that light.

"Angela?" Ben says. I whirl around.

"Sorry," I say. "I'm, uh, not feeling well."

Ben stands. Concern wrinkles his forehead. "Your head?"

I touch the still-tender bump. "Nope. I think I'm just a little tired is all."

"Right." Ben shifts from one foot to the other. "I guess I'll leave you to rest then."

"Yeah. See you."

I wait until Ben disappears down the hall, and then I head for the clock. I've seen that blinking red light before. I know what it means. I lean against the wall and look up.

A tiny black video camera hides behind the clock's metal cage, its lens aimed toward our dorm. I stare at it for a long moment, my heart hammering in my chest. I should have known it was there. Everything that's happened over the past few days clicks into place, and it's so obvious that I hate myself for not understanding sooner.

Dr. Gruen watched us leave our dorm in the middle of the night. She arranged for Brody and Mateo to find us. And she set up the raid because it was the only way to look for Jessica's bear. She was probably watching the officers dismantle our room on the television in her office, waiting for a clue.

I walk to the girls' bathroom and back again twice before I find the others. Three more tiny black cameras with blinking red lights. One hangs from the ceiling outside the girls' bathroom, half-hidden by a light fixture. Another points down the hall to our room, nestled beneath a fire alarm. The third sits beneath a staircase banister, poised to film the steps leading up to the second floor. And those are just the ones I can find. There are probably more. Lots more.

I think of all the crazy things Cara's been saying since Dr. Gruen and Mary Anne first got here. They're FBI agents studying the future criminal element. They're making everything perfect for their experiments. They're watching us. Studying us. It all sounded so stupid at the time.

But now . . .

The red light blinks from the camera in the staircase, warning me that someone really is watching. Someone's been watching this entire time.

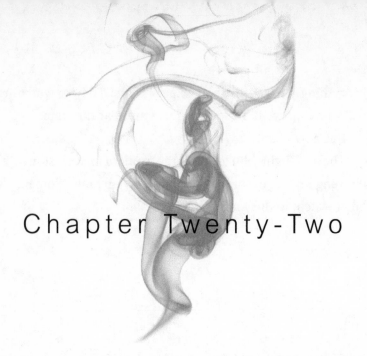

Chapter Twenty-Two

I yank the video camera out from where it's hidden beneath the staircase banister. It's small but heavy, and it fits perfectly in the palm of my hand. Smart has never been my strong suit, but I remember Mateo saying that videotaping minors without parental consent is illegal. Jail-time illegal.

I smile into the lens. Dr. Bitch is going down.

I press the Power button, and the camera's red light blinks off. Director Wu's office is on the second floor, just down the hall from the infirmary. Technically, we're not supposed to be wandering the halls on our own, but it's free hour. They leave the doors unlocked so we can go to the library or make a phone call or use the restroom. For the first time in days, I don't worry that the guards are going to swoop down on me the second I turn a corner. They barely even glance up as I walk past.

The second-floor hallway is empty. I hurry past the dorms and the infirmary and stop at the last door on the left.

"Director Wu?" I bang my fist against the door, still clutching the camera in my other hand. No one answers. I try the doorknob.

"Director, I—" I push the door open and the rest of my sentence dies in my mouth.

Director Wu's office is empty. *Really* empty. Someone's taken the faded couch, and the filing cabinets, and the giant wooden desk that stood in front of the window. Even the rug is gone. The concrete floor stares up at me, and the gleam of the sun on its surface is almost a smile.

I step into the office, crushing the smile beneath my foot. For one horrible second, I feel like Brunesfield is laughing at me. Like this is some sort of practical joke. Then the logical part of my brain kicks in, and I realize the director must have switched rooms, or ordered new furniture. The floor didn't open up and swallow her. She couldn't have just *disappeared*.

I turn in place, searching for any clue. But there's nothing. It's like the room was always empty. Like Director Wu never existed.

A flicker of movement catches my eye. I whirl around. Dr. Gruen stands in the doorway. Watching me.

"Miss Davis," she says, stepping into the room. A black dress hugs her frame, its square neckline emphasizing a sharp collarbone and stiff shoulders. She looks like she'd draw blood if you touched her. "Can I help you with something?"

"Where's the director?" I don't realize how upset I am until I hear my voice tremble. Dr. Gruen crosses the room, her pointed heels clacking against the concrete.

"Director Wu no longer works for this facility."

"No." I tighten my fingers around the video camera, wanting to throw it. "You're lying. What did you do with her?"

"*Do* with her?" A puzzled expression moves over Dr. Gruen's face. "We were impressed with Director Wu's work so we offered her a more lucrative position elsewhere. She left this morning."

Her eyes flick down to my hands, then back up to my face. "I see. You've found the video cameras."

A kind of giddy fear spreads through my body. "They're illegal," I say, holding up the camera. "You can't record us without our permission. It's the *law*."

"Taking video inside a minor's private quarters is against the law. But the hallway and stairwells belong to the state. They're fair game." Dr. Gruen leans against the window, folding her arms over her chest. "I didn't feel comfortable allowing Jessica to remain around members of the general population without a few precautions in place."

I don't know what to believe . . . No matter what she says, it still feels like an invasion of our privacy.

Dr. Gruen taps her fingers against her arm, considering me. Every nerve in my body becomes jagged and sharp. How can she be so calm when all I want to do is scream?

Finally, she sighs and shakes her head. "Miss Davis, I'm afraid our last meeting didn't go as well as I would have liked. You and I are on the same side, you see."

I'm not expecting that. I shift from foot to foot, not sure what to do with all the nervous energy running through my body. "We're *not* on the same side," I snap. "You said you wanted to help Jessica, but you're a liar. You're not helping her at all."

"No, I'm not."

There's a beat of silence. I frown, sure that I heard her wrong. "What?"

"You're right," Dr. Gruen says. "I never intended to help Jessica. Everything I told you about her trial was a fabrication. There is no trial. No police. Jessica was placed in this facility intentionally. So we could watch her."

The floor feels unsteady all of a sudden. I take a step backward, toward the door. "I don't understand."

"SciGirls was set up to work with pyretics just like Jessica. At this moment, we have ten in residence at our facilities. We know everything about them—how their abilities developed, where they came from. How strong they are."

Dr. Gruen licks her finger and rubs at an ink stain near her thumbnail. "But Jessica came out of nowhere," she continues. "Pyretic abilities are closely regulated. They don't spread genetically. Jessica shouldn't have been able to develop these abilities outside of the SciGirls program. We placed her here for further observation, to see if we could find some clue as to where her power came from. Unfortunately, Director Wu blocked my attempt at placing a camera inside your dorm, so we haven't discovered anything useful. Luckily, that's no longer an obstacle."

"You really think a stupid bear will tell you more about her powers?" I ask.

"Yes. I know you know where it's hidden, Miss Davis," Dr. Gruen says, "and I assure you I'm capable of delivering everything I promised in our first meeting. If you want to get out of here before your eighteenth birthday, then I don't see why a silly letter from your mother should stand in your way. I should also tell you that SciGirls is backed by some very powerful people. I've been authorized to make a more . . . substantive arrangement as well."

"Substantive? You mean, like, money?"

"I was thinking of something along the lines of a scholarship. SciGirls has relationships with several amazing schools across the country."

"College?" I press my lips together to keep from laughing out loud. Despite my dreaming, I know college isn't a real possibility for someone like me. If Gruen thinks I'm the kind of kid who could get into one of these "amazing schools," then she really hasn't done her research. "I'm not going to college," I say.

"No, I don't imagine you will. But your little brother, Charlie, has decent grades and test scores. A scholarship could mean the difference between four years of university, and night classes after he finishes his shift at McDonald's."

I freeze. For a long moment I can't think of anything other than my brother's name. *She knows my brother's name.* Then my brain starts working again, and I focus on what else she said: grades, test scores. Charlie's name *might* have been in my file, but she found the rest of that information on her own.

She's been watching him.

"How do you know so much about my little brother?" I ask, my throat dry.

"I do my research," Dr. Gruen says smoothly. "And I'd be remiss if I didn't remind you of all you have to lose. You see, Angela, we're going to find Jessica's bear eventually. We're going to get what we need from this place and take her away. Your stubbornness won't stand in the way of that. But time is an important factor here. Jessica is a very dangerous little girl, as I'm sure you've discovered."

I think of boiling water. Flickering lights. "You're worried she's going to hurt someone?"

"She's already killed her foster father," Dr. Gruen says. Her pale eyes fix on mine and I see something in them I've never noticed before. Pain, maybe. Or fear. "I'm worried that one of the girls here might be next."

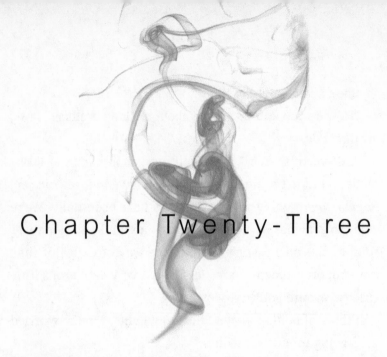

Chapter Twenty-Three

I hurry out of Director Wu's office, those last words repeating in my head like a song.

She's already killed her foster father. One of the girls here might be next.

I stop on the landing halfway between the second floor and the first. I want to scream and stomp and bang my head against the wall, anything to drown out Dr. Gruen's voice. She's lying. She's manipulating me. It's not true.

But it *is* true. Whatever else Dr. Gruen said, whatever lies she told, Jessica is dangerous. It doesn't matter that she likes baby animals and monster trucks and books. She has incredible power and doesn't seem able to control it. I think of the little boy lying in the hospital bed, tubes running up his nose. What if that was Cara? Or Issie?

I make my hands into fists and hard plastic digs into my palm. I look down. I'm still holding Dr. Gruen's stupid video camera.

Anger bubbles up inside me. Before I can think about what I'm doing, I pull my arm back and throw. The camera hits the wall, then bounces down the stairs, showering bits of broken plastic. It smashes into the first floor. Ruined.

I expect more raids over the next few days. I'm convinced that Officer Crane will appear at any second to rip apart our mattresses and dig through our lockers. Every footstep is Dr. Gruen coming back to threaten me with something new and terrible. Each flash of light is another hidden camera. Watching. Always watching.

I'm so twitchy that Issie asks me if I have a rash.

"Don't be embarrassed, girl. I got one last year," she explains, wiggling her shoulders. "Oooh, it made me all itchy and squirmy. I think it was from that crappy soap they used to have in the showers. The new stuff's *nice*."

"Yeah," I say. A few days ago Dr. Gruen replaced the watery liquid soap in the showers with this thicker, moisturizing stuff that supposedly feels like velvet on your skin. I wouldn't know, because I refuse to try it. So now I'm paranoid *and* stinky.

I go back to scrubbing dried tomato sauce from the stovetop in the kitchen. I've wanted to tell Issie about Dr. Gruen's cameras at least a hundred times, but something always stops me. Right now it's Officer Sterling. I can see the back of her head through the window in the kitchen door. She can probably hear every word we say.

My muscles burn as I work. The sauce seems to be glued down with some sort of special superhuman adhesive. I see something out of the corner of my eye and recoil—but it's just Issie.

"Here." She squirts a stream of soap onto the impossible tomato stain.

"Where's Her Highness?" I ask to cover my nerves. Cara never bothered showing up for evening chores today. She used to disappear all the time, leaving us to cover for her, but I thought she was over that crap by now.

"Who knows?" Issie says, elbow-deep in greasy water. "Gross. Do you smell that? Nasty."

"Is it the smell of my desperation?" I dig the sponge into the tomato stain. The kitchen always smells foul. Today the smell is a little . . . riper than usual, but that's probably because the trash needs to be taken out. "Just work fast so we can get out of here," I say, scrubbing away the last red flecks of tomato sauce. I triumphantly toss the sponge back into the sink, splashing Issie with water.

"Watch it!" she mutters, wiping the water from her face with the back of her arm. She wrinkles her nose again. "Seriously though, you don't notice that? Something smells *rank*."

I frown, and pull open a cupboard door. "You think something's gone bad?"

"I think something *died*."

One of the girls here might be next, I think. I picture Jessica's eyes turning black, the air growing hot and dry. "Seriously," I say. "When was the last time you saw Cara?"

"We *both* saw her in the yard for rec. Remember?" Issie turns and gives me a look. "Girl, what's wrong with you? I was *joking*. Nobody's dead. Jesus."

I close the cupboard. Issie's right. Nobody's dead. The kitchen always smells gross. This isn't unusual. I wipe my greasy hands on a towel and follow Issie around the room. We move the trash cans, but there's nothing there—in fact, Cara must've taken the trash out yesterday. A few crumpled paper towels lay at the bottom of the bins.

"Weird," I say, pushing the cans back into place. I'm trying to act calm, but I feel like every hair on my body is standing straight up. I rub my hands up and down my arms, trying to ignore my nerves. Lots of things smell bad. Sour milk, for instance. And bad meat. Mold.

Bloody clothes. Burning skin. Dead girls.

I cover my mouth with my hand, feeling like I'm going to be sick. Issie opens up another cupboard door while I search the fridge to see whether something's gone rotten. But nothing's expired, nothing's moldy. I smell an open carton of milk, then put it back and close the door. It's completely fine. *Shit*.

Desperate now, I yank open the door to the walk-in freezer. I half expect a frozen body to tumble out but no—it's empty. My eyes travel over shelves of frozen, saran-wrapped meat. I sigh and close it again. "Freezer's clean too."

Issie sniffs the air, then grimaces. "*There*," she says, pinching her nose. "It's coming from in there."

She points to the pantry.

A sour taste hits the back of my throat. Other than the freezer, the pantry's the only place in the kitchen large enough to hide something creepy. Like a body. I stare at the door, and everything in my body tells me not to open it.

"Maybe we should leave," I say. Issie frowns.

"Don't be dumb. Come on."

She reaches for the door. I cringe, waiting. I don't want to know what's inside.

She turns the knob, and pulls the door open.

Something tumbles out, smacking me in the shoulder. I scream, and jump backward.

A mop falls to the floor—the same mop I used to clean the Seg Block. Someone must've brought it back up here now that I'm done with my punishment. I'm so relieved I could sink to the floor and cry, but the feeling doesn't last long. The scent of old, rotting meat wafts over me, turning my stomach.

"Oh God," I say, gagging. I pull my T-shirt over my nose, but it doesn't manage to mask the smell. My eyes water. "Definitely coming from here."

The pantry is packed with food. Mostly dried goods, but there are also bags of potatoes and lemons, and stacks of canned fruit floating in sugary syrup. I keep my shirt pulled up over my face as I sort through them, wondering what could possibly have gone so bad so quickly. Issie squeezes in next to me.

"I'm going to kill Cara for skipping out on this," she mutters. I move a box of dried noodles and stand up on my tiptoes, sweeping my hands along the shelf.

"She's probably just—" The end of my sentence dies as my fingers brush something rubbery and thin—almost like a shoelace, but the texture's wrong. The hair on my arm stands up. I reach deeper. Now I feel something dense and prickly. *Fur.*

I jerk my hand back. Issie whirls around, nearly hitting me in the face with her elbow.

"What the *hell*?" she says.

"There's something up there," I say, pointing to the shelf. Issie grabs the mop.

"I'll do it," she says, shouldering past me. She swipes at the shelf with the mop handle, frowning. "I don't feel any—"

A small, dark object tumbles from the shelf, cutting her off. I dance backward, biting off a scream. Issie drops her mop and jerks away.

A mouse lies on the floor, burned and blackened. I cover my mouth with my hand. The last time I saw that mouse, Jessica was trying to feed it a Tootsie Roll. Now, raw, bloody meat peaks out from its fur in patches. Angry blisters cover its tail, and yellow pus leaks from its eyes.

Something cold hits the back of my throat. This mouse has been burned to death. I think of Jessica trying to coax it out of the hole in the wall and I swallow, again worried I might throw up.

Jessica is a very dangerous little girl.

Issie covers her face with her hands and stares down at it through the gaps in her fingers. "That's Ellen's mouse," she says. "Remember? The one Jessica called Sir."

"Yeah," I say. "Maybe."

"You think it crawled into the stove?"

"It must have," I lie. I grab a trash bag from under the sink and hurriedly sweep the mouse inside. "I'll take it out," I say. Issie waves me away.

"Go right ahead," she says, pinching her nose again. "Get that out of here."

Jessica sits at a circular table in the library, staring at a book on emperor penguins that's larger than she is. Her legs swing off the sides of her chair, her feet skimming the floor.

Officer Sterling stands guard at one end of the dank, crowded room. Two other girls pace between the stacks, quizzing each other with flash cards. Every single table is filled with girls and textbooks and dog-eared reams of notebook paper.

I stare at the study materials as I cross the room. The paper looks fresh, and the books are several decades newer than anything else in the library. Clearly they're gifts from Dr. Gruen, but no one looks suspicious or paranoid. I want to grab the books and throw them. I want to scream at all the other girls. Can't they tell that she's manipulating them? Am I the only one who sees who Dr. Gruen really is?

But I'm here because of Jessica, not Dr. Gruen. I still feel the stink of dead mouse on my skin, even though I dropped it in the Dumpster before coming here. No one looks up or makes a face as I walk past, so the smell must be in my head. Still, I find myself wiping my hands on my scrubs, trying to make it go away.

I slide into the chair across from Jessica. She puts her book down, and a goofy little-kid smile splits her face.

"Hey!" she says, too loudly for the library. Sterling shoots her a look. "Oops," Jessica whispers. "Sorry."

I wait until Sterling turns back around and then I lean across the table, trying to keep my expression normal. I can't let Jessica know how freaked out I am. She won't tell me anything if she's scared.

I press my hands flat against the table, like I'm trying to push it away. "We found . . . something in the kitchen," I say, finally.

"Yeah?" Jessica puts the book down and folds her hands on its cover.

"You remember Ellen's mouse? Sir?"

Jessica's face falls.

"Jessica?" I say, harsher this time. She fidgets in her seat.

"Did that guard catch him?" she asks in a small voice.

I frown. "No. The guard didn't catch him."

Relief passes over her face. "Good," she says, exhaling. She opens her book again. "Did you know emperor penguins mate for life?"

Officer Sterling starts walking toward me. I tap my knuckles against the tabletop, suddenly nervous. I bet Dr. Gruen told her to watch me. I wait for her to stop next to our table and demand to know what we're talking about.

But Officer Sterling passes behind me without a word. She heads to the stacks on the other side of the room to help Aaliyah get a book from the top shelf.

I lean forward again, barely speaking above a whisper. "Jessica, the mouse is dead," I say. Jessica looks up from her book, eyes widening.

"But you said—"

"Someone burned it to death."

Jessica's lower lip starts to tremble. "You think it was me."

"It was *burned* to death," I say again. "Who else—"

"I didn't do it," she whispers. It reminds me of how Charlie used to sound whenever he thought he was going to get in trouble for tracking mud into the house or getting a bad grade on a quiz at school. I keep my eyes glued to Jessica's face.

"Don't lie to me about this. Was it an accident? Did you get angry?"

"I didn't do it!" she says again. I cringe, and turn around. Officer Sterling is still helping Aaliyah. She doesn't seem to have heard us. I hold a finger to my lips, and shoot Jessica a look.

"I would never hurt a little animal," Jessica whispers.

"Jessica . . ."

"You *have* to believe me. I've been practicing! I can control it now."

Doubt flickers through me. She sounds so earnest. I want to trust her. But then I think of the mouse's raw skin, the blisters on its tail.

"I promise," Jessica says. "I *didn't*."

"Evening, ladies." Ben's voice comes out of nowhere. I turn too quickly and my neck cramps.

"Crap," I moan, grimacing. Ben crouches next to our table.

"You okay?" he asks.

"Peachy." I try to catch Jessica's eye, to tell her this conversation isn't over. But she takes one look at Ben and slides her penguin book off the table, cowering behind its cover.

"Can I talk to you for a second?" Ben asks.

"Yeah, sure." I doubt I'll manage to coax Jessica out from behind her book, so I push my seat back and follow Ben to the other side of the room. I study Jessica over his shoulder. She's still hiding, her knuckles turning white from gripping the book cover so tightly.

"Angela?"

"Sorry." I turn to Ben. He's studying a book on the table next to him, absentmindedly running a finger along the cover. "Everything okay?" I ask.

"What? Yeah." He tries to flip the book open and knocks it off the stack instead. It hits the floor with a slap.

Two girls across the room glance up, then lean their heads together and giggle.

"Jesus," Ben mutters, kneeling to pick up the book.

"Why are you being such a spaz?" I ask.

"I don't know." He drops the book back on the table and shoves his hands into his pockets. I wait.

"You wanted to talk to me, right?" I say, after a moment.

"Right. Yes." He clears his throat, looks down at his shoes and then back up at me again. "I wanted to give you something, actually."

He hesitates, then pulls a cassette tape out of his pocket. "Here."

"This is for me?" I turn the cassette over in my hands. "What is it?"

Something about my expression relaxes Ben. He exhales, and his shoulders loosen.

"Just listen to it," he says. Then he nods good-bye and hurries out of the library.

I stare down at the cassette. It's blank, no label or anything to tell me what it is. I press it between my palms and it still feels warm from being inside Ben's pocket.

Curiosity gnaws at me. I want to hurry back to my dorm and pop it into my tape player. But I can still smell that dead mouse on my scrubs. I shiver, and turn back to Jessica's table.

It's empty. The oversize book on emperor penguins lies on the chair where she'd been sitting.

Chapter Twenty-Four

Issie's lying on Jessica's bunk when I get back to our dorm. I set Ben's tape on my locker and bite my lip to keep from frowning. I was hoping Jessica had come back here. No such luck.

"Where did you run off to?" Issie asks, putting the flash cards down on the bed.

"Library." I sit on the bunk next to her and pick up the cards. They're still stiff and new, like she'd just slid them from the pack. "Invertebrates," the top card reads.

"Where did you get these?" I ask, flipping through the deck.

"Dr. Gruen," Issie says. "She's scheduled the SciGirls test for tomorrow afternoon, so everyone's cramming."

"*Tomorrow*?" My voice catches. I thought I had more time. Issie takes the cards out of my hands and pushes herself off the bunk.

"Yup," she says. "I was just about to head to the library to study."

I glance into the hall. I can't see the blinking video-camera light from this angle, but I know it's there, recording everything I say. It's now or never. I stand and hurry across the room to close the door.

Issie's eyes go wide. "What are you doing? If a guard sees—"

"Listen," I cut in. "Issie, you can't take the SciGirls test."

Issie frowns. "Why wouldn't I?"

"I don't trust Dr. Gruen." I clear my throat and glance over my shoulder, through the window in the door. I almost expect to see the doctor standing behind me, listening to everything I say. But the hall is empty. "She's not what she seems."

"You're joking, right?" Issie slaps the deck of flash cards against her palm with a little more force than necessary. "Or haven't you noticed the new sports equipment, and the better showers, and—"

"What about all the extra demerits? And girls spending the night in the Seg Block—"

"God, is *that* what you're worried about? Dr. Gruen explained all that the last time I met with her. They have to be harsher with us because SciGirls only accepts the best. It's for our own good."

"But don't you think that's—"

"Look. I have to meet Aaliyah," Issie says, coldly. "Can you move?"

"Issie, wait."

Issie squares her shoulders, propping her hands on her hips. "Don't make me go through you."

I shift to the side, and Issie pushes the door open. She pauses before starting into the hall. "Have you heard yet?"

"Heard what?" I ask.

"Cara's in the infirmary," Issie says. "Been there since before dinner."

My stomach drops. "*What*? Why?"

Issie shrugs. "No one knows. But that's why she never came to evening chores."

My heart starts beating faster. Jessica would never hurt Cara. But Jessica's not the only dangerous girl in this place. Cara's knife flashes through my head, the blade glinting. I picture someone thrusting it into her gut, and suddenly I feel cold all over.

I hurry past Issie and start down the hall.

"Ang," she calls after me, "they're not letting anyone in to see—"

I turn the corner and can't hear her anymore. I take the steps two at a time and slip past Officer Crane while she has her head turned.

The lights in the infirmary are off. Darkness pools in the corners and seeps across the floor. The only brightness comes from the two large barred windows on the far wall. The last few beams of sunlight bounce off the snow and catch on the bleached-white sheets, making the empty sickbeds glow like ghosts.

"Cara?" I whisper, making my way to the only occupied bed. Cara rolls over.

"What are you doing here?" she asks. It's too dark in the room to see her clearly, so I kneel next to her bed and wait for my eyes to adjust to the light.

"What happened? Did Peach—"

"Quiet," Cara says, sitting up. I can just make out her face. She looks fine. Not a bruise in sight.

I frown, and open my mouth to ask another question, but Cara raises her hand, stopping me.

"Wait," she whispers. I glance over my shoulder to see what she's looking at. A shadow looms in the hall just outside the infirmary door. Cara's eyes flick back over to mine. "Officer Crane's gonna take a smoke break soon," she explains.

We wait in silence for one minute. Two. Then Officer Crane's shadow moves away from the door, and I hear a window at the end of the hallway creak open. Cara relaxes behind me.

"We have a couple minutes before she comes back," she says. "What are you doing here?"

"Issie told me you were hurt."

Cara groans. "I'm *fine*. God, I should have known you guys wouldn't be cool."

I seriously consider punching her in the face. "Then why are you here? You missed kitchen duty."

"That's what you're pissed about? Kitchen duty?"

"Cara!" I snap.

"Fine. Jesus. Calm down." Cara peeks into the hallway again, but Crane still isn't back.

"Okay," she starts. "Remember that meeting I had with Dr. Gruen the other day?"

"About your demerits?"

"Right," Cara says. "Get this. Dr. Gruen told me she'd wipe my slate clean if I took the stupid SciGirls test." Cara snaps her fingers. "All my demerits gone, just like that. Don't you think that's weird?"

I think about what Issie just told me, that Dr. Gruen made our punishments harsher because SciGirls only accepts the best. "It sounds like she's trying to trick people into joining."

"Right? Why is she so desperate to get people into her stupid club? I thought it was supposed to be all competitive," Cara says. "And it looked like lots of girls were signing up anyway. So I snuck into the activity room to use the computer and check this SciGirls thing out. But they block all the good websites. That's why I had to pretend I was sick."

I frown. "You lost me. What does playing sick have to do with anything?"

Cara lowers her face to her hands, groaning. "Don't you *ever* pay attention? There's only one computer in Brunesfield that doesn't have a firewall blocking the best websites. And it's sitting right there."

She nods at an ancient computer in the corner. "What do you want to bet Nurse Ramsick uses WebMD?"

"So you pretend to be sick, and when everyone's gone, you sneak onto the computer." I pinch the bridge of my nose, my head spinning. Only Cara would go all Sherlock Holmes over something like this. I don't know if I'm impressed or deeply disturbed.

Cara lowers her voice. "Get this, there's no mention of SciGirls anywhere on the Internet."

I shift my weight, suddenly aware of the stress I'm putting on my knees. "Maybe they just don't have a website?"

Cara cocks an eyebrow. "*Everything* has a website. But say they didn't. If they were really all about helping underprivileged girls get involved in science, there'd be stories in the news about it. Or someone would have mentioned them on a forum, or in the comments section of some article. But there's *nothing*. Not even an address on Whitepages.com. It's like someone went through the entire Internet and erased them."

"Or like they never existed in the first place," I say. Fear prickles along the back of my neck. I already knew Dr. Gruen was a liar. She changed her story every time she mentioned SciGirls. But it hadn't occurred to me until just now that SciGirls might not be real at all. Those nurses could have been actors; the girls in the brochures fakes. Dr. Gruen could have made it up.

"And then I found this." Cara pulls a crumpled piece of paper out from under her pillow. It's folded in half, and all I can see is a faded black-and-white photograph of a woman's torso. She has her arms folded across her chest, and a green rubber bracelet dangles from her wrist. "*SciGirls*", the bracelet reads.

I smooth the corner of the photograph out with my thumb. "So it does exist."

Cara leans forward, mattress springs creaking beneath her. "This is from an *obituary*. The woman was a Jane Doe someone dumped at this hospital upstate—Underhill Medical Center. When the doctors performed the autopsy to see what killed her, they found out that the body had been—" Cara hesitates, grimacing— "that she'd been tampered with."

My stomach turns. "*Tampered* with?"

"Experimented on," Cara says. "It's all in the article. They found traces of weird drugs in her blood, and sections of her bones and muscles had been removed. One of the doctors said it reminded him of the experiments the Nazis did back in the forties, which is weird because that's completely illegal here.

"I did a little more research after that. Turns out a lot of girls have disappeared in the past few years. They've been vanishing on their way home from correctional facilities all across the country, only no one ever thinks to look for them. They figure they're just runaways."

I almost interrupt. Dr. Gruen said SciGirls never recruited from juvenile detention centers. She said this opportunity was unique. That we were lucky.

But then I realize—it was a lie. Just like everything else was a lie.

"And that's not all." Cara takes the photograph out of my hands and unfolds it, revealing the young woman's dark skin and eyes and her thin, elfish face.

"Looks like someone we know, doesn't it?" Cara says. I pull the paper away from her, fingers trembling.

The woman looks exactly like Jessica.

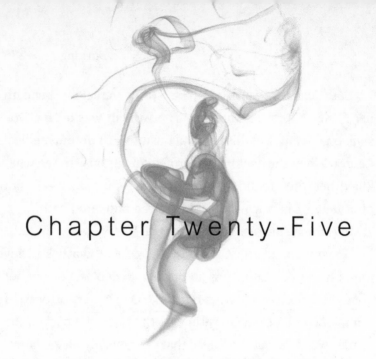

Chapter Twenty-Five

I stare down at the article in Cara's hands. The woman in the photograph has Jessica's long, thin nose, her sharp chin, and dark eyes. She could be her mother or older sister. Dr. Gruen's voice echoes in my head: *She shouldn't have been able to develop pyretic abilities outside of the SciGirls program.*

Sweat gathers between my fingers. Jessica was never in the program, but this woman was, and they were clearly related. Dr. Gruen said pyretic abilities weren't passed genetically, but Jessica became a pyretic anyway. No wonder she's studying her.

It doesn't make sense to me, but one thing, at least, is clear. SciGirls isn't what Dr. Gruen said it was. I hide my hands in my lap so Cara won't see that they're shaking. Every single word out of Dr. Gruen's mouth was a lie. She doesn't care about any of the girls here.

And I trusted her. I helped her.

"Oh my God. *Issie*." I stand so quickly that I lose my balance and have to grab on to Cara's bed to steady myself. "She's taking that test tomorrow. We have to warn her."

"Quiet!" Cara shoots me a look, then jerks her chin at the door. I glance over my shoulder, suddenly certain I'm going to see Dr. Gruen standing behind me. But the doorway is empty. Cara tugs on my arm, and I sink back down to my knees.

"Crane will be back any second," she says in a low voice. "Issie can't join SciGirls. You have to make sure she doesn't take that test."

"What about the others?" I can't stop picturing all those SciGirls sign-up sheets, filled in with neatly written names. Those names belong to girls who won't ask questions about shady science programs. Girls you could threaten with demerits and punishment until they signed up for whatever you wanted them to. Girls who don't have people waiting for them to come home.

Cara levels her eyes at me. She speaks very slowly. "You know you can't tell anyone else, right?"

"But we have to warn them!"

"We *can't*. What do you think Dr. Gruen will do to us if she finds out we know about this? You and I could disappear so easily. No one would look for us."

Silence stretches between us. *Tampered with*, I think. *Experimented on.* If this were a fairy tale, Cara and I would come up with a plan to thwart Dr. Gruen's evil scheme and save the day. We'd be heroes.

Helplessness settles over me, and it feels thick and cold, like a blanket soaked through with icy water. This isn't a fairy tale. There's nothing I can do to help the girls who signed up for SciGirls. I can't even help myself.

"Can I take this?" I reach for the article, but Cara pulls it away.

"What? Why?"

"I want to ask Jessica if she knows who this woman is."

"We can talk to her together."

"No," I say, too quickly. Cara narrows her eyes. The dim light turns her pupils amber. Like a fox.

"You're not telling me something." Cara folds the photo in half, her fingers making a crease in the paper. I press my lips together. I want to tell her the whole story. I roll the words around in my head, trying to figure out how to start.

Then something in the room shifts, like a stone dropping through water. I sit up straighter, the hair on the back of my neck prickling. My eyes move over the ceilings and the shadowy corners, searching for the telltale red flash of one of Dr. Gruen's video cameras. I don't see anything, but I still feel watched.

Cara clucks her tongue. "Friends don't keep secrets," she says.

"I have to go." I stand, but hesitate next to her bed. "Can I have the photo?" I say in a low voice. "Please?"

"Fine." She holds out the photo. I grab it, then frown. This isn't a page printed off the Internet. It's an actual newspaper clipping. The edges have frayed, and creases crisscross the photograph as if it's been handled many times.

"Cara," I breathe, turning the article over. "Where did you get this?"

"You have your secrets," Cara says, sinking back into the hospital bed. "And I have mine."

I sneak out of the infirmary, but the feeling that I'm being watched follows me all the way to my room. Every creak and footstep makes me flinch. I've tucked Cara's newspaper clipping into the waistband of my scrubs and it lies flat against my skin.

No one can see it, I tell myself. But I practically run down the stairs, and I breathe a sigh of relief when I see that the hall to my room is empty. I'll feel safer when the article is hidden.

I find a note on my pillow when I reach my dorm:

All-night cram session in the library 2nite, thanks 2 Dr. G!!!. See u at brkfst. —xo Issie

I sink down onto my bed, reading the note again. Brunesfield has never let inmates stay out all night before. I wonder how many girls are crowded inside the library, how many guards Dr. Gruen has stationed around the room. Anger bubbles up inside me. I crumple Issie's note into a ball and throw it. It skids over the concrete floor, disappearing beneath Jessica's bunk.

"Shit!" I flop back on my bed. I can't talk to Issie about SciGirls with so many people around. Even if we found a private corner, I'd have no way of knowing whether Dr. Gruen hid one of her tiny video cameras inside a book or underneath a shelf. The only place in Brunesfield that I know is safe is *this* room. If Dr. Gruen had a camera here, she'd have found that damn bear by now.

I roll onto my side, and stare at the wall across from me. I wonder if the teddy bear is still hidden in the hole behind Cara's poster. Things would be a lot easier if I just took it to Dr. Gruen. I'd get the hell out of Brunesfield, and I wouldn't have to worry about Issie getting into SciGirls, or evil experiments, or the dead woman in the photograph who looks just like Jessica. I would be with Charlie, and this could all fade away. Like an unpleasant dream.

My heart gives a strange lurch. I ignore it, and sit up. Those are shitty reasons to betray someone, and I'm a shitty person for even thinking them. I crawl out of bed and start to pace. The room is so small that I can only take two steps across before I have to turn around, but I can't just sit here freaking out about SciGirls and waiting for Issie to come back. I need a distraction or I'll go crazy.

My eyes fall on the cassette tape sitting on top of my locker. I'd forgotten about it, but now I can't help remembering the hint of red that colored Ben's cheeks, and the way he couldn't quite meet my eyes when he gave it to me. I grab the tape and my ancient Walkman, and crawl back into bed. Then I slip my headphones over my ears and wait.

The tape buzzes to life. For a long moment there's only staticky silence. Then someone clears his throat.

"Uh, hi, Angela," Ben says. Hearing his voice makes my throat go dry. I sink back onto my pillow, hugging the tape player to my chest.

"I looked for that audiobook you wanted," he says. "*The Amber Spyglass*, remember? Would you believe they don't have it at the library? *Or* the bookstore? *And* it's back-ordered online."

I can't believe he remembered I wanted to read that book. There's another long, static-filled silence. I dig my teeth into my lower lip. I hear a sound like pages turning. Ben clears his throat again.

"The library had the paperback, and I thought . . ." He laughs. "You know it took me forever to find blank cassette tapes? Anyway, here goes."

"*In a valley* . . ." Ben's voice is deep and steady, and I can't listen to him read without feeling the words rush through my entire body. I look down at my tape player, shocked. He couldn't have read the entire book out loud.

He keeps reading. I hear another page turn. The tension loosens from my shoulders, and a very small part of my fear drains away. I close my eyes, letting Ben's voice lull me to sleep.

The smell of smoke wakes me hours later. I bolt upright, and the tape player slides off my chest, the headphones ripped from my ears. Ben's tinny voice echoes through the room for a second before I snatch the player and shut off the recording.

Smoke drifts past my nose. *Jessica*, I think. I assumed she was in the library with Issie, but she must have snuck out. I blink the sleep from my eyes and pull Cara's photo out from under my mattress, where I hid it for safekeeping. No one will interrupt us in the bathroom this late at night. I'm still rubbing my eyes as I creep to the door and ease it open. The concrete floors chill my feet, but I barely notice the cold.

The bathroom feels icier than usual. No light dancing on the walls. No smoke billowing toward the ceiling. The girls must be studying down in the library, but I can't hear them from up here. Still, I try to walk lightly, just in case my footsteps carry through the ceiling. The smell of fire hangs in the air, reminding me of bonfires clawing at summer skies, of fall nights lit by piles of burning leaves. I step into the room, cringing when my toes hit the damp tile floor.

"Hello?" I whisper. I take another step forward. "Jessica?"

No answer.

I peer around the wall that separates the toilets from the showers. Dark tile stretches before me, and shallow pools of water gather in the dips in the floor, and in the corners near the walls. The thin windows near the ceiling reveal a moonless sky. There aren't even stars out tonight.

Fear tickles the back of my neck. Something's different. Wrong. I huddle near the wall, searching for anything that looks out of place.

A faucet drips. A door moves on its own, the creak of its hinges like a gunshot in the silence. I stiffen, and take two quick steps forward to peer into the stall.

No one there.

I swallow. I must be going crazy. It's just a dark bathroom. I turn to go, when I hear movement behind me. I whirl back around.

A shadow flickers beneath a stall door.

I cross the bathroom on the balls of my feet, and place my hand flat against the door. Juvie girls don't get locks on our bathroom stalls. A little push, and it swings open.

Two girls huddle inside the stall, wound together so tightly I can hardly tell where one begins and the other ends. My face flushes. I take a quick step back.

"Shit!" I avert my eyes. "Sorry!"

One of the girls lifts her head. It's a moment before I recognize her face beneath the dark tangle of hair. My voice freezes in my throat.

"*Cara?*"

Cara untangles herself. The other girl tries to slip away without looking at me, but I recognize her wispy, brown hair and pale skin.

"Mary Anne," I say. Mary Anne hesitates, flashing me a nervous look.

"Don't tell Dr. Gruen," she whispers. "*Please.*" Then, before I can say another word, she slips past and hurries out of the bathroom.

I turn back to Cara. "I don't understand," I say. "Are you and Mary Anne . . . together?"

It never occurred to me that Cara liked girls, but that's only because it never occurred to me that Cara liked *any-one*. She's all sharp edges and attitude. Most days she barely seems to tolerate Issie and me.

Cara stares at the words carved into the side of the bath-room stall: *Aaliyah is a slut, Jesus luvs you.* "I didn't think you'd find out," she says.

"Clearly." I bite off the end of the word and it comes out sharper, angrier than I mean for it to. "Why didn't you tell me?"

Cara digs her fingernail into the grooves of a jerky heart. She carves out a sliver of plaster and lets it flutter to the floor. I cross my arms over my chest, ignoring the goose bumps scattered across my skin.

"Cara, what the hell?" I say. Anger ripples across Cara's face. It tightens her features and pulls at her skin, sharp-ening her edges. I'm certain she's going to tell me to fuck myself, and stomp off.

But then her shoulders slump, the anger passing like a storm. She lowers her head to her hands.

"I don't know." She rubs her eyes with her palms and looks back up at me. "Mary Anne is . . . cool. And funny. I knew her back in high school and I always thought she was cute, but we never really talked." The ghost of a smile flick-ers across Cara's lips. "I know it sounds strange but it's just *easier* in here."

"But she's in SciGirls," I say. "She works with Dr. Gruen."

A hard look slides over Cara's eyes. "I know, but Mary Anne isn't like that. She's the one who told me there was something weird going on."

"Cara . . ."

"No, really. Remember that day she came by our dorm to drop off the brochures?"

I nod. "You said she was trying to recruit you."

"She was trying to *warn* me. She hid a note in one of them." Cara pulls a scrap of paper out of the waistband of her scrubs. "I know I should have thrown it away, but I just couldn't believe it was real. Look."

The note is blank except for three columns of hastily scribbled numbers. I touch the edge of the paper, frowning. "What does it mean?"

"It's a code. Back in school I used to pass notes to people like this. The lines of numbers correspond to a word in a book. See, the first number tells you what page to go to, and the second tells you the paragraph—"

"And the third tells you the word, right?" I close my eyes and pinch the bridge of my nose. Already this is giving me a headache.

"Exactly," Cara says. "Anyway, Mary Anne remembered that I used to do this, so she wrote me one. This corresponds with the SciGirls brochures. It says, "Don't trust her.""

"Dr. Gruen?" I ask. Cara nods.

"I wrote back to her later that day, asking her to tell me what's going on. But she said we were being watched, that it wasn't safe. So we kept passing notes back and forth like this for, like, a week. She told me about the raid, and warned me not to get a flu shot."

A chill shoots up my spine. "What was in the flu shot?"

"She doesn't know," Cara says. "That's the problem—she doesn't really *know* anything. But she kept noticing these really weird things happening. Like, a bunch of SciGirls disappeared a few weeks ago, and Dr. Gruen won't talk about where they went. And Gruen lies to the girls she's recruiting. She tells them the program is prestigious, and that they're going to get to do all these amazing things. But Mary Anne said that, after they take the test, she never sees those girls again. They're just *gone*."

"So why didn't she just leave?" I ask. "No one's forcing her to be in SciGirls."

"She was scared! She knew something really bad was going on. I told her that if she wanted to help, she needed to find real proof—something she could take to the police. We knew there was nothing about SciGirls online, but Mary Anne thought there might be something in the local newspapers. She said that Dr. Gruen has been recruiting around this area for years. It's impossible that no one noticed, and it's harder to get rid of evidence when it's in an actual newspaper and not just words on a screen. She's been going through the archived papers at the library for the past few days. That's where she found that article about the woman who'd been experimented on."

I nod. I'm glad I know where the article came from, but I'm still curious about Cara and Mary Anne. How long have they been together? And has Cara always liked girls? Did she not trust me enough to tell me? I'm not sure how to ask any of these questions without sounding judgmental, so I keep quiet. I hesitate for a second, then drop my hand on Cara's arm. Her shoulders tense.

"You're going to be weird around me now, aren't you?" she asks, shrugging me off.

"Jesus, Cara. That wasn't weird, it was supportive."

"I don't want you to be supportive. I want you to be normal." Cara slumps against the bathroom stall, hanging her head. "Things don't have to change. It's not like I'm—"

The air around us shifts, like when a noise you didn't even notice suddenly goes silent. Cara stiffens. I turn, pressing my back against the bathroom stall so no one can sneak up behind me. We watch the empty bathroom for a full minute, but nothing happens. I exhale, and allow my shoulders to loosen. We're just being paranoid. There's no one here.

"The wind," I say. Cara doesn't look convinced.

"We should get back," she whispers. "*Now*."

Together we creep back down the hall and slip into our dorm. I pull our door shut behind us, taking solace in the low, hollow sound as it clicks. Cara kneels on the floor, fishing a bobby pin out of her hair.

"*You* were the one messing with our lock," I say.

"Sometimes I meet up with Mary Anne at night, if she's working late with Dr. Gruen." She jams the pin into the keyhole and wiggles it around until she hears a click.

"I thought it was Jessica," I explain. Cara shoves the bobby pin back into her hair.

"Girl, did you really think that tiny little thing could work *these* locks?" she says, nodding at Jessica's bed. She starts climbing the ladder to her bunk, but I frown and glance down.

Jessica lies huddled in the bunk below, her breathing slow and steady. I think of the smoke that woke me from my sleep, smelling of bonfire and burning leaves. It had seemed so real at the time, but Jessica's *here*, not setting things on fire in the bathroom.

So who was?

Chapter Twenty-Six

"Miss Davis."

The voice is so low that, for a moment, I think it's part of a dream. I groan and roll over, my eyes flickering open. A long, thin shadow stretches across my floor.

I jerk upright. Dr. Gruen stands in the doorway, the golden rose glinting in the early-morning sunlight. The bed across from me creaks. Cara moans.

"What the—" she starts, but Dr. Gruen raises a hand, silencing her.

"Don't get up, ladies. I just need to borrow Miss Davis."

I swallow. "Why?"

Dr. Gruen stares at me with those cold blue eyes. "Follow me."

I crawl out of bed. Cara's gone completely white. It occurs to me that she's scared. I've never seen her scared before. The sweat on the back of my neck feels suddenly very cold.

I look around the little dorm, wondering if this might be the last time I see it.

Jessica stares out from the bunk across from me, her dark eyes wide with fear. She's got her hands all bunched up near her mouth, and she's written the word "hope" across her knuckles.

I look down at the wobbly letters. In the nearly two years since I started coming up with four-letter words to write on Issie's hand, I had never once thought of "hope."

"Miss Davis," Dr. Gruen says. Her voice harder, this time.

I follow her out of the room and down the hall, clenching and unclenching my hands as we walk. Something's going to happen. Something bad. I feel it in the back of my throat. I stare at the bloodred soles of Dr. Gruen's shoes, and think of one hundred different ways she could destroy my life. I should be scared, but I just feel numb. I wish I'd gotten to see Issie again. And Ben.

Gruen turns down the hallway that leads to the visitors' center. I frown. I never have visitors.

"Who's in there?" I ask. Dr. Gruen places a hand on the doorknob.

"Come look," she says. She pushes the door open.

Charlie sits at a long, plastic table, staring at his hands. His hair has grown longer and he's started twisting it back into cornrows, like some of the older boys in our neighborhood. My heart climbs into my throat. Someone has taken the old Charlie and stretched him out, leaving this newer, ganglier model behind. He looks exactly like he did the last time I saw him, and impossibly different.

He can't really be here. This is an illusion.

"You have fifteen minutes," Dr. Gruen says. She steps out of the room, and the door clicks shut behind her. I don't watch her go. I can't peel my eyes away from my little brother.

"Charlie," I gasp. He looks up, and a smile like sunshine unfolds across his face. A sob claws at my throat, but I choke it down. I cross the room in two large steps and throw my arms around him.

Brunesfield fades into the background, like an unpleasant dream. I hold my brother tight. He's almost as tall as I am now, and there are muscles in his arms that weren't there before.

"Ang, you're gonna break me," he says.

"Sorry," I say, letting him go. He shuffles backward, shoving his hands into his sweatshirt pockets. I make a face. "Are you wearing *cologne*?"

"No." Color brightens his cheeks. "It's my shampoo. I don't have to use that Herbal Essences crap you buy anymore."

"So you're buying manly shampoo now?" I sniff his hair. "What is that? *Old Spice*?"

"Stop." He laughs, swatting me away. I sink into the chair across from him and lean over the table.

"Have you been getting my letters?" I ask. His grin falters.

"Yeah. Sorry I haven't written more," he says. "You know Mom . . ."

"Don't apologize." I make my smile hard, trying not to think of my mother's angry handwriting. *Leave your brother alone.*

"Anyway, things will be different when I bust out of here," I say. Charlie stares at his hands. His smile fades into something small and private. Like I'm telling him a story he's getting too old to believe.

"Yeah," he says. "Definitely."

The doubt in his voice opens a deep, ugly space inside my chest. "How's Mom?" I ask to change the subject. Charlie shrugs.

"Good, I guess."

"She working?"

Another shrug. "Sometimes. She ain't doing too bad, really."

"*Isn't,*" I correct him. I don't care how the other boys in the neighborhood talk; I won't let Charlie sound ignorant.

Charlie smiles, sheepish. "Sorry. She *isn't* doing too bad. She has a part-time job at a bakery."

"How long?"

Charlie chews on his lower lip. I know he's trying to decide whether to tell me the truth, or lie so I think things are better than they are. "Only two weeks," he says, opting for the truth. "But it's going really well! The manager likes her."

I frown. There's only one kind of manager who ever likes Mom, and he's usually bored and wearing a wedding ring. "The manager a guy?"

Charlie shakes his head. "Nah. It's this old lady who's owned the place forever. I think it could be okay."

I nod and work my mouth into a hopeful smile. Mom's never been able to hold a job for more than a couple of months. It always starts out fine, but then something goes wrong. She'll become convinced that the manager doesn't respect her, or that the job is below her abilities. She'll stop showing up on time. Or at all.

When she's out of work, things get real bad. She drinks earlier in the day, and watches old movies in bed, the volume turned up loud to tell us she doesn't want to be disturbed. She'll forget to buy groceries, and Charlie and I will have to figure out how to make a loaf of bread last a week.

That thought sends a shudder through my body. Because it hasn't been Charlie and me dealing with Mom, not for the past two years. It's just been Charlie. He looks so hopeful right now. Like he wants me to tell him I'm proud of him.

"That's really good, bud," I say. I reach across the table and take his hand.

"She's doing better. You'd be surprised," Charlie says. "She's seeing this guy from my school now, Dan. He's the PE teacher. He's nice."

I try not to let the surprise show in my face. Boyfriend with a job is new. I bite my lip to keep myself from asking whether he has a wife. "That's really great," I say, instead.

"Yeah," Charlie says. "I just want you to know that things are okay. In case . . ."

"In case what?"

He picks at his fingernail. "In case you can't come back."

His words hit me like a shot to the heart. I grip his hand tighter. "Charlie, I'm coming back. You *know* I'm coming back."

"Yeah." He narrows his eyes, just slightly, and in a second I see exactly the kind of man he's going to be. It's like watching one of those nature programs where things grow in fast-forward.

He looks like our dad.

"But in case you can't," Charlie adds, slowly. "In case something happens, I don't want you to worry. I'm fine."

The tears I'd been trying not to cry come to my eyes and spill over onto my cheeks. I close my eyes. Stupid.

Charlie turns his hand over in mine and squeezes me back. I stare down at our entwined fingers.

"It's okay," he whispers. "It's okay, I'm okay."

I nod. "I know you are," I say.

Chapter Twenty-Seven

Charlie and I spend the rest of our fifteen minutes talking about school (him) and telling funny stories about Cara and Issie (me). I learn that he's planning on trying out for the basketball team this spring, and that he got third place in a schoolwide essay contest, and that Jason isn't his best friend anymore because now Bradley is.

I listen to it all, enthralled. It feels like a long, cool drink of water after spending years in the desert. Charlie's life is so normal. I take note of details and specifics so I can recount his visit for Cara and Issie. I don't want to get anything wrong. I don't want to forget anything.

Fifteen minutes passes too quickly. I hear the door click open and my stomach plunges. I swivel around in my chair.

"Just a little longer," I beg. "Please."

Dr. Gruen's face is a mask. She shows no emotion. No sympathy.

"You may have a minute to tell your brother good-bye," she says. It'd be stupid to waste time arguing with her, so I turn back around and take Charlie's hand.

"I'll write you," I promise.

"Me too," he says. "I'll try."

I give him another quick, tight hug, thankful he's not old enough to shrug me off yet. "I'll come home," I whisper into his ear. "I promise."

"I know," he says.

And then Dr. Gruen's behind me, telling me to stand, and I'm sliding my chair away from the table and trying not to cry as I walk away from my little brother.

Dr. Gruen shuts the door to the visitors' room. My head is still filled with Charlie, but then I look up at her pale, pointed face, and the memory switches off like a television.

Officers Sterling and Crane stand behind her. They stare straight ahead, hands clasped at their backs. Fear hovers at the edge of my mind but I steel myself, refusing to let it in.

"How did you find my brother?" I ask.

Dr. Gruen considers me, her mouth a thin, straight line. "The address was in your file," she says. "Of course."

"But how did he get here?" I ask. "My mother—"

"I have resources, Miss Davis."

Resources. My eyes flick back over to the closed door. I imagine my little brother on the other side, waiting for someone to take him back home. My mouth feels dry, but I make myself open it. "Why?"

Dr. Gruen purses her lips. "I've made my intentions quite clear. You're the one who's been playing games."

I think of the word "hope" dancing across Jessica's knuckles. I hear her whisper in the dark. *Don't let them take me.*

"I told you," I say. "I don't know where that damn bear is. I've tried—"

"*I don't believe you!*" Dr. Gruen's voice cuts through the stillness of the hallway. Officer Sterling flinches, but doesn't look at me. "You may not understand the importance of 'that damn bear,' as you call it, but I assure you it's essential to the work I'm doing."

Dr. Gruen grabs my shoulders and jerks me forward, her face inches from my own. It's the only time I've ever heard her raise her voice. Her eyes flash, and a strand of blond hair falls over her forehead. For a second, she looks unhinged. Then she tucks the strand of hair back behind her ear.

"What do you think I'll do to your brother if you don't bring me what I want?" she asks.

Horror washes over me, and it feels cold and thick, like mud. "I won't let you touch my brother," I say, but fear makes my voice tremble.

A cruel smile twists Dr. Gruen's lips. "Do you have any idea how easy it was to get to him?" she says. "Your idiot mother didn't even ask for identification before handing him over to a complete stranger. Tell me, how much time could pass before she'd think to call the cops? Too much, I bet. Canada's only a couple of hours away by car. And then *poof*." Dr. Gruen snaps her fingers. "He disappears. You never see him again."

She wants me to cower. Beg. But I'm used to threats, and I learned a long time ago that crying gets you nowhere. I push my anger and fear as far down as they'll go and look her straight in the eye.

"You don't scare me," I say.

Dr. Gruen shakes her head, disgusted. "I should," she says. She takes a step back, nodding at Officer Crane. "Take her."

Crane shoves me against the wall, pressing the side of my face up against the cold concrete. I press my lips together to keep from crying out. Sterling twists my arms behind my back, and metal bites into my wrists. Handcuffs.

"What are you doing?" I ask, finding Dr. Gruen's eyes.

"It occurred to me that you might need some time to think about your situation," Dr. Gruen says smoothly. "It's probably best to put you someplace free of distractions. Luckily, Officer Brody informed me of an open room in the Seg Block."

Fear drops through me like a stone. "You can't do that," I say.

"You'd be amazed at what I can do," Dr. Gruen says. Sterling drags me away from the wall, and I stumble toward the door.

"Stop!" I shout. "*Please.*"

An amused smile crooks Dr. Gruen's lips. She's enjoying this.

The guards drag me away from the wall and force me through one security door, and then another. Dr. Gruen's heels click against the concrete floor, following us down the staircase and through the twisting basement halls. I hold my breath as we round the corner to the Seg Block.

Ben will be there, I think. *Ben will help me.*

But Ben isn't sitting on the rickety metal stool at the end of the hall. Brody is. The flickering fluorescent lights bounce off his pink skull. He flashes me a cruel smile and jabs the security button with his thumb.

"Fresh meat," he mutters, as Sterling and Crane steer me through the buzzing door.

"Go to hell," I spit.

The guards drag me past pink walls and small, dirty cells. Horror claws at my chest. The girls down here still haunt my dreams. Their shrill screams echo through my head. I see them run their dirty tongues over their glass doors and scratch at the walls until their fingers bleed. I can't stay here. I can't be like them.

Officer Crane fumbles with the keys at her belt. She unlocks the cell and slides the door open.

"Go on," she says, pushing me forward. My knees give out, and I collapse onto the floor, next to the dirty mattress shoved up against the wall. My legs shake, but I leap up and lunge for the still open door.

Dr. Gruen steps in front of me, blocking my way. She lifts one thin hand to the door.

"I suggest you use this time to think about your options," she says in that low, too-sweet voice of hers. "Jessica is an infection. If we don't stop her, she'll wipe out everyone here."

Then, without another word, she closes the door in my face, leaving me locked in the cell. Alone.

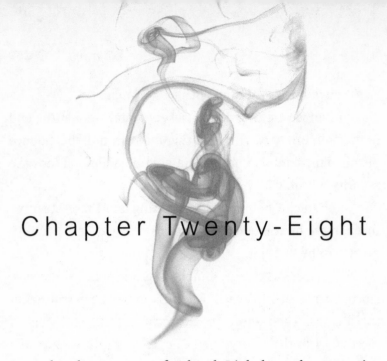

Chapter Twenty-Eight

Sweat breaks out on my forehead. I inhale, and oxygen rips through my throat and lungs like knives. I push myself to the corner of the room and pull my knees to my chest. I wrap my arms around them, trying to make myself as small as possible. The walls inch closer every time I blink.

This can't be real. Dr. Gruen can't leave me here. It's a trick. My breathing calms a little, and my head clears. She's coming back for me. She has to.

Minutes tick past. Cold creeps in through the walls and coaxes goose bumps from the back of my neck. I tighten my arms around my knees, shivering. It's a trick. Dr. Gruen thinks she can break me, but she can't. I won't let her.

"Always knew you were one of us, pretty," someone whispers. I flinch. It's Karen, the girl I met my first day here. I hear her crawl across the floor of her cell. Her breath sounds ragged. Like her lungs are paper bags.

"Pretty girl," she whispers. Her nails scratch the wall. "Talk to me, pretty girl."

"Shut up." I cover my ears with my hands. In a cell farther down the hall, someone laughs, the sound sharp and cruel.

"One of us," another girls says. I dig my fingers into my skull and start to rock. Another girl joins in, and another after that. I don't want to hear them. I don't want to believe what they say.

Their voices merge together, until I can't hear anything at all.

Hours pass before the girls get bored and stop calling to me. I lower my hands and press my face against the cloudy glass door of my cell. The light in the hall looks different. Darker. It must be late. I sigh, and crawl over to my dirty mattress. I don't want to touch it, but I remind myself that Jessica slept in this cell too, and that makes me feel a little better. I climb onto the mattress and curl into a ball.

I close my eyes and try to sleep. It's impossible. I can't sleep here. A million things race through my head. I think of Issie taking the SciGirls test, and I worry about what'll happen to Cara and Mary Anne if Dr. Gruen catches them together. No wonder the other girls here go crazy. How can you stay sane when you're locked up with only your thoughts to keep you company?

Mostly I think about Jessica.

Jessica is an infection. She'll wipe out everyone here. The words chase themselves through my brain, repeating like song lyrics you can't get out of your head.

I think about the photographs Dr. Gruen showed me. That tiny house. That sad family. I think of the newspaper article Cara found, the woman who looked like Jessica. The woman who died in a fire.

I roll over, uncomfortable. I can practically feel the cold tile floor through the lumpy mattress.

Still, my eyes grow heavy. I picture flames eating away at raw wood siding and a field of tall grass burning in the wind. I picture the little boy with tubes running up his nose. But it's not Jessica's little brother. It's Charlie.

"It's okay if you never come back," he whispers, just before I fall asleep.

I wake to the sound of footsteps. Light seeps through my closed lids. I groan and rub at my eyes. Every part of my body aches.

The footsteps come closer. Suddenly I'm wide awake. Alert. I sit up on the mattress. Whoever's coming walks slowly. Thick-soled boots hit the concrete floor at steady, even intervals.

Ben, I think. I push myself to my feet and stand, trying to smooth my short curls with my fingers. I'm very aware of the smell in here. I hope *I* don't smell like that.

The footsteps move closer. They pass the other cells without stopping. What if he's here to let me out? Relief bubbles up in my chest, and I have to bite down on my lip to keep from sobbing. I stumble across the cell and press myself against the glass door, anxious to see his face.

Brody stops in front of my door, a smirk twisting his thick, cruel lips. He's holding an aluminum tray in one hand.

"You," I say. I stumble backward, nearly tripping over the corner of my mattress.

"Morning, angel." He flips the food slot open and slides the tray into my cell.

"Where's Be—Mateo?" I ask. I'm surprised by how rough my throat feels. It's only been a day, and already I've forgotten how to use my voice.

"*Officer* Mateo has been reassigned." Brody stands up and loops his thumbs through his belt. He wrinkles his nose, considering me with those beady, watery eyes. "Dr. Gruen thought it would make more sense for me to oversee you."

I move away from the door, wanting to put as much space between myself and Brody as possible. But the cell is small, and I haven't taken more than two steps before the hard, cold wall is at my back. Brody's smirk twists into a cruel smile.

"How long do I have to stay here?" I ask. He shrugs. It's a lazy gesture, he barely even lifts his shoulders.

"The doctor didn't say," he says. "But you should get used to it. If I have any say, you're never getting out."

He wiggles his fingers at me in a mocking wave, then steps away from the door. I sink to the floor, listening to his footsteps echo down the hall. Every single *thud* reverberates inside my chest, like a warning.

Never the footsteps seem to say. *Never never never never.*

You're never getting out.

Chapter Twenty-Nine

Days last forever if you don't know when they end. Or begin.
I must sleep, but I'm not sure when or for how long. It feels
like I'm always waiting. I wait for hours. Days.

The other girls whisper horrible things that creep through
the walls like bugs. "Pretty girl," they say. And "You're just like
us." Sometimes they scream. The screams are the worst.

I watch the light in the hall fade. It creeps over the concrete floor like the tide. Hours pass, and then the light comes
back again. Fingers of yellow crawl over the floor. Slowly at
first. Then fast. I stretch my hand across the glass, trying to
touch them.

Time passes. I'm half-awake and half-asleep when the
security door at the end of the hall buzzes open. I hear low
voices and footsteps. I press my face against the glass, but I
can't see who's coming.

Keys jangle. A girl at the end of the hall giggles.

"Quiet!" a voice says. "Hands in diamonds."

Brody. The girl stops giggling, and metal clinks against metal: handcuffs.

He's taking her, I realize.

The whole process repeats about fifteen times. Once for every girl in the Seg Block. I hold my breath, waiting for Brody to come back for me.

The minutes stretch into hours. He doesn't come back.

I close my eyes, and I cover my ears with my hands. He can't just leave me here alone. He *can't.*

But he does. I wrap my arms around my knees and rock. The silence is even worse than the screams.

I don't belong here. I whisper those words to myself again and again.

But I don't believe them. Not really.

I always knew this was where I'd end up.

A sudden buzz interrupts the silence. The far door creaks open.

The security door. Brody's coming.

Every muscle in my body tenses. I scoot to the far corner of my cell. I do this every time Brody brings me food. It's easier to ignore him when I'm as far from the door as possible.

Footsteps sound on the concrete. I shut my eyes.

The footsteps stop in front of my room. Keys jangle at my door, and my eyes pop open.

"How are you feeling, Miss Davis?" Dr. Gruen says, opening my door. I stare at her for a long moment, trying to work out whether I'm hallucinating.

"How long have I been here?" I ask. Dr. Gruen considers me, her eyes flashing. She brushes a wrinkle from her black dress.

"Four days."

Four days. I close my eyes, forcing myself to breathe. It felt like longer.

"Have you had ample time to think about your situation?" Dr. Gruen asks. I nod without opening my eyes.

"I get it," I say. "I'll give you what you want."

"Good." I hear the smile in her voice, and my eyes flicker back open. "You have until tomorrow."

She steps away from my cell, leaving the door open. Her heels dig into the concrete floor as she walks away. The sound makes me cringe.

I scramble to my feet and follow her, keeping my eyes straight ahead so I don't have to look at the empty cells. I swallow, my throat cottony dry.

"Where did you take them?" I ask.

"Don't concern yourself with that right now," Dr. Gruen says, unlocking the security door at the end of the hall. "You might want to gather your things when you get back to your dorm."

"Why?"

Dr. Gruen glances over her shoulder, considering me. She rests a hand on the security door, her fingers tapping the wood. Index, middle, ring. Ring, index, ring. Like she's playing an invisible piano.

"Because you're leaving," she says, after a moment. "Bring me what I want, and you're out of here tomorrow."

Chapter Thirty

In the end, it's easy.

The dorm is empty. I hesitate at the doorway, but just for a moment. Then I walk over to Jessica's bunk and I peel the poster away from the wall above her bed. Her teddy bear's right where I left it. I pull it out of the hole and shove it into my pillowcase, then toss the pillow back onto my bed.

There. Done. When Dr. Gruen stops by tomorrow morning, I'll just hand her the pillow. I won't even have to think about it.

I'm supposed to head to the cafeteria for evening chores, but instead I crawl onto my bed and wrap my body around my pillow. I spent the past four days yearning for other people, but now the thought of them makes me cringe. I listen for the distant sounds of laughing and voices, but I hear nothing. It's like all of Brunesfield is empty. Like I'm the last one here.

I close my eyes. If I concentrate, I can feel the teddy bear inside the pillow, its blackened arms and legs protected by layers of cotton.

A second passes, and I jerk awake. Darkness presses in around me. I hear the low, steady sounds of breathing and realize the others are already asleep. I must've slept through dinner.

I shift in bed, tugging my blanket up past my chin. It's probably better like this. If I'd been awake when the others came in, I might have felt compelled to say good-bye or explain. Now I don't even have time to pack. I roll onto my side and tug Cara's newspaper article out from under my mattress and tuck it into the waistband of my scrubs. I lie on my back for a moment, thinking, but there's nothing else I want to bring with me.

A beam of light sweeps into the room. I close my eyes before it hits my face. I feel the brightness behind my closed lids, and imagine Ben on the other side of the door, pointing the flashlight at me. He hesitates for a beat, then the light disappears, and I hear his footsteps walking away.

I open my eyes. My tape player sits on the locker at the foot of my bed, headphones wrapped around it. I stare at it for a long moment. I was wrong. There is something I want.

I kick the blankets away from my legs and crawl out of bed. I hesitate at the door, worried it might be locked. But the handle turns. I glance at Cara's bunk: empty. I'm not the only one sneaking out tonight.

I follow Ben's bobbing flashlight down the hall and around the corner. He's a silhouette in the darkness, his body a jumble of black shapes. I think of how angry he was the last time he found me sneaking around at night, and I almost run back to my dorm.

Dr. Gruen's the one who stops me. Her voice echoes through my head. *Gather your things.* It doesn't matter if Ben gets mad at me. I'm leaving tomorrow. I'll never see him again.

I stop in the middle of the hall and clear my throat. "Hey."

Ben turns, his flashlight beam sweeping over the floor in a wobbly arc.

"Angela," he whispers. He crosses the hall in two long strides. His hand closes around my shoulder and every nerve ending in my skin explodes. "Jesus. I was so worried about you."

I lift my hand and brush a strand of hair back from Ben's forehead. Just to see if I can. His hair feels softer than I expected, and thick. He moves his thumb along the line of my jaw. I lean into him, and the rest of my body disappears. All that exists is the few inches of skin where he's touched me.

"I thought you left with the others," he says.

"Others?" I stiffen, and take a step back. My eyes adjust to the flashlight. Purple bruises shadow the skin below Ben's eyes. It looks like he hasn't been sleeping. "You mean the girls in Seg?"

"No." Ben frowns, and jerks his chin at the dorm next to him. "Didn't you notice?"

"Notice . . . ?" I look through the dorm window and see empty beds, the mattresses stripped of sheets and pillows. I whirl around to check the dorm behind me. It's empty too. I cross the hall without thinking, and press my face against the glass window in the door.

A cold, hard lump forms in my throat. Ellen used to sleep here. A stack of library books sits next to the foot of her bed, abandoned.

"A bunch of vans arrived a few days ago," Ben explains. "They took all the girls who signed up for that SciGirls test. None of them came back, so I guess they all passed. There are only a few girls left."

"No." I think of the article tucked in the waistband of my scrubs. The Jane Doe dropped at the door of some hospital upstate, a SciGirls bracelet dangling from her wrist. "Issie."

I was just in our dorm. I *saw* her. But that's not true. I heard breathing so I assumed she was above me. It could have been anyone.

For a long moment, I'm not sure how to make my legs move. I stumble for a few feet, then muscle memory takes over and I'm running down the hallway. Ben says my name in an urgent whisper but I don't turn around. I don't stop running until I've reached our dorm and thrown open the door.

Moonlight spills in from the barred window at our ceiling. All I see is silver. I hold my breath as I step into the room, and blink to help my eyes adjust to the light. The top bunk comes into focus.

I see a shape below the blankets, a tangle of dark hair on Issie's pillow.

"Oh God," I whisper. Someone touches my arm and I flinch, but it's just Ben. He holds a finger to his lips, and pulls me back into the hall.

"I tried to tell you," he says, closing the dorm door. "She didn't take the test."

I exhale and sink back against the wall, but guilt pounds at my chest like a fist. Issie's still here, but dozens of other girls have been taken, and who knows what Dr. Gruen's going to do to them. I knew this was going to happen, but I didn't think it would happen like *this*. It didn't occur to me that they would all just . . . disappear.

"I should have warned them," I whisper.

"Warned them?" Ben meets my eyes and it feels like the rest of the world has been put on Mute. "Angela, what's going on?"

A scream rips through the hallway before I can answer. We stare at each other for a moment, frozen. Then Ben jerks away.

"I think it came from here," he says, tearing down the hall.

We hurry around one corner, and then another. I'm so focused on keeping up with Ben that I don't notice we've reached the bathroom until we're standing in front of it.

"Hello?" Ben pushes the bathroom door open. He switches his flashlight on and the dim light illuminates grimy tile, and a shallow puddle of water.

Terror hits me in the second between stopping in front of the door and stepping into the bathroom. The air in here is wrong. It's too thick. Like breathing in sand. Silence hangs over us, heavy as a blanket, and I feel the spaces where the scream ripped through it, like a wound ripping through skin.

"Ben," I whisper. "Wait."

He doesn't turn around. He steps forward, his flashlight beam dancing off damp tile. He hesitates next to the wall that separates the toilets from the showers. I hold my breath. All the strings inside my body tighten, threatening to snap.

Someone sniffles. The sound barely stirs the air, but it sends every hair on my arms standing straight up. I drift forward and around the wall, ignoring Ben when he hisses at me to stay back.

Cara crouches on the cold floor, her knee covering a bit of blackened tile. She's shaking so badly the air seems to quiver around her. She's curled her hands around her face, her mouth hanging open in a silent scream.

"Cara," I start. I take another step forward and the words freeze on my tongue.

Mary Anne's body lies across the tile in the middle of the room. I stare at her and for a long moment I don't understand what I'm seeing. It's like she's wearing a mask. Half of her face still looks perfect—skin smooth and pale, lips holding the hint of a smile. Eye closed, like she might be sleeping.

The other half is pure horror. Fire burned away the flesh on her nose and around her eyes, and burns creep along her cheeks and over her forehead. The skin that's still left is black and puckered, and so thin I can see the muscle and bone twisted beneath it. A few singed strands of hair still cling to her scalp. The rest is gone, burned to ash beneath her head.

Mary Anne's open eye stares at the ceiling, lifeless. Blood spills down her cheek like a tear.

Chapter Thirty-One

No.

My mind screams that word. The rest of the world comes in and out of focus, like a dream I'm trying to wake from. I'm dimly aware of the acid taste at the back of my throat, and of Ben moving around me. He shouts something, and pulls his walkie-talkie from the holster at his belt.

My knees buckle. I put a hand out, steadying myself against the wall.

"Angela?" Ben says, and, just like that, the world slams back into me. Cara doubles over, sobbing and shaking. The smell of burned flesh hangs in the air. Voices crackle from Ben's walkie-talkie.

A memory unfolds in the back of my head: Peach screaming from her shower stall. Red burns unfolding across her shoulders. Jessica flashing me a private smile. Looking proud.

My stomach turns. I double over, catching myself seconds before my knees slam into the floor. I heave, but nothing comes out but air.

"Angela?" Ben says, again. He touches my shoulder. I'm suddenly aware of the thin veil of sweat coating my skin. I shake my head, edging away from the body.

"I have to go," I murmur, stumbling out of the bathroom. I try to run, but my knees knock together. Nerves make my legs weak. They feel like they could dissolve beneath me.

I tear down the hall and into my dorm, slamming the door so hard that it cracks against the wall. Issie sits up in bed. She groans, rubbing her eyes.

"What the hell?" she says. I walk straight to my bunk and grab the pillow. The teddy bear's legs shift below layers of fabric and cotton.

I turn. Jessica stares at me from her bunk. I think of Mary Anne's ruined face, her blackened skin, and fear jolts through me. Jessica blinks, and bunches her blanket up under her chin.

"You said you could control it," I whisper. I'm trembling so badly I almost drop the pillow.

Issie leans over the side of her bunk. "What's going on?"

I don't answer. I stare at Jessica, waiting for an explanation. It occurs to me that it's probably not safe to stand here. Nerves thrum inside my chest, but I hold my ground. Cara deserves to know what happened to Mary Anne. *Why* it happened.

Jessica sits up. Her blanket falls to her lap. "I didn't do anything," she whispers. "I swear."

"Liar!"

Jessica's face crumples. *Good,* I think. I squeeze the pillow so tightly that the muscles in my hand burn. The bed shakes as Issie climbs down the ladder.

"What the hell?" she says again. She crosses the room, reaching out to comfort Jessica.

"Be careful," I warn. "She's dangerous."

The lights in the hallway blink on. Issie glances at me, then up at Cara's empty bed. The color drains from her face.

"What happened?" she asks.

Officers Sterling and Crane appear at the door to our room before I can answer. Issie stiffens, and Jessica crawls out of bed. I stare at the officers' uniforms. It seems strange that they're on duty so late.

Dr. Gruen walks up behind them. She has Cara by the arm, but Cara stares at the ground, refusing to meet our eyes.

"Sit," Gruen says. Cara jerks her arm away and shuffles across the room, dropping down on the bed next to me.

Dr. Gruen folds her hands in front of her. She's traded in her usual structured black dress for a pair of dark lounge pants and a black T-shirt. Black-framed glasses perch on her nose.

Her eyes linger on me. "A tragedy has occurred this evening," she says.

Cara releases a choked sob and doubles over, clutching her stomach. Issie frowns. Dr. Gruen's eyes stay pinned on me.

"And the worst part," she continues, "is that it was preventable."

That last word vibrates through the air long after she stops talking. *Preventable.* Issie and Cara both look up, confused. I feel their eyes turn to me, and my cheeks flare.

"What is she talking about?" Cara murmurs. My throat feels suddenly dry. I don't know how to look at her, not when I know I'm partially responsible for killing Mary Anne.

"Where is it?" Gruen snaps. I don't have to ask what she's talking about. I hold out the pillow, my hands shaking.

"Inside," I whisper. "There's a rip in the seam."

Dr. Gruen's lips curl with something like hunger. She nods at the two officers standing at my door.

"Take the little girl," she says. "Bring the rest of them to my office."

Chapter Thirty-Two

Sterling leaves us in the office and steps outside, closing Dr. Gruen's door with a barely audible *click*. Her key grinds against the lock, and the dead bolt slams into place.

Cara covers her mouth with her hands. Sobs rattle her thin shoulders.

Guilt drums through me in static bursts. It's a low buzz at the back of my head, like fluorescent lights, how you don't hear them humming until you do, and then they're all you hear.

I did this. I knew what Jessica could do and I didn't tell anyone.

"Is someone going to explain what's going on?" Issie asks.

"Dr. Gruen's assistant is dead," I say. Issie looks at Cara, and then back at me.

"You're fucking with me," Issie says.

I say nothing. Cara presses her lips together, and tears crawl down her cheeks. The humor fades from Issie's face.

"I don't understand," she says. "How?"

A fresh burst of shame flares through me. I hug my arms to my chest, feeling like I might explode. Like a lightbulb, spraying the room with glass and pops of fire.

Cara and Issie slept in the same room as Jessica. They shared meals with her, they laughed at her jokes. If anyone had the right to know what she was capable of, they did.

And I kept it a secret. Like a coward.

Cara cuts her eyes at me. She takes a shaky breath, lowering her hands. "Mary Anne said you were working with Dr. Gruen. That you two had a deal."

"It wasn't like that," I say.

"You know something," Cara shouts. "I know you do."

I can't look at her so I twist my fingers together and stare at my ragged cuticles.

"Jessica," I say.

A muscle in Cara's jaw tightens. "What?"

"It was Jessica." I take a deep breath and look up, forcing myself to meet Cara's eyes. My body feels charged. I want to jump into cold water. Instead I have to stand here, guilt written across my face in neon.

"Remember when I burned my fingers?"

From there, I tell them everything. How I followed Jessica to the bathroom in the middle of the night, and watched her set the teddy bear on fire. How she told me she was practicing, that she could control it. And Dr. Gruen, pressuring me to give her up. To spy on her. Tell Dr. Gruen what I saw.

Cara interrupts me halfway through the story. "Bullshit."

"There are others like her," I continue. "Dr. Gruen told me they're called pyretics. I know it sounds crazy—"

Cara rounds on me, eyes flashing. "Crazy? You're telling us that little girl sets *fires* with her mind. No wonder they sent you to Seg."

For a moment, I'm dumbstruck. "Are you kidding?" I ask, when I find my voice again. "You're the queen of conspiracy theories—"

"That's different! The government covers up all sorts of—"

"Shut *up!*" Issie shouts, quieting us both. She chews on her thumbnail. "This is bad."

"Don't tell me you believe her," Cara snaps.

"Don't matter if I believe her." Issie takes her thumb out of her mouth and starts picking at her cuticles. "Take a look around. Half the girls here have already been whisked away in creepy murder vans. Now the ones left behind are starting to die. You planning to be next?"

Cara presses her lips together. After a moment, she shakes her head.

"We need to get out of here," I say to no one in particular.

"Exactly what I was thinking," Issie says. "Think the window opens?"

I release a startled noise, like a laugh, but hollow. The shell of a laugh. "Right," I say. "We can head to the woods."

Issie wedges her body into the narrow space between Dr. Gruen's desk and the window. She digs her fingers into the frame and pulls. The window doesn't budge.

"Help me," she grunts.

I frown. This doesn't feel like a joke anymore. "What are you doing?"

"Getting the fuck out of here. Now help me get this window open."

"We can't do that." I look at Cara for backup. The worry line on her forehead deepens. She chews her lower lip.

"Maybe we could break the glass?" Cara asks.

Issie purses her lips. "I bet that'd set off an alarm," she says. "Do you see a lock?"

"Stop!" I shout. I stand, nearly knocking over my chair. "This is crazy. We can't just break out and run off to the woods."

"Why not?" Issie turns around. I shake my head, not sure where to start.

"We'd get caught, first of all," I say.

"You said the woods were too deep," Cara says. "Remember?"

"That was a *story*. It was made-up! Just something I told you before we went to sleep."

Issie cocks an eyebrow. "Seemed pretty real to me."

"It's like twelve degrees outside," I point out. "We'll get hypothermia."

"We'll start a fire," Cara says.

"You don't even like being outside during rec time!" I rake a hand over my hair, feeling unhinged. They can't honestly think this is a good idea. We'd freeze to death before we even made it to the tree line.

The look in Cara's eyes makes me nervous: it's shifty and calculating. I'm not even sure she wants to run. I think she just wants to do some damage.

I touch her arm, and she flinches. "Cara, think about this," I say.

"Mary Anne's *dead*," Cara spits back. "And the rest of us are being carted off to God knows where to be used as human guinea pigs."

Issie turns toward Cara, one hand still resting on the window. I wonder if Cara told her about the experiments, and the woman from the article. Maybe that's why Issie didn't take the SciGirls test.

"You don't know what's going to happen to those girls," I say, but even I can hear the doubt in my voice.

"Why are you fighting this so hard?" Cara asks. "You saw the article. You know it's true."

"Even if it is, this plan is crazy!"

"Do you have a better option?" Cara's eyes flash dangerously, and I realize she's been holding something back. She's got an ace up her sleeve, and she's decided that now is the time to play it. "You can't exactly go home, right?"

"What are you talking about?" I say, steeling myself. Cara bites her lower lip—at least she has the decency to look embarrassed—and pulls an envelope out from the waistband of her scrubs. My mother's tiny, perfect handwriting stares out at me.

My voice feels thick. "Where did you get that?"

"You can't go home," Cara says. Her hands shake, making the envelope tremble. "Why didn't you tell us? Why did you just pretend everything was okay?"

I grab for the envelope but Cara dances backward, holding it above her head.

"That was *private*."

"You lied to us," Cara says. "You said you were going to go back home, to be with Charlie, but your mom won't let you. You aren't welcome there."

"*Stop*." I grab for the envelope again, halfheartedly. Cara holds it away.

"You aren't going to be with Charlie," she says. "You aren't allowed anywhere near him."

"Cara . . ." Issie says. Her eyes bounce from Cara to me.

"So where are you going to go, Angela?" Cara continues, ignoring her. "You can't go home. You can't stay here."

"Shut up!" I feel a sob rising in my throat, and I push it down. Juvie girls don't cry. I make the pain hard. Turn it into something I can use.

Cara's got a lot of attitude, but I'm bigger than she is. I get in her face, so close that she has to tilt her head to meet my eyes. She backs up, hits the wall. To her credit, she doesn't blink.

"That doesn't belong to you." My voice is a low rumble. I rip the envelope from Cara's hand, and her eye twitches. It's a small enough movement that no one else would notice. But I've known Cara for a long time. She's scared.

She narrows her eyes. Tries to look tough.

"Guys, stop!" Issie starts to wedge her body between us, but Cara squares her shoulders, blocking her.

"You don't want to take me on," she says. I lower my face so I can look her right in the eye.

"Try me."

"Stop it!" Issie says. "You're *friends.*"

I feel the air shift before I hear her coming. It's like how the pressure changes when the subway goes underground; there's a pop in my ears, and then something pressing against me, making my skin itch and buzz. I step away from Cara, and her eyes widen with triumph. She thinks she scared me off.

The office light flickers. Issie frowns. "What the—"

The door flies open, hinges creaking. Jessica stands in the hallway just outside, staring hard at the concrete floor. The air around her crackles.

She raises her head to look at us. Her eyes are a perfect, oily black.

Chapter Thirty-Three

I grab Cara by the arm and pull.

"*Move.*" We both stumble backward, into Issie. A trail of fire blazes along the floor where Cara stood, flames moving like liquid. They claw higher, burning first blue, then orange, before vanishing in a cloud of black smoke.

Jessica sinks to the floor. Her shoulders slump. Dr. Gruen stands over her slouched body, her expression carefully arranged in a look of mild interest. She plucks an invisible piece of lint off her dark pants and her eyes narrow, very slightly, in disgust.

"Officer Brody?" Dr. Gruen brushes her hands together and steps into the room. Brody lingers in the hallway, but he straightens at the sound of his name. All the pink has drained from his ratlike face, and he looks like he's trying very hard not to pee his pants.

"Yes, ma'am?" he says. Dr. Gruen jerks her head at Jessica.

"Detain her."

Officer Brody slides the nightstick from his belt. "On your feet," he barks, but I notice that his voice wobbles, just a bit. Jessica curls her hands into fists and Brody takes a quick step backward, swearing.

"She's trying to control it," I explain. Brody glares at me. I expect him to say something foul, but he just nods.

"You think she's cooled down now?" he asks. I frown at him, trying to figure out if the pun was intentional. Dr. Gruen pinches the bridge of her nose.

"She's just a little girl, officer," she says.

Jessica looks up. The black has left her eyes, and the air around her feels still. Safe. I nod at Brody.

"I didn't do it," Jessica whispers. She's looking at me, her lower lip twitching, and I feel a sudden pang in my chest. Brody grabs her arm and hauls her to her feet.

"I saw the body," I say. Cara flinches at the word "body," then tries to cover it by propping her hands on her hips. I don't know if she believes what Jessica's capable of now or if she just wants someone to blame. I know what her temper's like, and I'm sure she wants to rip Jessica's head off for what she did to Mary Anne. The only thing stopping her is Brody, and he won't stop her for long.

"I didn't hurt anybody," Jessica says. Brody twists her arm behind her back, and pain flashes across her face.

"Interesting," Dr. Gruen murmurs, bringing a hand to her chin. "She didn't remember killing the mouse either."

Something stirs in the back of my memory, but I can't quite grab hold of it.

"Watch them," Dr. Gruen snaps, giving Brody a look. "I have something to attend to before we can arrange for their departure."

My skin prickles. *Their* departure. "We're going somewhere?" I ask.

Dr. Gruen stares at me with her clear, alien eyes. "I took the liberty of signing you all up for SciGirls," she says. "You leave tonight."

I wait for the shock to hit me, but it never does. *Bring me what I want, and you're out of here tomorrow*, Dr. Gruen told me. But she never said where she was sending me. I hold her gaze for a long moment, dread settling in the pit of my stomach. "You were never going to let me go home, were you?"

Dr. Gruen cocks her head, and, for a moment, the look on her face reminds me of a mother explaining to her child that yes, sometimes puppies bite. She turns and sweeps out of the office without answering my question, pulling the door shut behind her.

"Looks like it's just us now, ladies," Brody says. He taps his nightstick against the closed door. He's trying to scare us, but he's not the one I'm worried about. Cara moves forward.

"I'm going to kill you." She levels her eyes at Jessica, her voice trembling. "You little *freak*. I'm going to *tear you apart*."

"Cara." I reach for her arm, but she jerks it away. I sneak a glance at Jessica. There's no black in her eyes, no air vibrating around her.

"I didn't do it," she says, meeting Cara's gaze. I can't help but feel a rush of pride. Much larger girls haven't been able to look Cara in the face in the middle of a fight. "I didn't. I swear."

Brody kicks the back of her ankle, and Jessica crumples. Her knees hit the floor with a slap that makes me cringe.

"Quiet," Brody snaps. Jessica wraps her arms around herself. A satisfied smile spreads across Cara's face. Brody points his nightstick at her.

"You too. No fighting," he says. Cara lifts her hands in front of her chest in surrender.

"Yes, sir," she says.

Brody relaxes, but I notice how Cara's jaw clenches and her shoulders tighten. She's not giving up so easily. I think of the story she told me about how she ended up in here, how she hid in the dark with a hammer, how she waited for that perfect moment for hours. Cara's not stupid. She'll watch Brody for as long as it takes. The second he isn't paying attention, she'll lunge.

"I didn't do it," Jessica whispers, almost to herself. I feel another tug at the back of my mind. *She didn't remember killing the mouse either,* Dr. Gruen said. I roll my lower lip between my teeth. Jessica didn't forget that she killed the mouse. She swore she didn't do it. And why would she have killed the mouse at all? She loves animals. She said the mouse reminded her of home.

Issie touches my arm. "Are you okay?" she asks.

"Hands to yourself!" Brody barks.

I think of how I swept the mouse into the trash, how I held my breath while I tied the plastic closed.

"How did she know?" I whisper. Issie tilts her head toward me.

"What are you talking about?"

"Dr. Gruen wasn't in the kitchen when we found the mouse. And I threw it away right after. No one knew about it but us."

"What mouse?" Cara asks, but Issie motions for her to be quiet.

"Why does that matter?" Issie asks.

"It matters," I whisper. I smelled smoke the night I found out about Cara and Mary Anne. But Jessica was in bed, sleeping. Dr. Gruen said there were others like Jessica. Kids who set fire to dolls and action figures.

Objects help them to focus their power, she'd told me. *Like a token, or a good-luck charm.*

There's that nagging again, that feeling that I've forgotten something. I turn, my eyes darting over Dr. Gruen's bookcase. I run my fingers over Dr. Gruen's books. I saw something here. A clue.

"Davis, enough!" Brody shouts. Out of the corner of my eye, I see him step forward, nightstick raised. Cara stiffens, and Issie swears under her breath.

"Angela!" Issie shouts. I hold up a hand.

"Wait." I drop to my knees, my fingers powdered with dust from the shelves. An image flashes through my head: Dr. Gruen's fingers stained black with ink.

Only what if it wasn't ink? What if it was ashes?

I see it out of the corner of my eye: a blackened tree branch, twisted and ugly. It sits on the top shelf, half-hidden by the flat-screen. I thought it was art the first time I saw it. I stand, and pick it up. Flakes of dead wood crumble away, staining my hand black.

Dr. Gruen said there were others—pyretics—who could set fires, just like Jessica. I'd always pictured *kids*, boys and girls Charlie's age. But kids grow up.

"What is that?" Issie says, but my mouth has gone dry as dust.

"It's a token," I say, when my voice comes back to me. "Jessica didn't kill Mary Anne. Dr. Gruen did."

Chapter Thirty-Four

"Give it up, Davis." Brody clutches the nightstick so tightly his knuckles turn white. I'm seconds from feeling metal slap the back of my hand.

"Dr. Gruen is pyretic, like Jessica," I explain, clutching the blackened tree branch to my chest. "That's how she knew about the mouse. Issie and I didn't tell anyone, but Gruen knew because she burned it to death and left it for us to find. So I'd think Jessica was dangerous."

"Davis, I'm warning you!" Brody shouts.

"And Mary Anne?" Cara asks. Her voice is pure, cold fury. I've never been scared of Cara before. "Why did she have to die?"

"Maybe Dr. Gruen found out about the two of you," I say. "Or maybe she killed Mary Anne so I'd turn on Jessica and bring her what she wanted. She—"

Brody comes out of nowhere. He backhands me, his knuckles digging in just below my cheekbone. I crash to the ground, and my head smacks into the concrete. Pain blossoms through my skull.

Brody kneels in front of me, and rips the branch out of my hand. "Warned you," he mutters. Lights flicker before my eyes. I taste blood on my lip.

Cara whips around. She moves her arm in a smooth arc, something silver glinting from her hand. Brody stumbles backward. A thin red line appears on his cheek. He lifts a hand to touch it, and the line smears. Blood.

"Bitch," he spits. He rocks forward, but Cara jabs the knife at him before he can take a single step.

"Don't come any closer," she says. Blood coats the thin blade. A drop slides down the edge and spills to the floor.

"Cara," I breathe. "Don't."

Cara doesn't move, but her eyes move over to me. "Issie was right," she says. "We have to—"

Brody darts forward and grabs Cara's arm. He twists it behind her back, cranking her hand around until something snaps. The knife slips from her fingers and clatters to the ground. Cara whimpers. Brody pushes her against the wall. He keeps one hand on her wrist and the other pinched at her neck.

"There's a good girl," he hisses into her ear.

I can't seem to catch my breath. All the things I've been afraid of these past few weeks hit me in the same horrifying, surreal moment. This room feels too small, smaller than our dorm rooms or the cells in the Segregation Block. I press my hand against the wall so I can be sure it isn't inching nearer. Closing in on me. The air seems to grow warmer. Like an oven.

The edge of Brody's sleeve begins to smoke. I stare at it for a moment, sure that I've finally cracked, that I'm hallucinating. Fire curls out of the fabric. Brody flinches, and glances down at his sleeve.

"What the hell?" He shakes his arm, like the flame is a bug he can brush away. But it crackles, and grows. Brody's face pales. He stumbles backward, letting go of Cara's arm.

Jessica stands behind Brody, her fists at her sides. She rocks back and forth, her eyes black.

"Jessica, *no*." I stand, ignoring the pain beating against the back of my head. Jessica doesn't look at me. She rocks faster, and the air around her buzzes, electric. The overhead light blinks on, and then off again.

Flames appear at Brody's feet. They lick the rubber soles of his boots and crawl up over his shoes before leaping to the hems of his pants.

"No." Brody dances backward. He shakes his feet and stomps on the floor. The fire thickens. The smell of burning fabric and singed skin fills the small room.

"*Jessica!*" I yell, but I don't think she hears me. Her hair twitches, then lifts away from her head, surrounding her in a halo of black hair. Brody starts to scream. The fire spreads up his leg in a solid wave of flame. I clutch my chest, awed and horrified all at once.

"Make it stop!" I hear the *click* of metal as Brody starts to unbuckle his belt. The fire moves from his pants to his arms and the smell of burning skin grows stronger. Brody's flesh puckers and boils and turns a deep, angry red. Smoke clouds around us. It's so thick that it makes me cough. I pull my shirt over my nose. My eyes water.

Brody drops to his knees. I can't see his face anymore. It's hidden beneath clouds of smoke, and the growing wall of fire. I push myself into the far corner of the office. I hadn't even realized I'd been edging backward, hadn't noticed how badly my knees trembled. I shut my eyes and throw my hands over my ears. I can't take any more.

It's a long moment before I realize the fire's dying. Flames shiver and flicker out, leaving behind blackened skin and the tattered remains of Brody's uniform.

I hear a dull thump as Jessica drops to her knees. Smoke hangs in the air between us, obscuring her face, but I can tell that her eyes are normal again. The danger has passed.

Brody's body slumps before her, still as death.

Chapter Thirty-Five

"No," Jessica says. She bunches her fingers around her mouth, hands shaking. "No. *No.*"

"Is he . . . dead?" Issie chokes out. She steps closer to Brody's body, wrinkling her nose at the smell.

"It was self-defense," Cara says, her voice fast and shrill. "You saw the way he hit Angela. Jessica was just trying to—"

Issie silences her with a look. "Nobody's gonna believe *that* was self-defense."

Jessica starts to rock. "No," she whispers, again.

"Stop, all of you." I move out from behind the desk and crouch next to Brody. The stink of burned flesh rolls off him in waves, and I have to hold my breath to keep from vomiting. I hesitate just for a second, then raise my hand to his neck. I press my fingers into the skin below his jaw.

At first, nothing. The bottom falls out of my stomach. I move my fingers to the left. And then the right.

And there it is—a faint *bomp, bomp, bomp* against the tips of my fingers. Relief makes my knees buckle. I grab hold of the edge of Dr. Gruen's desk to steady myself.

"He's alive," I say. "Barely."

The room around me goes still. Jessica stops whispering, and stares at Brody with wide, tear-filled eyes. Issie makes the sign of the cross over her chest.

"*Jesucristo*," she says. "What should we do?"

"We leave," Cara says. "*Really* leave. Now."

She looks at me. I press my lips together, saying nothing. I think of Charlie learning to ride his bike in Prospect Park. Charlie, who uses pine-scented shampoo now, and has muscles like a man. If we leave like this, I won't ever see him again. We'll be outlaws. Fugitives.

And if we stay . . . I glance down at Brody's blackened face. He looks dead. If I hadn't felt his pulse myself, I never would have believed he could be alive. He might still die. Seventeen-year-olds charged with murder are tried as adults. And that's if we manage to avoid SciGirls.

A sob rises in my throat, but I push it back down. Juvie girls don't cry. If I stay, I might get to see my brother again, someday. But I'll spend the rest of my life in prison. Or worse, I'll be taken to SciGirls and become some crazy doctor's experiment.

"Cara's right," I say, looking away from Brody's body. "We have to go."

* * *

I push the door open. I expect to see Officer Crane standing guard outside the office, or Dr. Gruen heading down the hallway. But there's no one. Early-morning light pours in through the narrow windows, casting dusty gold stripes over the floor. I exhale, and motion for my friends to go. Issie mutters something under her breath in Spanish as she slips past me. It sounds like a prayer.

I think about praying. But, if there is a God, he gave up on me a long time ago. I pull the door closed behind me, holding the latch to keep it from clicking. And then I follow Issie and Cara and Jessica down the corridor.

I don't remember any of our silent trek through those empty halls and down the twisting staircase. It's like someone erased that part of my memory. All that's left is the hushed sound of footsteps, figures moving through shadows, and the smell of smoke, which drifts along beside us like an old friend.

Then I turn the corner and see Ben at the end of the hall. He leans against the security door, staring off into space. Dark circles shadow the skin below his eyes, and his hair flops over his forehead in messy waves. He looks scared.

The world slams back into me in full color, the volume turned up high. I have to physically restrain myself from running to him.

I'll never see him again either, I think, and then I swat the thought away, like a fly. If I really thought about that, I wouldn't be able to make myself leave.

Ben looks up. He jerks forward, then freezes when Issie, Cara, and Jessica stumble down the stairs behind me.

"If another guard sees you down here . . ." His eyes narrow in concern. "Brody . . ."

I glance at Cara, and something passes between us. Issie lowers her head, whispening another Spanish prayer.

Ben swallows. His Adam's apple rises and falls in his throat. "What happened to Brody?"

"He hit Angela," Cara says. Ben's face tightens.

"He *what?*"

"I'm fine," I insist. "But we have to get out of here. *Now.*"

Ben's walkie-talkie buzzes to life at his belt.

". . . be on alert . . ." a female voice says. I strain to listen, but it doesn't sound like Dr. Gruen. Officer Crane, maybe. ". . . four girls have escaped their dorms. I repeat, four prisoners are loose in the halls. Be warned, they are extremely dangerous, and possibly armed . . ."

The voice fades to static.

"What did you do?" Ben asks, looking at me. Above us, the fluorescent lights begin to flicker. Nerves creep down my arms and my legs. I turn to Jessica, but her eyes are clear. She's not doing this.

Dr. Gruen's coming.

The story I'd been about to tell turns to ice in my throat. I don't have time to explain everything that's happened and, somehow, convince Ben to believe me. I grab his arm.

"We're in trouble," I say. "*Please.* We have to get out of here."

Ben opens and closes his mouth. Some emotion I don't quite recognize flashes through his eyes. I'm going to lose him.

"*Ben*," I say. His face softens at the sound of his name. He looks over my shoulder, at Cara and Issie and Jessica.

"Come on," he says, swallowing. "I might know a way."

The lights blink on, and then off again. Ben leads us down a dark, narrow hallway that I've never seen before. He pulls a thick door shut behind us and fumbles with a key ring clipped to his belt.

"This should give us some time," he says, jerking a key into the lock. He turns, and the dead bolt slides into place with a heavy jolt.

"Hurry," I whisper. Ben clips the key ring back to his belt and we start to run.

The hallway twists through a part of Brunesfield I didn't know existed. There are no windows, and the only light comes from the naked bulbs dangling from the ceiling. There's an unmarked door every few feet, and I find myself glancing back at them as we run, wondering where they lead. Our shadows stretch across the concrete floor, and our ragged, gasping breaths echo back at us from the concrete walls.

"Here," Ben says, skidding to a stop in front of a metal door emblazoned with the word Exit. Issie, Cara, Jessica, and I stumble up behind him. He thrusts a key into the lock and pushes the door open with a grunt.

Icy air slides in through the crack. I wrap my arms around my chest, suddenly aware of how woefully unprepared we are to run away. We don't have coats, sweatshirts, hats. Even our shoes are ridiculous, just thin slip-ons that won't last more than a few days in the bitter northern cold.

Ben seems to realize this at the same moment that I do. He glances over the four of us.

"You're going to freeze to death," he says.

I'd thought the same thing myself, but saying it out loud won't help anything. "We have to go," I say, instead. Ben holds up a finger.

"Wait. Just a second."

Before I can respond, he's dashing down the hallway, throwing doors open at random. At the third door, a smile curves his lips, and he pumps a fist into the air.

"Jackpot," he says. He reaches inside and pulls a stack of bright orange sweatshirts out of a closet. He hands them to Cara, then digs around again and tosses us wool hats and extra pairs of socks.

"You're a god," Issie says, pulling a sweatshirt over her head. I yank a sweatshirt over my head, and tug a pair of socks over Jessica's hands, like mittens.

"Thank you," I say to Ben.

The light at the end of the hall explodes, showering the floor with broken glass. Fire crackles from the ruined bulb at the ceiling. The next light bursts, and then the one after that, until every light in the hallway has cracked. Ben pushes us through the door.

"Go," he says. "I'll find a way to stall."

"Something could happen to you," I say. "Dr. Gruen—"

"Don't worry. I'll be fine."

Cara races through the door, Issie at her heels. There aren't any barbed-wire fences or security gates back here. Ben brought us to an exit only guards use. Empty white fields stretch before us, and the snow is so bright and so clean that it dazzles me. The woods leave a dark mark on the horizon. They look close, but we'll need to book it in order to make it to the trees before anyone realizes we've escaped.

Jessica slips through the door. I move to follow her, but Ben catches my arm, holding me back.

"Where are you gonna go?" he asks.

"I don't know." I feel heavy. Like someone dipped my feet into lead. "Somewhere far."

Ben nods, and everything that's lovely about him seems suddenly heightened. His messy hair curls around his ears, and there's a night's worth of stubble on his cheek, but it's perfect. Like looking at a painting.

This must be what love feels like, I think, almost giddily. The singers got it wrong. It's not like falling; it's like lying in the grass. Like the sun warming your skin.

"Be safe," Ben says.

I knot my hands around the front of his shirt and tug him toward me. He looks surprised, but just for a moment. Then he leans into me, his nose brushing against mine.

He tastes like coffee and oranges. His stubble scratches my cheeks, and his hands move along my waist, pulling me closer. I want to disappear inside this kiss, but Dr. Gruen's coming, and my friends are waiting, so I move away. Icy air finds the space where his lips were, and the sensation is so awful that I almost cry.

Ben takes my face in his hands. "I'll find you," he promises. "When things settle down here, I'll come after you."

I hear something behind him that might be footsteps. Ben glances over his shoulder, then at me.

"Go," he says. "Now."

I take a step back. I start to run.

Then we're all running, and Ben is farther and farther and farther away.

And then he's gone.

Chapter Thirty-Six

At first I don't notice the cold. My heart beats like a drum, and everything is sweat and adrenaline and fear. The sun peeks through the trees, sending long shadows over the grounds. I think of the glare the light leaves on the windows early in the morning, how it bounces off the snow until it's so bright you can't even see your reflection in the glass. I hope it's enough to keep us from being spotted. Snow crunches beneath our feet. It's so crusty and hard we don't even leave footprints.

I stop running a few feet from the tree line and double over, my breath forming white clouds. Brunesfield looms behind us, all shadow and gloom. Two round windows stare out at me from the second floor, set above a row of barred windows that look like teeth. They give Brunesfield a giant, snarling face.

I'm not just putting Dr. Gruen behind me. I'm leaving my tiny cell, and scratchy sheets. I'm leaving the stuffy kitchen covered in grease where Issie and Cara used to read my brother's letters to me. I'm leaving concrete floors, and girls who scratch the walls of their cells until their fingers bleed. I'm leaving Ben.

I'm leaving it all.

"Where are we going?" Cara asks.

We've been on the run all day and all I've come up with is "far." I lick my lips, and the wetness freezes in the corners of my mouth. We've been eating snow so we don't get dehydrated, but I still feel dried out. I wipe my mouth on my sweatshirt sleeve. If I let the moisture turn to ice, it'll crack my skin. The corners of my lips already feel tight and brittle.

"Pretty," Jessica whispers, looking up. The sun has just started to dip behind the trees, painting the gray sky with flames of orange and pink. It'll be dark soon.

"We should find somewhere to camp," I say. The cold seeps into my skin, making my lips slow and clumsy.

"Like a cave?" Issie says. Her lips are nearly blue.

"Bats sleep in caves," Jessica adds. "And bears."

I cut my eyes sideways, studying her. I don't want to tell them the truth. That when we first started running, I kept checking to make sure Dr. Gruen wasn't behind us. I expected to see her weaving through the trees in one of those tailored black dresses. Stopping to dig a high heel out of the snow.

It took me hours to realize that Dr. Gruen didn't need to chase us. We'll freeze to death the minute we stop moving. She just needs to wait.

"We aren't going to find a cave." My voice shakes with every word. "But if we stay out here, the cold will kill us."

There's a beat of silence. Cara and Issie exchange a look over Jessica's head. This was never part of the story.

"We need to keep walking until nightfall," I continue. "The movement will keep us warm. Or, warm enough. We'll make a fire as soon as it gets dark."

I'm worried about the fire. I've listened to enough audio-books to know that you don't make a fire when you're on the run. The flames draw predators, and the smoke will alert anyone who can see it to your presence.

But if we don't find a way to get warm, we'll die. The darkness should mask the smoke. As for predators . . .

The wolves in the woods aren't any worse than the wolves in here.

I start walking again, trying to ignore the fear prickling the back of my neck. I wish I knew whether that was true.

We spend our last hour of sunlight gathering bits of wood for a makeshift shelter, and clearing away snow. Jessica scurries around the clearing, looking for sticks, while Issie and Cara lean whatever she brings them against a tree, wedging the edges into a fork in the branches. Most of the twigs are too small, and the larger ones don't want to behave. They stand straight for a minute, then tumble over as soon as you touch them. Jessica has started speaking in a whisper, like she's worried that talking too loudly will disturb the trees.

I clear away snow for a fire pit, and gather the driest logs in a pile. I'm so cold I can't feel my toes. I keep thinking of this documentary about frostbite that Charlie and I watched years ago. I imagine black creeping over my skin. I picture my toes falling off my feet and rolling around inside my socks like marbles.

By the time the shelter is finished, a silver moon hangs high in the sky and the temperature has dropped twenty degrees. I hadn't realized numb could be painful, like flames of ice. The shelter itself is complete crap. Gaps the size of my fist separate the sticks, and it isn't strong enough to protect us from a squirrel attack or a heavy wind. But it's the best we're going to do.

"Jessica," I whisper. "It's time. Can you help us make a fire?"

Jessica picks up a thick, log-like branch that we abandoned because it wasn't long enough to use for the shelter. It isn't that big, but she can barely get her skinny fingers around it. She lowers herself to the ground, twisting her legs beneath her.

She glances up at us, her eyes darting and nervous.

"It's okay," I say.

Jessica sets the branch on the snow in front of her and folds her hands in her lap. For a long moment, nothing happens. I burrow into my sweatshirt like a turtle. Issie pulls her sleeves over her hands and bounces in place. Cara stares at Jessica's thin frame, a worry line creasing the skin between her eyebrows.

Jessica's eyes darken. Issie stops bouncing, and Cara takes a quick step back, colliding with me. Jessica starts to rock. She hums, and the sound is low. Tuneless.

A thin ribbon of silver smoke drifts away from the log. Fire crackles to life, turning the bark black. Issie whoops in triumph, and Cara swears loudly. But she's smiling.

"That was amazing," Cara breathes.

Jessica looks up at her, and the darkness in her eyes ripples and fades. "Thank you," she says.

There are no wolves that first night. We wake early, and spend most of the next day heading deeper into the woods, trying to ignore how weak we all feel. I want to be strong for the others, but hunger makes me slow and stupid. It's too late in the winter to find any last berries on the tree branches. We see wildlife here and there. A bird's feathers cast shadows against the gray sky. A thin rabbit darts into the bushes. But we aren't hunters. We can't catch them.

"Could she do something?" Issie whispers to me. Jessica trails behind us, singing under her breath. We've been walking for most of the morning, but we can't go much farther. We're all sluggish and clumsy.

Issie turns to Jessica. "Can't you, like, hit one of the little bunnies with a fireball?"

Jessica stops singing. "I'm not going to hurt a bunny."

"Yeah, it's not like a laser, Issie," I add.

"Why not?" Issie frowns. "She's got good aim."

"Rabbits are fast."

"So? She's like a little superhero. She can take a rabbit."

"It doesn't work like—" I start, but Jessica interrupts me.

"I'm not going to kill a *bunny*," she says.

Cara stops walking. "But you could," she says, narrowing her eyes. "You could hit one if you wanted to."

Jessica jerks her shoulders up and down. "I dunno."

Issie smirks at me. "Told you."

"Bunnies are really smart," Jessica adds. "That's why people keep them as pets. You can train them to do tricks, and they can jump, like, a *yard* off the ground and—"

"Jessica, we have to eat something," I say. Jessica squares her jaw. Stubborn. "We could die out here," I add. She exhales, and looks back down at her feet.

"We should practice first." Cara picks up a thin twig. She tosses it into the air in front of Jessica.

The twig drops to the ground. Cara cocks an eyebrow.

"I wasn't ready," Jessica mumbles. Cara shuffles over to the twig and picks it up again. She hesitates, holding it out in front of her.

Jessica makes her hands into fists. She takes a deep breath. The black oozes over her eyes almost immediately. The air around her thickens.

"Cara," I say. "Throw it now."

Cara tosses the stick into the air. Jessica's head shoots up, her dark eyes following it through the sky. The stick bursts into flames. The still-burning splinters rain down on us, then flicker out when they hit the snow.

Issie whistles through her teeth. "Damn."

We only catch one rabbit that day, but it feels like a feast. We eat it around the fire after nightfall, juices running down our chins. I pick the meat off with my fingers and run my tongue along the bones. It tastes smoky and rich, better than anything I've ever eaten before.

Issie huddles next to me, her body blocking the wind. She lifts a rabbit bone to her mouth and, for a second, our campsite almost feels cozy. I half expect her to flash a smile and beg me to tell the story of us.

She rips a chunk of meat off the bone with her teeth. "I saw you making out with my boyfriend," she says, swallowing.

Guilt hits me like a jab to the chin. I don't even see it coming until the pain explodes through my head. "Issie . . ."

"Don't bother lying." Issie licks the juice from her fingers one by one. "I saw you. With my eyeballs."

I stare at my feet. Issie's dental floss has started to unravel and my toe pokes out, my skin practically blue with cold. A bubble of laughter rises above the crackling flames. Jessica and Cara crouch together on the other side of the fire, discussing something I can't hear.

"It just happened," I say, wiggling my bare toe to keep warm. "I didn't want to hurt you."

"Girl, it'd take an act of God to hurt me." Issie tosses a rabbit bone into the fire. The flames spark. "I'm talking a tornado or a hurricane. Something with wind and shit."

I frown. "So you're not mad?"

"Mad?" She wipes the leftover juice on her scrubs. "You know he wasn't really my boyfriend, right? That's just something I said because he's a hot piece of *culo*."

I raise an eyebrow.

"Ass," Issie translates. "See, unlike you, I don't think I don't deserve nice shit just because I made some mistakes. That guard has been into you forfuckingever. I'm glad you got him."

Issie pulls her sleeves down over her hands. "Or had him, I guess," she adds. "Even for a little while."

I want to hug her, but juvie girls don't hug. "Thanks," I say, instead.

"Anytime."

Wind moans through the trees, making the branches shiver. I clear my throat. "Ben told me you didn't take the SciGirls test."

"Oh *Ben* told you that, did he?"

I throw a rabbit bone at Issie's shoe. She laughs, and kicks it into the fire.

"Why didn't you?" I ask. Issue shrugs.

"I thought about what you said while you were in Seg. About how you had a bad feeling about SciGirls and Dr. Gruen. I shouldn't have blown you off when you told me that. You've always had my back."

Issie picks up a stick and uses it to poke the fire. "Did you know that everyone who took the test made it into SciGirls? Dr. Gruen made it sound like the program was this big deal, like it was really hard to get in. The whole thing was just a trick to get us to sign up."

"Yeah," I say. "She was good at that."

Issie tosses the stick into the fire, sending embers into the snow. "Do you think they're okay?" she asks. "Aaliyah and Ellen and the others?"

"I don't know," I say. For a moment we're both silent, watching the fire burn.

"Ang, tell me you brought the photo," Cara calls. She and Jessica have stopped talking and now both stare across the fire at me, expectantly.

"I brought it." I lean forward, and slip the newspaper article from my waistband. I edge around the fire, crouching next to Jessica.

"Did Cara tell you who we think this is?" I ask, holding out the paper.

"My mom," Jessica says. Her voice barely lifts above the spitting and crackling sound of the fire. She jiggles her knee.

"Don't be nervous," I say. Jessica nods, and takes the folded article from my hand. She holds it in her lap for a long moment, then breathes in deep, and unfolds the paper.

I can tell the woman in the photograph is her mother before she says a word. Her knee goes still, and her lips part, slightly. She stares at the photograph, mesmerized.

"Do you remember her at all?" Cara asks. Jessica swallows.

"She liked plants," she says without looking up. "We had them all over our house when I was little. She used to sing to them." She smiles. "It was funny."

"Do you know if she was like you?" Cara asks. "If she could . . ." She nods at the crackling fire. Jessica frowns, the flames dancing in her black eyes.

"I don't know." She folds the paper twice, clutching it like she might bite you if you tried to take it away.

"Maybe it's genetic?" Issie says. I shake my head.

"Dr. Gruen said it wasn't. No one knew how Jessica was infected." I point to the article. "That photograph looks *exactly* like her. If her mom could start fires too, then genetics would have been the first thing they tested."

"Can you think of anything else?" Cara asks. "Anything weird that happened when you were little?"

Jessica thinks for a second. "I got burned once," she says. "It was pretty bad. We had to go to the hospital."

"Maybe that's how it spreads," Issie says. "Like, if you get burned and don't die—boom. Superhero powers."

I press the tips of my fingers together, recalling the tender pink wounds I got from the tray. "I got burned, and I don't have superpowers."

"Your fingers were barely hurt," Cara points out. "Jessica said she had to go to the hospital."

I catch Cara's eyes over the flickering light. "So you think you have to be really badly burned for the power to pass over?"

She shrugs. "Maybe."

Something blinks in the darkness behind her. I freeze, a piece of rabbit halfway to my mouth. Cara frowns, then turns to look over her shoulder. I see it again—two dots of light. Eyes.

It's too dark to see the wolves clearly, but I can make out the shaggy outlines of their bodies, and I can tell by the sound of their footsteps that they're big. Bigger than I thought they'd be.

They hover in the woods around us for the rest of the night, but they never enter the circle of fire.

I wake to the sound of helicopters. I can't see them—it's still dark—but I hear an engine roar and the sound of propellers beating against the sky. A spotlight flickers through the trees. I watch it sweep over the woods. It's miles away from us, but it won't be long before it comes closer.

It won't be long before we're found.

Chapter Thirty-Seven

"I'm hungry," Cara says.

"No shit," I say. My stomach rumbles beneath my sweatshirt. We're *all* hungry. We agreed it would be too risky to let Jessica start a fire this morning, even if that meant going without food. I keep checking over my shoulder, listening for the sound of helicopters.

"Just keep going," I add. We're moving so slowly it barely feels like walking, but my muscles scream with pain every time I lift my leg from the ground.

"Go where?" Cara kicks a pile of snow, spraying the path in front of us. Gray light filters down through the tree branches, and the sky above is solid white. A blizzard's coming.

"Don't," I warn Cara, my voice hard. She glances over her shoulder at me, lifting an eyebrow.

"Don't *what*? We're walking in circles."

I bite back a groan. I don't have the patience to deal with Cara right now, not with hunger clawing at my stomach and fear making my muscles weak.

"You wanted this, remember?" I say. "You practically blackmailed me into leaving with you."

Cara huffs and turns back around. "I never wanted *this*."

"You're welcome to try to do better," I say.

Cara shakes her head. Under her breath, she says, "Like you'd ever let someone else be the leader."

"What does that mean?" I snap.

Cara shrugs jerkily and hugs her arms to her chest. Mary Anne's vegetable charm bracelet dangles from her wrist. "Just stating the facts," she says.

Issie stops walking. "*Guys,*" she says.

"No, really." Heat rises in my cheeks. "Cara thinks she'd be a better leader. So let's let her lead."

"*Anyone* would be a better leader."

"Guys!" Issie shouts.

"Go for it, Cara. Show us how great you are at navigating a frigid, frozen forest with no tools and no food and no—"

"Angela!" Issie grabs me by the shoulders and spins me around. "Shut the hell up and *look!*"

I'm so angry and cold and scared that, for a long moment, I don't see anything. Issie points at a thick patch of trees covered in snow. A squat log cabin sits behind them, not even fifty feet away.

Cara blows air out through her teeth. "Oh."

"Maybe Issie should be the leader," Jessica says.

We approach the cabin like it's a wild animal about to dart away. Excitement hammers at my chest. *The door will probably be locked,* I tell myself. *Or else the owner's here. I bet he already called the police.*

But the cabin looks empty. There's no smoke drifting from the chimney, no car in the drive. The windows are dark. I put my hand on the doorknob. And turn.

It creaks open.

"Holy shit," Cara breathes. We hover together on the doorstep, both of us too nervous to make the first move. Jessica slips past us, and wanders through the door like she belongs.

"Screw this," Issie says, and follows her inside.

The cabin is small. Just one room, with a tiny kitchen shoved up against the far wall. There's no heat, but the temperature rises a few degrees as soon as we step through the door.

"Look. A fireplace," Issie says, teeth chattering. She tugs a flannel blanket off the futon in the corner, and wraps it around herself.

"It's not dark yet," Cara says, collapsing on the futon. She props her legs up on a small wooden trunk.

"What's in there?" I ask. Cara reluctantly moves her feet, and I pop the trunk open. A stack of neatly folded blankets sits inside, looking so warm and cozy that it makes me want to cry. I toss one to Cara, and one to Jessica, and drape a third over my shoulders, shivering. The heat has started to climb back into my arms and legs.

"No fire," I say, closing the trunk. "But look around for anything we can take with us. Food, blankets, winter clothes. Anything we can carry."

"Take?" Issie says. She and Cara share a look, and she tugs her blanket tighter around her shoulders. "We're not staying?"

"They'll find us here," I explain. I cross the small room, and push aside the flannel curtain covering the window. The woods outside look quiet. I don't see helicopters dotting the sky, or hear the distant sounds of propellers. But it's only a matter of time.

"We can't leave this place." Cara leans forward, and the futon groans beneath her. "Angela, we could have *died* out here!"

"They're going to check this cabin the second they find it. We'll get *caught*."

"Well, maybe . . ." Cara stops talking. She bites her lower lip.

"Maybe what?" I ask. She doesn't answer. I sink onto a rickety kitchen chair, stunned. "Maybe we *should* get caught? Maybe we should go back to Brunesfield? I know that's what you're thinking."

Cara lowers her chin to her chest and covers her face with her blanket. "I didn't mean it," she says, her voice muffled by flannel. "I'm just cold and tired and hungry. And those *wolves*."

"Wolves don't usually attack humans," Jessica says in a small voice. "They're too scared."

I twist around to tell her *enough* with the animal facts already, but something about her posture stops me. She's crouched next to the fireplace with her back to us, her shoulders stiff.

Cara leans forward. "You okay, Jess?"

Jessica swipes a hand across her cheek. "This is my fault."

"It's not your fault," I say. Cara cocks an eyebrow. She doesn't say a word, but I know exactly what she's thinking. Maybe this isn't Jessica's fault, but she's the reason we're all here.

"You were all fine before I got here," Jessica whispers.

"Girl, none of us were *ever* fine," Issie says.

"We can't stop," I say. "We can't go back."

Cara peeks out from under the blanket. "I know."

"That doesn't mean we have to leave now," Issie points out. "We should rest for a few hours. Regain our strength."

I shoot her a look, and she raises her hands in a gesture of surrender. "Look, Ang, you're right, they'll find us if we stay here. But your troops are not doing well. Morale is down. Let us get our energy back, will you?"

The past few restless nights catch up to me all at once. I feel the exhaustion deep in my legs. It climbs up my body, and it doesn't relent until I lower my head to the kitchen table.

"Fine," I say, letting my eyes flutter closed. "A few hours. But no fire."

Hours later, I groggily open my eyes. At some point, someone moved me to the futon and weighed me down with blankets. A fire crackles and spits a few feet away, thawing my hands and feet. I yawn, and burrow down into the futon mattress, halfheartedly trying to place the heavy, rich smell that hangs in the air.

Food.

I'm suddenly wide awake. I sit, and the blankets fall to my lap.

"What the hell—"

"We waited until dark," Cara explains, cutting me off. She's bent over the stove, stirring something with a long wooden spoon. Sweat dots her forehead. "I know you said no fire, but they won't see the smoke in the dark, right?"

I'm not entirely sure that's true. We're in a house, not hiding out in the middle of the woods. I felt okay about the tiny little fires we set to keep ourselves warm. But this is different. Bigger.

My stomach tenses. The smell of the food makes me feel dizzy. We haven't eaten anything since the rabbit last night. It's probably more dangerous to keep running on empty stomachs.

I stretch my arms over my head. Jessica stands on her tiptoes in front of the stove, peering into a large pot. Issie's behind her, giggling as she pours some salt into water.

"We found dry pasta," Issie explains when I come up behind her. "And tomato sauce and canned beans."

"Yum," I say. The smell is garlicky and rich. My mouth starts to water.

"We got those too." Cara nods at a pile of clothes and shoes stacked by the back door. "We only found two coats and one pair of boots. We'll have to split them up and trade off every few hours."

"That's great," I say. I wiggle my toes, thinking about how much easier it'll be to trek through the snow when I can actually feel my feet. I wander back to the window. A faded map hangs on the wall. I trace a finger along the twisting roads.

"See the little red circle?" Cara calls from the kitchen. "We think that's where the cabin is."

I squint, leaning in closer. "Do you think that's the high—" My foot gets caught on a cord twisting across the floor. I trip and stumble into the window, catching myself with one hand.

"What the hell?" I mutter, leaning down. The cord trails toward the wall and disappears. My voice catches in my throat. I drop to my knees and dig below the futon. My fingers brush against plastic.

No. It can't be this easy. I grab the object and pull it out, placing it on my lap.

A telephone. A landline, still plugged in to the wall. Heart hammering in my chest, I remove the phone from the cradle.

A dial tone echoes in my ear.

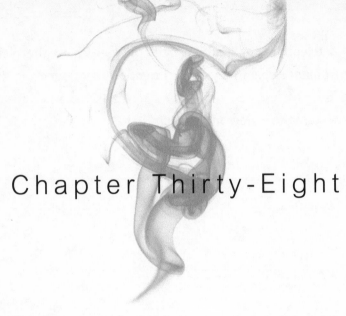

Chapter Thirty-Eight

"*Muchas gracias*, Daniel," Issie says into the phone. "*Hasta pronto.*"

She places the receiver back onto the cradle. We all stare at her. Waiting.

"It'll take him three hours to get here," she says. "He's in Sunset Park for Sunday dinner, but he's leaving as soon as he figures out what to say to *mamá*—"

"He's really coming?" Cara says, cutting her off. "Your brother's gonna pick us up?"

Issie rolls her eyes. "I *told* you. He owes me. He said he'll call this number when he's close, and that we should hike up to the highway to meet him. His friend Pedro lives in Brooklyn, and he has an extra room where we can stay till we figure stuff out."

"Pedro has an extra room," I repeat. A laugh bubbles from my mouth. "Seriously?"

Issie frowns. "What's the matter?"

"It's just so *easy*," I say. "I thought we were going to get eaten by wolves, but no. We're getting a ride to Brooklyn, and some guy named Pedro is going to let us crash with him."

A smile unfolds across my face, but I don't say what I'm really thinking. Charlie's in Brooklyn. I might see my brother again, after all.

Cara slaps my wrist with a tomato sauce–covered spoon. "We can still get eaten by a wolf on the way to the highway," she points out.

The next few hours pass in a blur. We finish cooking and eat mounds of spaghetti in happy silence. The noodles taste stale, and there's a strong whiff of tin can to the sauce, but I'll be damned if it's not the best meal I've ever eaten. I won't admit I'm finished until I've licked the plate clean.

When we're all done eating, Cara starts the dishes while Jessica and I fold the blankets and place them back inside the wooden trunk. Issie douses the fire with water, leaving a soggy black mess at the bottom of the fireplace.

I unhook a tiny broom and dustpan from the rack of tools next to the firewood.

"Really?" Issie says, when I hand her the broom. "You think they're going to know we came through here because we left some ashes in the fireplace?"

"I don't know," I admit, dropping the dustpan on the floor next to her. "But I don't want to take any chances."

It's only a matter of time before they realize we've made it out of the woods. Dr. Gruen isn't stupid. Eventually, she'll find this cabin and check the phone records and figure out exactly where we've gone. I just hope we have a head start.

Jessica stops folding. She cocks her head like a bird. "What's that noise?" she asks.

I don't hear anything, but I stop what I'm doing and listen anyway. Cara hums while she dries the last of the dishes. Issie scrapes the metal dustpan along the bottom of the fireplace.

"Guys, quiet for a second," I say. Cara frowns, and places the saucepan she's holding on the counter. Issie twists around to look at me.

A staticky sound floats in through the walls. Goose bumps climb my arms. It sounds like beating wings. I go over to the window and push back the curtains.

A black helicopter hangs in the sky like a wasp, barely visible in the dark. It's so close that I stumble away from the window, worried it might see us.

"Shit," I say. "*Shit.* A helicopter."

Cara knots her fingers in front of her chest. "What are we supposed to do?" she says.

I gnaw at my lower lip. According to the clock on the oven, it's been three and a half hours since we called Daniel.

"He should have been here by now," Issie says. She crowds in next to me at the window and carefully peeks around the curtains.

"Maybe he just forgot to call," I say. "We could head up to the highway now and wait for him, just in case."

I realize how stupid that plan is almost as soon as the words leave my mouth. Of course we can't wait for Issie's brother by the side of the highway. We're four girls wearing bright orange sweatshirts in the snow. The helicopter would find us in seconds.

I kick the side of the futon. Hard. Pain shoots through my foot, but I ignore it. This is bullshit. We're so close.

Issie stiffens. "Someone's here," she says.

I push past her, and yank the curtains aside.

Dr. Gruen stands in the snow several yards away, her body silhouetted in the moonlight. She stares through our window. Shadows fall across her face, but I can still make out the oily black depths of her eyes.

Chapter Thirty-Nine

"I know you're in there." Dr. Gruen doesn't raise her voice. She could be warning us about running in the halls or talking back to a guard. "Give me Jessica, and the rest of you are free to go."

I step away from the window. I feel shaken, like my world is a snow globe someone's turned upside down. Now that the snow has settled I see things as they really are. Dr. Gruen led us here. We were never going to escape.

Jessica cocks her head, like she's listening to music the rest of us can't hear. "I have to go with her now," she whispers. "Don't I?"

"No." I grab her hand. I have the sudden childish urge to yank the curtain closed and hide. Like, if I can't see Dr. Gruen, she isn't there.

"Yeah, don't be stupid." Issie pushes past me and looks through the window herself. "My brother's coming. We just need a way to get out of here without Crazy Bitch seeing us."

Outside, Dr. Gruen lifts her arm and taps the skinny watch fastened to her wrist. "You have five minutes."

Five minutes. Issie steps away from the window, letting the curtain slide back into place. Cara sets the saucepan she'd been holding down on the counter. We exchange a look and I know we're all thinking the same thing.

Five minutes isn't enough time for a plan. It isn't enough time for anything.

Jessica clears her throat. "She only wants me," she says, in a voice so quiet I almost don't hear her. "The rest of you would be safe."

Cara snaps her fingers. "There's a back door," she says. She wipes her damp hands on her pants and crosses to the cabin's far wall. A large upholstered chair sits in the corner. "It's behind this. I found it when I was looking for the coats."

Cara grunts and throws her shoulder against the chair, sliding it about two inches to the left.

Issie cracks her knuckles. "I'm like two and a half of you. What are you even doing?" She squeezes in next to Cara and together they slide the chair away from the door.

"Come on," I say, taking Jessica by the arm. She casts one last glance at the window before I steer her to the back of the room.

Issie kneels in front of the door and jiggles the handle. Locked.

"Shit," she mutters. She claws at the keyhole with her fingernail. "There isn't a dead bolt. We need a key."

"Key?" I wipe my sweaty hands on the back of my scrubs and glance at the digital clock on the stovetop. Two minutes have already passed. We don't have time to look for a key.

"Move," Cara says. She pushes Issie out of the way and crouches in front of the door. Under her breath, she whispers, "Easy enough." She slides a bobby pin out of her hair and jabs it into the keyhole, squinting.

"How the hell did you sneak that past the metal detectors?" Issie asks.

"Stole it off Sterling," Cara says, chewing her lower lip. She pulls the pin out and twists the end, then forces it into the hole again. "Told her she had lint in her hair."

"Ballsy," Issie says.

I look back at the clock. Another minute has ticked past. I pinch the skin on my wrists and, when that doesn't calm me down, I pace. Two steps to the left. Two to the right.

Jessica stares at the window. She knots her fingers together, humming a fragment of the song she'd been singing earlier.

"Don't even think about it," I say. She glances up at me, and a blush creeps over her cheeks.

"Hurry." Issie bounces in place. Cara wiggles the pin inside the hole. I hear a *click*, and my heart stops.

Cara pumps a fist into the air. "Got it!" she whisper-shouts. She twists the knob and the door creaks open. Icy air crawls in through the gap, and kisses the bare skin at my ankles.

"Highway's just through the trees," Issie says. She grabs a coat from the stack on the floor, and wiggles into it. "If

Daniel isn't there, we can hitchhike to the nearest gas station and call him from a pay phone."

"Hurry!" Cara says, slipping out the door.

Jessica glances at the window. "She'll follow us," she says.

"We'll run really fast." I nudge her toward the door. She crosses her arms over her chest.

"When antelope are being chased by lions, they don't go back if one of them falls or gets hurt. It would put the whole herd in danger."

"Yeah, well, you're not an antelope," I say, reaching for Jessica's arm. She wriggles away.

"I can give you a head start," she says. "You can make it to the highway."

"We have to *go*," Cara says.

I glance at the clock as the fourth minute ticks past. "We don't have time for this, Jess."

"I can *distract* her," Jessica says. She squares her jaw, and I have a sudden flash of Mary Anne's mangled face, of orange flames dancing toward the bathroom ceiling. Jessica's not planning on quietly going along with Dr. Gruen. She's going to fight.

And if I leave her here alone, she's going to die.

I look at Cara.

"Angela, no," she breathes. Behind her, Issie stiffens.

"What's going on?" she asks.

"Angela's going to stay," Cara says.

"I'm not leaving her alone," I say. I sneak another look at the clock. "Now *go*. You're running out of time."

Issie's eyes flicker over to Jessica, then back to me. "When you get away, head for the highway," she says. "Hitchhike to the nearest gas station. Cara and I will be waiting. *Promise me.*"

"I promise." I start to push the door closed, but Cara reaches inside and grabs my arm.

"I'll write to him," she says. She grabs my wrist, and I feel my first spark of fear, like static electricity leaping from her skin to mine. It's gone in a heartbeat, and then Cara's racing through the snow and disappearing into the trees with Issie.

Out of the corner of my eye, I see our final minute tick past.

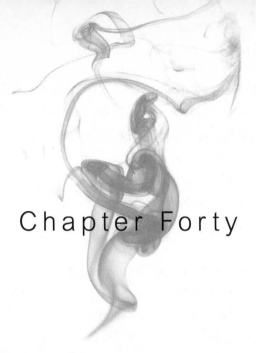

Chapter Forty

A trail of fire blazes through the front window, hitting the rickety wooden table in the corner. Glass explodes into the room, and flames crackle around us. I drag Jessica to the floor, shielding her with my body. Razor-sharp shards shred my shirt and bite into my back. Smoke the color of oil fills the room.

Dr. Gruen pushes the front door open and steps inside.

"Time's up," she says.

Jessica pushes me, and I roll into the wall, smacking my hip so hard I cringe. Fire erupts from the floor where our bodies just were, setting the rug alight. Smoke grows thick around us. It claws at my throat, making me cough. I scramble off the floor, pulling my shirt over my nose and mouth.

The air thickens. I think it's the smoke, at first. Then I smell something metallic, and everything seems to sizzle. It's like touching a live wire. Like standing near power lines.

Jessica pushes herself to her feet. Her eyes fade to black. A line of fire flickers across the floor, inches from Dr. Gruen's pointed heels. Heat fills the small wooden room. I scoot closer to the wall. Sweat breaks out on my forehead and drips down the back of my neck.

Dr. Gruen cocks her head in a vaguely reptilian gesture. Jessica's flames grow higher, becoming a wall that separates her from us.

"Impressive," Dr. Gruen murmurs, grinning. "Though not entirely smart, strategically speaking. It'll take a lot of power to hold that for more than a few minutes."

Jessica's arms tremble.

I stand, and search the room for a weapon. The heat makes my skin feel itchy and tight. Flames dance around my feet, and my knees wobble. Twice I have to prop a hand against the wall to keep from falling. I rip open cupboards and drawers until—*hell yes*. Knives. I grab the two with the biggest blades and shuffle toward the wall of flames.

Fire licks at the ceiling, leaving black scorches on the paint. Dr. Gruen paces, shoulders hunched, like a caged animal. Flames curl from the floor at her feet, but they spark and die when they reach Jessica's wall of fire.

"Adorable," she says through gritted teeth. She's not grinning anymore.

I tighten my grip on my knives, ignoring the sweat gathering between my fingers and the wooden handles. I cast another glance at Jessica. Her knees knock together.

The fire flickers. Spaces appear between the flames.

I launch myself at Jessica, shoving her out of the way a second before a line of fire shoots through a gap in the wall. It hits my leg, and pain like I've never felt before flares through my skin. I think of melting flesh and seared bone, of meat roasting. Tears spring to my eyes, and it's a long moment before I can catch my breath. The muscles in my hand spasm, and one of my knives drops to the ground.

Jessica's wall melts into a cloud of black smoke. She falls to her knees, her chest rising and falling as she struggles to breathe.

I sneak a look at my leg. Blackened, crusty skin peeks out from the holes in my scrubs, the edges red with blood. I move, and pain shoots through my thigh. I close my eyes and try to roll the pain into a little ball. Something small that I can deal with. It flares and burns inside me, making me dizzy.

"What happened to letting the rest of us go free?" I choke out.

Dr. Gruen examines her fingernails, like she's looking for leftover soot. "That was a calculated lie," she says. "None of you were ever going to be allowed to go free."

None of you. I think of Cara and Issie racing through the snow and silently pray that Issie's brother is waiting for them right now, that he whisks them away somewhere Dr. Gruen won't ever think to look.

"Your fates were sealed the moment Jessica set foot inside Brunesfield." Dr. Gruen picks something out from beneath her thumbnail. "Jessica can manipulate heat and fire, even though she was never part of the SciGirls program. That

means the ability can be transferred between individuals."
Dr. Gruen wrinkles her nose. "Like an *infection*."

Jessica lurches forward onto her hands. Dr. Gruen examines her crumpled body with cold detachment. Like she's an insect.

I pull my leg to my chest and try to stand. The pain turns my stomach. "And you came to stop her from giving it to someone else?" I ask.

"Infections need to be contained, Miss Davis. If Jessica's talents can be transferred, it's imperative that we know how. Brunesfield acted as a kind of quarantine, filled with would-be victims who had no families and no value to society. But after weeks inside that horrible facility, her pyretic ability hadn't transferred to anyone. We're still no closer to understanding how the infection spreads or where her power came from."

Dr. Gruen sighs, and turns to face the ruined window. "We have the bear, though. That's something. I just hope it will tell us what we need to know. Now it's time to dispose of the mess."

Her words chill something inside me. I tighten my grip on my knife, worried I might vomit. Dr. Gruen lifts her hand.

A cloud of smoke appears on the horizon. It makes me think of volcanoes erupting. Atom bombs being set off. The smoke billows in clouds so thick and dark they look solid.

"What?" I frown at the sky. Black tendrils reach across the blue, fading with the wind.

Dr. Gruen turns on her heel, brushing her hands together. "I couldn't just leave it there," she explains.

"That was Brunesfield?" My voice cracks. It's a trick. She's playing with my emotions. Trying to throw me off guard. Brunesfield isn't gone. All those girls can't be—

Oh God. *Ben.*

Something inside me snaps clean off. I pounce, slashing. The knife feels like an extension of my arm. I cut through the air, and the blade slides cleanly into its mark.

Dr. Gruen rears back, her hand flying to her shoulder. Blood oozes through her fingers. I've never enjoyed violence before, but the sight of Dr. Gruen's blood fills me with a horrible, animal glee.

She *deserves* this. I'm going to make her pay.

"What did you do?" Dr. Gruen gasps. She takes her hand away from her shoulder, revealing the mangled skin below her ripped shirt. I lunge hungrily, but Gruen sidesteps and stumbles on an overturned chair.

"I'm going to kill you," I say, tightening my grip on the knife. I no longer feel the burn on my leg. I feel powerful. Dangerous. Fear flashes through Dr. Gruen's eyes. Then it hardens. Turns to anger. She opens her hand, and flames dance up from the floor.

The fire spreads quickly across the tiny house. I leap aside, and it explodes against the back wall. Paint bubbles and pops. The wood buckles. A chunk of flaming ceiling drops to the floor and explodes in a shower of sparks and wood.

Jessica finally lifts her head, her eyes darkening. A wave of fire ripples across the floor, heading straight for Dr. Gruen.

Gruen's eyes grow black, but Jessica's flames reach her before she can do anything. They dance around her feet, and climb into the air, surrounding her in a cage of flickering sparks.

The fire leaps to the ceiling, and flares through the cabin. Something shifts above us, and another chunk of wood crashes to the floor. I drop my knife, and leap backward. A flaming beam swings from the ceiling, and smacks into Jessica's back. She drops to the ground like a rock.

"No!" I scream. The smoke makes my eyes water. Dim shadows move around me, and I think I hear the sound of Dr. Gruen's heels clacking against the wood. Suddenly the flames flare, growing higher. Hotter. I look around, but the fire surrounds us. We're trapped.

"Best of luck, Miss Davis," Dr. Gruen calls, gingerly stepping out of the wreckage. I hear a sound like a helicopter's propellers, and Dr. Gruen calls to someone I can't see, "Wait for the fire to die down, and then bring me the little girl. Leave the other one for the wolves."

I drop to my knees. Every part of my body aches and burns. Moaning, I drag myself across the floor, to where Jessica lies pinned beneath a burning wooden beam.

Soot coats her face. I release a sound that's halfway between a sob and a gasp, and her eyes flicker open. She finds my face, but her gaze is cloudy, and she can't quite focus.

"Jessica," I whisper. A flame sputters, and wood rains down on us. Sparks hit my face and arms. I cringe away, but it's no use. The fire's everywhere.

Jessica groans and eases her arm out from beneath the wooden beam. I take her hand. Heat presses in on us. It crawls down my throat.

"Get up," I whisper, my voice a croak. Flames climb the walls and spread across the floor. "The house is going to fall down. We have to run."

I prop my free hand against the wooden beam trapping Jessica's body but, no matter how hard I push, it doesn't budge. A sob escapes my lips. I try again, but my arms give way, and I collapse onto Jessica's chest.

I'm so tired. My eyelids droop, but I force them open. I have to stay conscious. We have to *move*. More blackened bits fall from the ceiling. I imagine pushing myself to my feet. Hauling the burning beam off Jessica's chest. But the commands never quite make it to my arms and legs. I lie there, paralyzed.

I feel fingers on my skin. They gently push the hair from my forehead.

"Tell me a story, Angela," Jessica whispers. Flames crackle and scream around us. I squeeze Jessica's hand, trying not to notice how weak it is. How she doesn't squeeze back.

"Once upon a time," I say, "there was a wolf who wore a necklace made of children's teeth."

My father's stories echo through my head. I tell of monsters that gamble away their souls at the racetrack, and serpents who live in shower drains. I tell the stories long after Jessica has stopped moving and breathing, until the smoke chokes my lungs and clouds my head, and I can no longer speak.

Epilogue

I open my eyes.

The sun hangs high in the sky above me. I squint and shy away from its light. For a long moment, I don't move. I worry that if I flex my fingers or toes I'll learn that I don't have any feeling in them. That I've lost them.

Or maybe I'm already dead. Maybe this is hell.

I don't feel dead. Heat rushes through my veins, spreading into my hands and down my legs. I stretch my fingers. I wiggle my toes. With a groan, I push myself up to my elbows.

The cabin lies in pieces around me. Shredded wood and broken glass blanket the snow. I groan and push a blackened piece of wall off my legs, glancing around frantically, searching for her, afraid of what I already know. She's dead, and they took her body, I'm on my own.

I push aside more pieces of wood and broken furniture until I locate a singed coat that's two sizes too large for me, and a pair of rubber boots that might be for gardening. My canvas slip-ons have melted onto my feet. I cringe and peel the layers of fabric away quickly, like a Band-Aid, leaving strips of raw red skin behind.

Time blips. I don't remember walking away from the ruined cabin, but all of a sudden I'm wandering through the woods in my too-large boots, and slipping on the snow, and grabbing tree branches to steady myself. My breath forms icy clouds, but the cold seems to stop at my skin. Strange.

The highway's closer than I expected. I've only been walking for a few minutes when I stumble onto a stretch of black asphalt. I wrap my arms around my chest. I wait.

A spot appears on the horizon. A truck.

I stick out my thumb. The truck rumbles to the side of the road and pulls to a stop in front of me. A man leans his head out the window. He has a face like a basset hound, covered in a layer of white scruff. I tug the coat tighter around my shoulders, praying the driver won't recognize my juvie uniform.

"Okay, miss?" he drawls. "You look like you could use a hospital."

I frown. I don't feel like I need a hospital. I wonder, for the first time, how long I spent lying in the snow under the ruins of that little log house, how I survived the cold. It felt like hours but it could have been days. Weeks.

"Yeah. I could use a ride," I say. The man nods and throws open the passenger door. I hurry to the other side of the truck and scramble inside.

I slam my door shut, catching my reflection in the side mirror.

Burns cover my face, leaving my skin raw and puckered. I stare at myself, certain there's something wrong with my eyesight, or with the mirror. But no. This is real. One of my eyebrows has vanished, and the remaining flesh looks shiny, like it's been polished. Black scorch marks stain my lips and cheekbones. I touch them with the tips of my fingers. Fascinated. The fire ate everything beautiful and familiar. I look like a stranger.

Black tendrils reach out from my pupils and spread over the whites of my eyes, like oil through water. I hold my breath. The air around me vibrates. The paint along the edges of the mirror starts to bubble.

"Where to?" the driver asks. His words are a switch. The black fades from my eyes. The air goes still. I stare at my horrible reflection for a long moment, not sure I trust myself to speak.

"Miss?" the driver says.

Paper crinkles beneath the waistband of my scrubs. Cara's newspaper article. I slip it out from my waistband and unfold it. It's blackened along the edges, but the article's still readable. I scan the type until I find the name of the hospital where Jessica's mother was left. Underhill Medical Center. I run a finger beneath the words.

Revenge missions have to start somewhere. This place is as good as any other.

"There's a hospital upstate," I say. "Underhill Medical Center. Do you know where that is?"

The driver squints down at the clipping. Then, "That's up north a bit. You have family near there or something?"

"Or something," I say.

The driver nods. "No problem." He flashes me a kind smile.

The truck pulls away from the side of the road. I exhale and look back at my reflection. I study every whirl of my melted skin, the black scorches on my lips, my newly singed hair. Dr. Gruen made me into a monster, I think as the truck picks up speed. Just like the ones in my father's stories.

So maybe it's time to become one.

Acknowledgments

Thank you thank you thank you thank you to Mandy Hubbard, agent of my dreams, for finding *Burning* such a wonderful home, for glittery Christmas cards, and for the perfect gif at the perfect time, as well as a hundred other things that are much harder to put into words. If I could put a gif in these acknowledgments, it'd be that one of Dawson ugly crying. So picture that when you read this.

Thank you to Mary Kate Castellani for understanding why monsters are more interesting than heroes, and for loving Angela as much as I do. You've been a dream to work with. Big ole, sloppy, heartfelt thanks go to the rest of the Bloomsbury team, all of whom worked tirelessly to get this book out into the world. Publishing people are angels with books instead of wings. Or maybe the books are like their wings? Sorry, that's a weird metaphor but Mary Kate didn't edit this part so what do you expect?

Thanks to my mom, who called me after she finished and read her favorite lines over the phone. And my dad, who never reads anything but who read this book, and Ron, who talks about these characters like they're real people. Thank you to the rest of my family, who fight over the ARCs I send home. You make me feel like a rock star instead of a weirdo author who sometimes forgets to put pants on. (I'm definitely wearing pants now. Wait . . .)

And last, thank you to whoever is reading these acknowledgments right now. It takes a special reader to make it this far into a book. I used to go to the library and turn right to the acknowledgments and think about how cool it must be to be a writer. And now that I am a writer, I still read the acknowledgments of my favorite books simply because I never want them to end. Whichever you are, thank you. Seriously.

Prep school gets a twist of supernatural
suspense in **Danielle Rollins**'s next thriller.
Read on for a sneak peek!

"Charlotte, wake up." Zoe leans over me. She's so close that her dark eyes look like a single Cyclops eye in the center of her head. Her jet-black hair sticks up at odd angles.

I blink. It's still dark. Moonlight streams through the windows behind us, doing little to illuminate our messy, crowded dorm. Zoe didn't unpack so much as explode into the room when she moved in. Boxes of rolled-up vintage movie posters and makeup and fencing equipment are everywhere.

I hear whispering on the other side of our door. Footsteps.

"Charlotte?" Zoe says again.

"What's going on?" My words blur together—*wasgonnon*? I groan and raise a hand to brush the hair off my forehead, but there is no hair on my forehead. It takes one slow moment before I remember that I cut it all off two weeks ago. I swear I can still feel it, like a phantom limb. Phantom hair.

Someone giggles in the hall outside our dorm. More

footsteps. It isn't unusual for the girls of the Weston Preparatory Institute to sneak out at night. It's easy to trip the lock on the door leading to the courtyard. But they don't usually sneak out all at once.

Zoe leans back onto her heels, the floorboards creaking beneath the weight of her knees, and I'm finally able to focus on her face. She looks like she's not sure she should've woken me. We're just roommates, after all, not friends, and we haven't been roommates for long.

She's standing, but, since she's not quite five feet tall, her head is just a few feet above me. Zoe Hoang is French Vietnamese, tiny with giant eyes and big lips that never seem to smile. I sit up in bed and we're practically eye to eye.

"Is everything okay?" I ask.

"No," Zoe says, her speech taking a trace of French accent. "Something happened."

Anyone else would make her say more, but I learned long ago to be comfortable with mystery. My old roommate, Ariel, never bothered with *where* or *why* when she woke me in the middle of the night. She'd just crook her finger and smile, and I'd come, like a puppy. Like a shadow.

I pull a robe on over my T-shirt and follow Zoe out of our room, down the hall, and outside. It's almost like old times, almost like Ariel's the one hurrying through the darkness ahead of me. Only Ariel never hurried. She walked like she had all night to sneak through the school. She dragged her fingers over the doors lining either side of the hallway, daring someone to open one. To find her. I let myself smile and, for a minute, I actually see her. Her red hair falls in tangles down her back, and she's wearing that vintage slip she loves—the lime-green one with the broken strap, no matter if it's freezing outside or if there could be boys wandering around. Especially if there could be boys.

Dry leaves crunch beneath my toes, and wind claws at my ankles. I shiver, my teeth chattering. My robe is too thin and there's a hole at the elbow. I've always hated the cold. It hits me harder than it does other people. It seeps into my skin and curls around my bones. Girls in pajamas flit past us through the trees, their voices trailing behind them like scarves. Moonlight paints their bare arms and legs silver.

I wrap my arms around my chest, holding the warmth close. Ariel would love this. The trees, the dark. The mystery. I start to turn, a joke for her on my lips. But then I don't. It's been a month. I've almost stopped talking to her.

Zoe glances over her shoulder to make sure I'm still following. We're deep in the trees now, and I can't really hear the other girls' voices, but I feel them moving around us. I yawn, still half asleep. Red light flashes through the branches and, for a second, I think of sunlight. Then it flashes blue.

"No." I stop walking. My hands go to my chest and I press them there, flat. My fingers find the skin at the edge of my T-shirt.

Zoe turns. "Are you okay?"

I nod, but my voice cracks, betraying me. "Is it Devon?"

Devon, my second-best friend since we were sophomores, which feels like forever and ever ago instead of eighteen months. Or first-best friend now, I guess, with Ariel gone. Devon disappeared two days ago, but everyone, even her teachers, thought she hitchhiked into the city to go dancing or see a concert. It wouldn't be the first time, or even the fifth time. We were never worried—just pissed she didn't invite us.

Zoe hesitates. "I don't know," she says carefully. "I just heard that the cops were here. They found . . . something."

She darts through the trees. I walk slower, aware of the wet on the leaves beneath my feet, the wind on the back of my neck. I hear Ariel's voice in my ear, but it's a memory of a voice, not a real one.

Why are you so surprised?

The trees open onto a clearing. Police tape weaves between the branches, a shocking spot of fluorescent in the middle of all the black and gray and brown. I see faces, but most of the girls don't creep close enough to be recognized. Dean Rosenthal kneels in the dirt, and her assistant, Mr. Coolidge, stands behind her. He has one hand pressed to his mouth. The emotion on his face is raw in a way that makes me blush and avert my eyes. I feel like I've just seen him in his underwear.

Their bodies form a barricade, blocking my view of what they're staring at. I hesitate behind Zoe, but just for a moment.

"*Charlotte*," Zoe says, but I'm already moving closer, ducking below the police tape. She grabs my wrist, her tiny hand surprisingly strong. I shake her off. An arm lies across the leaves. Brown skin and long, tapered fingers with bright red nails. The last time I saw those hands, they were wrapped around a tumbler of whiskey in her daddy's office.

Now Devon holds a syringe. Her knees are bent, like she'd crumpled to the ground after it happened.

Doesn't she look perfect? I imagine Ariel saying. I nod, because wouldn't it be just like Ariel to say something so horrible? But she's right. There are no marks on Devon's body. No blood.

"Like she's sleeping," I whisper. I close my eyes and wrap my arms around my chest. Devon isn't lying here in the dirt. Devon is dancing at a party in the city. Devon is drinking martinis and flirting with a thirty-year-old businessman who hasn't guessed yet that she's only eighteen. Devon is wearing a ridiculous dress that shows off too much skin and that she bought with the credit card she stole from her mother. She's not here.

When I open my eyes again, they settle on a shape in the trees across from me. I recognize Jack by his height, which is nearly two feet taller than everyone around him. His hair bleeds into the shadows, his pale skin a spot of brightness in the night.

If he's out, the rest of the boys' dorm is out, too. I pull my robe tighter around my body, suddenly self-conscious.

Jack takes a few steps forward, and red and blue lights flash across his face. His shaggy black hair is messy with sleep, and his faded T-shirt strains against his broad chest. He finds me in the dark, his gaze lingering for a second too long. Heat creeps up my neck and spreads over my cheeks.

There's a part of me that doesn't want to look at him, in case Ariel sees.

But Ariel's dead. So that's impossible.

Much later that night, when I'm back in my dorm and Zoe's breathing has deepened, and even the moon has fallen asleep, I roll onto my side and curl my knees toward my chest. And I cry.

Devon is dead. Devon, who told me that red lipstick made me look fierce, and who once brought a kitten to the animal shelter, a kitten so tiny and weak we'd had to feed her with an eyedropper. Devon, who always sat with me at lunch when Ariel was being a bitch and giving me the silent treatment, even though we both knew she liked Ariel better.

Devon followed Ariel to that dark place knowing I would never be brave or strong enough to meet them there.

I cry silent sobs. The ones that claw at your throat and dig their way up from your chest no matter how you try to choke them back down. The ones that hurt, deep.

If Ariel were still here, she'd slip into my bed and knot

her fingers through my fingers and lean her forehead against my forehead, like she did that night last year when I found the baby bird someone had run over with a bicycle. I replay that night in my head. How I squeezed my eyes shut because I was crying, and I don't cry in front of anyone.

"Charlotte," Ariel said. She traced a finger down my cheek, catching a tear beneath her fingernail. "I know your secret."

"Shut up," I said, hiccuping.

"You act all tough, but you're soft inside. You're a kitten."

The words tiptoe through my head on feet made of needles. They dig their points into the soft tissue of my brain. It was a conversation we had a lot, when Ariel was alive. She was the only one who saw the real me. She told me that "nice" wasn't something to be ashamed of, but I think she never really listened to herself say that word.

"Nice." It doesn't even leave an imprint on the air after it's been spoken. It doesn't slash at you, like "daring," or enchant you, like "magnetic." It's empty. A bubble that glitters and gleams, then disappears when you apply too much pressure.

Nice girls don't kill themselves. Nice girls get left behind. Nice girls cry in their beds alone.

I turn my head, letting my tears soak into my pillow. I want to sleep, but Devon and Ariel wander through my brain all night, refusing to let me. They laugh and dance and, for a moment, it's like old times, when we'd sneak out to the cave in the woods and drink and tell secrets. It's like it's supposed to be.

But then they disappear into the trees, and no matter how hard I look, I never find them.

"They're saying it was an overdose." Dean Rosenthal grabs a tissue from her desk, then leans back in her chair, dabbing at the corners of her eyes. She cried at the emergency assembly this morning, too. Her tears don't seem real. They're like props, like the tasteful strand of pearls around her neck and the sensible black heels she wears with her Chanel suits.

I am appropriately sad, the tears say. *I am having a healthy emotional reaction.*

"Who's saying it was an overdose?" I ask.

"The police."

"But Devon doesn't do drugs," I say.

Rosenthal raises an eyebrow, calling my bluff, but I don't correct myself. Like hell am I going to admit the truth to the dean of our school.

Rosenthal balls her tissue in one hand, shifting in her seat so she can look at me. *Really* look at me. The way adults look at teenagers who concern them.

Let's take inventory of what she sees: Eyes, dry. Hair, freshly (and badly) cut, probably done with a plastic razor in the girls' bathrooms. Too tall. Too thin (anorexia!?). Skin, ashy and pale. Deep circles under eyes. Not smiling.

In other words, I am *not* having a healthy emotional reaction.

Rosenthal clears her throat. "A few of your teachers mentioned that you haven't been turning in assignments. Since . . ."

"Yeah." I take a pristine crystal ashtray off Rosenthal's desk and turn it over in my hands. What's the point of an ashtray you don't use? Is it art? "I know. I'm trying to catch up."

"You were barely keeping up with your classwork before."

Before. Since. Rosenthal's become quite the pro at dancing around difficult subjects.

"I've always passed my classes," I say.

"Mr. Carver says you won't pass physics unless you hand in your take-home test today by three. Ms. Antoine says you've missed her last three classes, and you still haven't completed a ten-page essay on *Brave New World* that was worth seventy-five percent of your grade."

"But I'm getting a B in drama."

Dean Rosenthal pushes her glasses up with two fingers and pinches the bridge of her nose. "In light of . . . recent events, we think it might be best for you to take a break from Weston for the remainder of the year."

The air in Dean Rosenthal's office grows several degrees cooler. Weston isn't the kind of place you "take a break from." Not without sacrificing a pound of flesh. People donate entire buildings to get their children considered for admission. The entrance forms and tests and interviews take months to complete. There's a 3 percent acceptance rate.

Unless your mother is very important, of course. Like mine.

I place the ashtray back on Rosenthal's desk and fold my hands in my lap. "We?"

"Your mother and I."

A knife pierces my back and twists. I bite the inside of my lip to keep from doing something stupid, like forming an expression. My mother, who forced me to come to this idiotic school, has decided that I'm not good enough. My mother, who's always been hopelessly embarrassed by how very ordinary I am. How unlike the cutthroat, genius sociopaths who attend this place.

The logical part of my brain knew something like this would happen eventually. Growing up, Mother was always switching me from school to school. I attended three very different prestigious day cares, not to mention a rotating door of private grade schools and junior highs and summer camps. Weston is my second high school, and the place I've been the longest. I was kind of hoping it would stick. Silly, silly Charlotte.

"Did she say why?" I ask, and my voice doesn't crack. Thank God for small victories.

"Why?" Rosenthal frowns. A tiny wrinkle creases the skin between her eyes. "Charlotte, your two best friends committed suicide within a month of each other."

I stare at the wrinkle. It takes me longer than it should to recognize the look of sympathy on her face. I'm not slow or anything; it's just not the kind of thing you see at Weston. Pity, yes. But not sympathy.

"You were in a . . . a kind of a club with Devon Savage and Ariel Frank. Is that correct?"

I cringe. I hate the way she says Ariel's last name. Frank, with a hard *k*. It sounds like a cough.

"We were friends," I say.

"Friends who were in a club?"

"God, it wasn't a *club*. We're not seven years old."

Rosenthal leans back in her chair and folds her arms over her chest. "How would you describe it, then?"

I stare at the heavy velvet curtains covering the window behind her head. What is it with fancy private schools and *velvet*? Velvet and oak and marble and leather. Have there been studies done detailing how these materials are more conducive to an academic environment? Has someone made up charts and spreadsheets and highlighted things with yellow markers?

"Charlotte?"

"Ariel liked fairy tales," I say, pulling my eyes away from the curtains. "She used to joke that we were all like characters from the stories."

It wasn't really a joke. Ariel thought this was brilliant. "Weston looks like a creepy-ass castle," she used to say. "And we're the princesses they're keeping locked in the attic."

I don't know what story she got that from, but it was hard to argue with her. She was charismatic. She made things like pretending to be a fairy-tale princess when you were seventeen sound dangerous and exciting. She'd wake us after it got dark, persuade us to sneak out into the woods with her, and drink stolen wine straight from the bottle. She said our lives were going to be like fairy tales.

Across from me, Rosenthal nods. She's waiting for me to speak first. I could outlast her patience, if I tried. Years of wordless dinners with Mother have taught me to be very comfortable with silence.

"Devon was Snow White," I say, because I want to get this over with. "It was kind of an irony thing, because she's—she was black. Ariel thought it was funny."

"Who are you?"

I close my eyes, letting breath escape from my lips in a rush that's almost a sigh. "Cinderella. Because she had all those animal buddies."

Rosenthal stares for a moment, and then understanding passes through her eyes. "Ah, right. Your shelter."

I press my lips together, nodding. Weston is in the middle of the woods, and there are stray cats and lost dogs and injured bunnies that find their way onto the grounds. I used to hide them in our dorm until Ariel complained that it made our stuff smell like woodland creatures. Then I went to Dean Rosenthal to see about opening the shelter.

I don't tell her the rest of it. That I was Cinderella because Cinderella was loyal and kind and easy to manipulate. That Ariel teased me about it.

Photo © Caroline Donofrio

Danielle Rollins is the author of *Burning* and *Breaking*, in addition to the Merciless series and *Survive the Night* under the pseudonym Danielle Vega. She lives in Brooklyn, New York, and spends far too much money on vintage furniture and leather boots.

www.daniellerollins.com

@vegarollins